j

Brother, can you spare a dime?

Also by Ken Dalton

The Bloody Birthright

The Big Show Stopper

Death is a Cabernet

The Tartan Shroud

Brother, can you spare a dime?

Ken Dalton

Different Drummer Press

For more information concerning *Brother, can you spare a dime?*, email the author at ken@kendalton.com

ISBN 978-0-578-14039-1
1. Humorous—Mystery—Fiction. 2. Pinky—Delmont (Fictional character)—Fiction. 3. Bear—Zabarte (Fictional character)—Fiction. 4. Southport, North Carolina—Fiction. 5. Kona Coast, Hawaii—Fiction. 6. Beijing, China—Fiction. 7. Lhasa, Tibet. Fiction. I. Title.

ACKNOWLEDGEMENTS

This novel came together with the help and assistance of the following;

I salute the folks who live along the friendly North Carolina shores—the Kona Coast of Hawaii—the enigmatic land of China and Tibet. They made my visits to their areas an incredible joy.

To my artistic son, Hugh, who reads the first draft of the novel and then he creates the provocative covers that turns each Pinky and Bear Mystery into a work of art.

To Wendy Maxham, and the newest mystery member of my editing staff for another exceptional picky, picky, picky job of editing.

To Dr. Ye, and all the staff, nurses and Pharmacists, that dwell in the magical land of room 170, also known as the Kaiser Infusion Center, for giving me another year to write.

To the long suffering members of my writer's group:

Jon Gunner Howe

Norm Benson

Omar Eljumally

And the divine Sarah Andrews

Finally, to my wife Arlene, for remaining my lover and best friend and standing beside me through the self-imposed madness of writing.

This book is dedicated to Mary Hallock who died a few weeks before this book was completed. Mary was a friend, editor, and fellow author. I, along with your fictious friends, Pinky, Bear, and Flo will miss you and your spot-on counsel .

Chapter One

Bear Zabarte—Carson City, Nevada

I thought I had all my ducks lined up for a super afternoon of watching my Red Sox beat the crap out of the damn Yankees while I sucked down a few cold ones.

Flo would be gone all afternoon so she wouldn't get on me about tossing down too many brews—in fact, I should jump all over her for spending the afternoon at that woman's joint where she drops her weekly C note getting a broad to fiddle with her hair, while another broad plays with her finger nails.

So, like I said, I was ready for a couple of hours of peace and quiet when the damn phone rang. When Flo's home she answers the phone 'cause she says that I say too many bad words. What the hell was that broad talking about?

For example, my Pop told me it was okay to say shit 'cause the wife of one of those old Presidents told everyone that her husband said it. I don't remember his name, but he was the dude that took over when that other guy died and then he dropped the atom bomb on Japan. I remembered that 'cause the story of that dude trying to decide if he drops the bomb, or not, was really cool. So if saying shit's good enough for a President of the good old U. S. of A., I'm going to tell Flo she can pound salt and . . . Shit! That phone kept on ringing, so I hoisted my butt off the couch and answered it.

"Bear? Am I talking to my old high school chum, Bear Zabarte?"

It was a dude but I didn't get his voice. "Who wants to know?"

"It's Helmut!"

"Helmut? I don't know anybody named . . . hold on, I remember you now. You lived in Elko."

He said, "Yes, we rode on the same school bus together—spent four years in high school together—we both played tuba in the marching band."

I growled, "But at the senior prom dance you flashed your nasty side and turned into a back-stabbing bastard."

"Bear, I figured that by now you would have forgotten my youthful faux pas. But—"

I interrupted, "How could I forget the weasel that swiped my date just before the last dance, and after I had paid big bucks for the prom bid? Shit, I even dropped ten bucks on a really cool white orchid corsage."

"That was a long time ago, my friend. Please accept my sincere apology. Let us forget my prom blunder as if it were water flowing under a bridge. Before that incident we were close. Remember, you were one of the few who talked to me that first week on the school bus. My brother Ludwig and I were different from everyone else in Elko. We were the sons of German immigrants, and were surrounded by a veritable legion of Basque families. And I'm sure you recall that my brother was the only student in the school who was confined to a wheelchair. Each morning, you and I would lift Ludwig and his wheelchair into the school bus. Now—"

"Helmut, like you said, that was a long time ago. I have an important meeting starting in five minutes." Pinky would be proud of me. He'd say, 'Bear, you are finally thinking on your feet.' But between you and me, I don't have a clue what my feet have to do with good thinking.

"Bear, I need your help at once. Please drop everything and come to 2016 Mountain View Dri—"

"Helmut, watch my lips. I have to go to a meeting."

"Bear, I'm desperate. My brother, Ludwig Kaufmann, the brave senior from Elko High School who wheeled his chair across the stage to claim his high school diploma, is dead! And I am—"

"Helmut, that's shitty news about your brother. Hey, you've got a pot-full of things to do— like getting somebody to do something with your brother's body, and you've got to find him a cemetery plot, so you better get your ass in gear. Call me back someday."

"Damn it, listen to me. I'm at Ludwig's home and I'm standing in a pool of his blood!"

There goes my afternoon of baseball and beer. "So he didn't just croak from old age. How'd he die?"

"My guess is from the bullet hole in the middle of his forehead."

Jesus, this dude's talking murder. "Okay, you've got my attention but I still don't know why you called me."

"There is one more item, and it is important. I

think my brother's 1894 S dime could be missing."

"Ten cents? Is that the best you can do? Helmut, have you lost your marbles? Why worry about a stupid dime when somebody just murdered your brother?"

"Bear, that dime is worth two million dollars."

"Two million for a stupid dime?" Flo was right. We live in a crazy world. "That's nuts."

"My old friend, according to a recent article in a magazine for coin collectors, *The Numismatist*, in June of 1894, the San Francisco Mint had a little silver left over, just enough to produce twenty-four 1894 S dimes. They planned to make more dimes later that year, but for reasons unknown, no more dimes of that year were minted in San Francisco. Bear, think of it, the mint superintendent, John Daggett, accidentally, or on purpose, minted the rarest coins in America."

"How rare is rare?"

There is some controversy on that exact question. Some say there are nine 1894 S dimes, some say ten, but regardless, the seven proof coins we know of are all worth in the neighborhood of two million dollars."

"What's a proof coin?"

"Proof means a special early sample of a coin issue that's made to check the dies."

"Are you sure the coin is missing?"

"No."

"Can you take a look and see?"

"Bear, I don't know where Ludwig stored the dime, but considering the value, I am sure it would be kept in a safe place."

Shit, I should have quit while I was ahead.

4

"Helmut, for a second let's forget all about the coin story. I have couple of important questions for you."

"Go ahead, but there are a couple more tales about the 1894 S that I'm sure you'll find fascinating."

Like I really cared! "Do that later, okay? Now, answer my questions and give me the straight skinny. Did you make that hole in your brother's forehead?"

"No!"

One word answers were the shits. I glanced at the clock and the first inning would be damn near over by now. "Any idea who did?"

"I have a couple of ideas. Bear, I heard through the grapevine that you do investigative work for the famous attorney, Pinky Delmont."

"You're right, but Pinky only handles rich dudes accused of murder and you just told me that you didn't kill your brother."

"I'm afraid it's not as easy as that. When I arrived at my brother's house, I let myself in with my key because it takes Ludwig a long time to answer the doorbell. I called his name. He didn't answer so I went into the office where he conducts his business—he's a professional numismatist—a man who buys and sells rare coins. There he was, leaning back in his wheelchair. Ludwig's face almost looked as if he was asleep, if you could force yourself to ignore the bullet hole in the center of his forehead."

Damn! The first inning had to be over by now and I still hadn't popped the top off my first beer. "Helmut, I'm almost late for my meeting. Get your brain in gear. What the hell do you want from me?"

5

"Bear, you don't have to swear at me. I feel dumb enough without you orally berating me."

"What do you mean dumb? You and your brother were the smartest dudes at Elko High."

"That may have been true back then, but I sure wasn't the smartest dude today."

I was starting to get pissed off. "Come on, Helmut, cut to the chase. Why did you call me?"

"Without thinking, I picked up the pistol that lay on Ludwig's desk and then I stepped into a pool of Ludwig's blood. Bear, I'm a successful businessman, not a police detective, but between my finger prints on the gun, and the soles of my shoes soaked with my brother's blood, everyone will think I shot my brother. So now you know why I called you. I'm in an untenable position and desperately need your immediate help."

I said, "Okay, put a sock in it for a minute and let me think." Before I screwed anything up I knew I'd better call Pinky and find out what to tell this dude. "First, and this is important, don't move your feet or set the gun down. Give me your phone number and I'll call you back in a couple minutes."

I scribbled the number down and hung up. Then I hit Pinky's number and waited for Mabel to answer.

"Law office of J. Pincus Delmont."

"Babe, I need to talk to—"

"I'm sorry, Bear, but he just left for court."

That meant Pinky was sitting in his office and he didn't want to talk to anyone. "Babe, this is an emergency. I need to—"

"I told you a moment ago, Pinky is—"

"Mabel, do you still own that fluffy cat?"

"Why no. She died, but I didn't know that you had any feelings for my pet."

"I don't! Stop screwing around and put me through to the boss, or I'll come over there and pop an ice pick into your car's tires."

A second later Pinky came on the line. "What is so important that you dare interrupt my morning meditation?"

Jesus! That probably means he's drinking his coffee with his eyes closed. "Boss, I've got you a live one on the phone."

"Don't call me boss."

"Okay, Boss."

I listened to Pinky think for a couple of seconds, then he said, "Does your potential 'live one' have anything to do with an untimely death?"

"Yup!"

"Excellent. Now, to adhere to the ethics of my profession, and due to my deontological obligation as an officer of the court, from this moment on, our conversation will be conducted as if it were a hypothetical situation."

"What's a needle got to do with anything?"

"I beg your pardon?"

"Hey, you were the one that told me to use a hypodermic solution."

"A hypothetical situation, you dolt, not a hypodermic solution."

One of these days I'm going to ask Flo to tell me what dolt means, and if it's bad, I'm going to kick Pinky's ass around the block. "Calm down, Boss, and tell me what you want me to do."

"Damn it, tell me about the prospective client, but open your conversation by saying this is a

7

hypothetical situation."

"Okay, but this dude is waiting for me to call back. Boss, everything from now on is a hypo-something story. The dude's name is Hel—"

Pinky yelled, "No names, damn it."

"Okay. Somebody killed the made-up dude's brother with a single shot to the forehead. The made-up dude called me from his brother's office. He's got a gun in his hand. He's standing in a pool of his brother's blood. Boss, the made-up dude wants to know what to do next."

"Did you explain to the fictitious felon that a successful attorney requires a retainer in the neighborhood of $100,000?"

"Your retainer used to be $65,000. What happened?"

"Inflation, my boy, inflation. Back to my question. Does he understand the cost of retaining the best possible attorney?"

"I told him that if he's not willing to cough up the money, there's no Pink . . . whoops, there's no getting the best attorney in Northern Nevada. Boss, do me and Flo get a bonus for this?"

"Absolutely not!"

The cheap bastard! I would have settled for a couple of G's, but now me and Flo will figure out a way to skim-off double that. "Okay, what do I tell the made-up dude?"

"You have described a very delicate situation, so you had better write down my hypothetical solution for your hypothetical friend."

"Boss, Hel—"

"No names, my boy, We are discussing a hypothetical case—a friendly fabrication based on

8

fantasy. Do you have a pencil handy?"

"Fire away."

I scribbled off a pot-full of things the boss told me to tell Helmut, and then he said, "Finally, your hypothetical friend must go home and wait for a call from the police. Then, and only then, should your hypothetical friend contact me."

"Got it!"

I clicked off from Pinky and dialed Helmut's number.

"Bear, thank God, I thought you had given up on me."

I asked the first question on Pinky's list. "Helmut, does your brother live alone?"

"Yes. He never married."

"Does anybody come in to clean his joint?"

"Yes, a woman named Rosa."

"Is she there every day?"

"She cleans daily in the afternoon. She usually arrives around twelve-forty-five to one and leaves around five. After cleaning, Rosa fixes Ludwig's dinner and a sandwich lunch for the following day that she stores in the refrigerator."

I glanced at my watch. It was twelve-thirty. "You've got to get your ass in gear before that broad comes to work." I looked at the next thing on Pinky's list. "Is there a cloth that you can grab without taking a step?"

"Nothing within my reach."

"Are you still holding the gun in your hand?"

"I am and I my arm is getting very tired."

"Set the gun down on the desk and take your shirt off."

"My shirt? Bear, I don't see—"

9

"Damn it, do what I told you and make it snappy."

After a few seconds, Helmut said, "Okay, the gun is on the desk and I am holding my shirt in my hand."

"Good. Now wipe the gun clean and be careful you don't shoot yourself when you rub the trigger. Once the gun is spotless, hold the gun by the shirt and stick it in your brother's right . . . wait, was Ludwig right, or left handed?"

"Right handed."

"Put the gun in Ludwig's right hand and very carefully wrap his finger on the trigger."

I waited a few seconds, and then Helmut said, "Okay, that's done."

"Can you step outside the pool of blood?"

"Yes."

"Good. Now unlace your shoes and step clear of the blood stain.

"Okay."

Finally Helmut said, "I'm standing on the clean carpet in my stocking feet. What do I do next?"

"Pick up your shoes and move your ass out of your brother's house."

"Bear, what do you recommend I do with the bloody shoes."

Jesus, what a dork. "Dump them anywhere where the sun don't shine."

I glanced at my watch. Damn, it was twelve-forty and that cleaning broad could be walking in at any minute. "Helmut, you've got to get your butt out of there before that broad comes to work. But first, and this is real important, listen to me.

"After you ditch those bloody shoes, go home, sit down and wait for a call from the cops. When the cleaning broad finds your brother's body, the cops will be all over Ludwig's joint like maggots on a ripe road apple. Trust me, it won't take long for the cops to come after you but they'll hit you two different ways.

"If they call you on the phone and tell you your brother's dead, hustle your sorry ass over to Pinky's office and hire him to represent you. And you'd better take your checkbook 'cause Pinky won't even let you sit down in his office until you hand him $100,000.

"If the cops show up at your place, they're damn sure you've killed your brother. They'll arrest you, throw cuffs on you, and take you in to interrogate you. If that happens, clam up! Helmut, this is very important, don't say anything to anyone but Pinky Delmont.

"Either way the cops come at you, once you've hired Pinky, you have to tell him the whole scoop— how you found Helmut—how you picked up the gun—how you stepped in the pool of blood— everything. And then tell him how you suddenly got smart and figured out what you did was stupid, so you wiped the gun clean, picked up your bloody shoes, and vamoosed.

"And Helmut, listen up 'cause this is the most important part of all this crap. Everything we talked about during these phone calls was a made up story, like a movie, or a cool crime show on TV. If the cops ask you if you got any of these ideas from me, just tell them that you haven't seen me, or talked to me, since our little dust-up at the Elko

High senior prom. Now get your ass out of that house!"

Helmut hung up so quick he forgot to say goodbye.

I sat down on the couch, popped the top off a cool one, took a big swig, and turned on the TV. Damn it. It was the third inning and the Yankee's were ahead by three runs. I drained the first can and opened another. I wasn't really worried. My Red Sox were playing at Fenway, and in that ball park, a three run lead can disappear faster than a pair of bloody shoes.

Chapter Two

J. Pincus Delmont—Carson City, Nevada

An hour after an excellent lunch—a romantic date with my beautiful ex-wife, Willow Stone—I sat in my office and wondered if my subtle offer had been lost on Willow while we consumed the stunning Tiramisu. My reverie was shattered when my phone buzzed. "Yes?"

"Willow's on your line."

Ah, she had picked up my hint. The lovely Willow Stone, was an unequal amalgam of Scottish and Native American genes. Silken red hair. Hazel eyes. High cheek bones, and a whisper of freckles danced across her alabaster skin.

My stomach tightened as I considered what her answer might be to the question I dearly wished to ask, but first, I felt it would be prudent to remind her of my largesse. "My dear, I trust you have sufficiently recovered from the excellent mid-day feast personally chosen by the head chef, Roberto."

She chuckled, "Just barely. If I ate like that every day I would weigh three hundred pounds. Pinky, I had the feeling that there was more to our little lunch than a District Attorney and lawyer meeting to discuss a pending plea bargain."

"You are correct my dear. In fact—"

There was a knock on my office door. Mabel

peeked in and said, "I know you're on the phone, but there's a man who demands to see you at once. He doesn't have an appointment but he assures me that you'll want to see him."

Without question, these were the sort of interruptions that accompanied true fame. "Willow, just a moment. I have an office emergency." I held my hand over the transmitter and told Mabel, "Tell him that I am in the middle of an important phone call and . . . hold on, what is the man's name?"

"Helmut Kaufmann."

"Ah-ha! Mr. Kaufmann." So Bear's fictitious person was on the verge of becoming a fact. "Tell Mr. Kaufmann I will squeeze him into my busy afternoon schedule."

I took my palm off the transmitter. "Willow, at the moment, a situation has arisen and my normally smooth-running office has spun out of control. I need to rescue Mabel and spread some oil upon the troubled water. My dear, I am forced to beg your forgiveness and I will call you back as soon as the turmoil has subsided."

Before Willow could respond I hung up my phone.

I glanced at my office door and my secretary stood there as if she were a sentry guarding the entry to an unfathomable treasure of gold bullion. "Mabel, please show Mr. Kaufmann into my office and do not disturb us for any reason."

Kaufmann was firmly locked in his late thirties, at least six foot tall, but his current stature was shorter due to the pronounced slump of his shoulders. The man's chin rested on his chest, and his pale, pasty face exhibited all the signs of

14

extreme stress—an expression I am used to seeing as an attorney defending the wretched, and downtrodden—those poor souls who have been accused of murder.

I motioned to the chair in front of my desk and said, "My good man, please sit down."

As he sat his head slowly slid into his hands and he began to weep.

I said, "Mr. Kaufmann, I am extremely busy so I must ask you to compose yourself or leave my office and return when you can gain control of your emotional state."

He lifted his head, wiped a teardrop off his chin with the back of his hand, and said, "I apologize, Mr. Delmont, but you do not understand how close my brother, Ludwig, and I—"

I interrupted, "Mr. Kaufmann, before we discuss anything concerning the reasons for your fragile mental condition, we must complete the mundane business aspects of my retainer. I believe $100,000 was the amount quoted."

"I understand." He pulled a check out of his shirt pocket and placed it on my desk.

I picked it up and was pleased to note that it was a bank draft. The amount was for $100,000 and drawn on a business called Kaufmann Development. "Mr. Kaufmann, I am pleased to inform you that from this moment on, you are represented by J. Pincus Delmont, who many have ranked as the top defense attorney in Northern Nevada. Now a word of warning. Your retainer will allow me to listen your story. However, if your defense goes beyond a simple plea bargain, you must be ready, and financially able, to cover those costs."

The strain on the man's countenance tightened. "Mr. Delmont, I fear that bank draft represents all my funds at the present time. However, there's my brother's estate and I am the only living relative."

At the moment, I did not have time to get into the legal ramifications concerning Ludwig's estate after Helmut had been convicted of murdering his brother. "Helmut, let us hope that your original retainer will be sufficient to cover my time and costs."

The tightness in Helmut's chin began to relax, minuscule muscle by minuscule muscle. "Mr. Delmont, I am happy to hear that."

I said, "One last item of business. If I require additional funds for your defense, and you find yourself unable to supply those funds, my services on your behalf will immediately cease."

"I understand, Mr. Delmont."

"Please, call me Pinky. Now, inform me why you seek my services."

After listening to Kaufmann recount the identical tale that he had told to Bear I nodded. "That was an extremely interesting story, but what made you come to my office concerning legal advice?"

My phone buzzed. "Mabel, I told you that under no circumstances . . . Oh, I understand."

I faced Mr. Kaufmann and said, "I apologize, but I have to take this phone call to conclude what I can only describe as an extremely delicate negotiation. Would you be so kind as to step outside my office for a few moments? Mabel will get you a

16

cup of my personal blend of freshly ground coffee and when I have completed this call, my secretary will inform you that I will be ready for you to complete your tale."

The man removed himself from my office.

Waiting on the phone was the lovely Willow Stone, my favorite ex-wife. During my adult years I had married several women, but Willow was the only one that had offered me moments of true bliss. The instant my office door closed I exclaimed, "Willow, my dear. I was about to call you back and remind you that you are the only woman to whom I have given my heart."

"Pinky, I assumed by now that you had resolved your office emergency. Now, the annual County Law Enforcement awards dinner is next month, and I —"

I was stunned. I thought she called to accept my thinly veiled, but heart-felt proposal of marriage. I said, "You are my true love. And yet we parted. Why?"

"Pinky, that is not why I called, but if you insist, your sperm had low motility. The fertility doctor and I attempted to get you to change your diet, to increase your intake of zinc, but you—"

"My dear, that is but one side of the story. If I recall, around that time you decided to run for the office of District Attorney, and according to your campaign manager, the mental image of a pregnant, female, District Attorney would not provide the voters of our macho county the proper persona."

"Damn you! Before I hang up can I put you down for two tickets to the dinner?"

"Of course. In fact, make that four. I owe Bear and Flo a little bonus."

Willow said, "Now, if you will excuse me—"

"Before you hang up, I have a question to ask of you and I want you to think long and hard before you answer."

"Does this have something to do with my gut feeling that you were trying to ask me something during the tiramisu?"

"You never cease to amaze me. You are correct. For sometime I have been seeking a way to broach this delicate subject and—"

"Is it a subject concerning the ring box you attempted to hide in the palm of your right hand?"

Now that my true intensions were out in the open I waited for her affirmative response. "Guilty as charged, my love. Yes, I have in my possession a small box that contains a ring, a circular symbol of my undying love."

"And after I accept the ring, then what?"

"Willow, I feel the time is ripe for us to try matrimony again."

A cacophony of voices overwhelmed Willow's response, as if she were suddenly standing on the floor of the New York Stock Exchange. "Pinky, I had three people talking at me at the same time and I heard 'the time is ripe' but didn't get the rest. You'll have to excuse me but something important has come up on my end. I'll call you right back."

Click!

Damn her! I was a fraction of a second away from officially asking her to marry me, again, when she cut me off. Well, two can play at that game.

I buzzed Mabel. "After you send in Mr.

18

Kaufmann, call Bear and tell him to report to my office immediately . . . hold all my calls, and that includes calls from Willow Stone."

Kaufmann returned and sat down.

I said, "Now, explain why you seek my legal advice."

"I am here because Bear told me that if the police called to inform me of my brother's death I should—"

I slammed my hand on my desk. "Mr. Kaufmann, do not utter another word. As far as anyone outside this office is concerned, everything you are about to say, and everything you have said so far, is the first time I have heard the story of your harrowing day. Do I make myself clear?"

"I think so."

"That includes all you have done prior to my acceptance of your retainer check. You see, the attorney/client privilege is inviolable, so from the moment I accepted your retainer, everything we discussed from that point on is protected by the attorney/client privilege. Had I been aware of any unfortunate circumstances, or situations, prior to you retaining me as your legal representative, I fear that knowledge would not be covered under attorney/client privilege. Again, have I made myself clear?"

His eyes perked up. "Now I understand why Bear was so insistent that our little discussion over the phone was a fabrication. Right?"

"Mr. Kaufmann, may I address you as Helmut?"

"Please do."

"Helmut, from the moment you handed me

that check, we are now dealing with facts and only facts. Let us go through your day again. And be very careful that you do not leave anything out."

I turned on my tape recorder and as he rambled on about the pool of blood, and the weapon, my phone buzzed. I turned off the recorder, held up my hand to stop Helmut from talking, and said into my phone, "Damn it, Mabel, I told you to hold all my calls."

"I'm sorry, but Willow is on line one and demands to talk with you concerning official police business."

"Has Bear arrived?"

"He has."

"Send him in. Inform Willow I am presently performing one of those natural physical functions all civilized humans take care of in the bathroom and I will be able to talk with her in less then ninety seconds."

"Okay."

Bear burst in. "What's up, Boss?"

"Take Helmut to my Lake Tahoe condo on the California side, the same place where I sent you when Ice Connor was after your skin for pushing him into your swimming pool. As you will recall from your previous visit, there is five thousand dollars hidden under the rock on the right side of the fireplace for expenses. Do not contact me for any reason. I will call you on your cell. Now get out of here. The police will be here in a few minutes."

Bear said, "Can I stop by and pick up Flo?"

"No! And you just wasted ten seconds with your inane question. Get out of here."

Bear said, "Helmut?"

20

"Yes."

"Did you ditch the shoes?"

"I did."

"Where?"

"In my laundry hamper. I figured I'd wash off the blood and then give the shoes to the Salvation Army."

"Jesus, what a dork!" Bear grabbed Helmut's arm and pulled him through the back door.

I buzzed Mabel. "Put through Willow Stone."

Willow said, "Pinky, I've just been informed that a local coin dealer, Ludwig Kaufmann, was found dead. The police on the scene determined that someone had attempted to make Kaufmann's death look like a suicide so we're talking about first degree murder."

"My dear, that is interesting, but I fail—"

"I am not through. The deadman had a surveillance system on the front entrance of his home that recorded his brother, Helmut Kaufmann, entering and leaving the victim's home around the time of his death. Now here comes an interesting part, the Chief of Police is an amateur coin collector and he informed me that Ludwig Kaufmann was rumored to own a dime worth two million dollars."

An interesting tidbit of information that Helmut had neglected to mention during our brief conversation, but without question that coin would be part of his inheritance. I said, "My goodness! That is a large amount of money."

"Pinky, now I get to the best bit. The police did a quick background check on the Kaufmann brothers and discovered they both attended Elko High School the same time as Bear Zabarte. I sat back, put the pieces together, and concluded that our prime suspect, Helmut Kaufmann, could be in your office."

"Willow, my dear, there you are incorrect. And I take umbrage at your insinuation that I, an officer of the court, would—"

There was a knock on my office door. Mabel stuck her head in and said, "There's a Detective Henrietta Spaulding here and she just presented me with a search warrant."

I cried, "Willow, you issued a search warrant on me—the man who loves and adores you? Have you lost your mind?"

"Shut up and put Detective Spaulding on the line."

Mabel escorted a feminine detective into my office. As I handed the phone to her I cried to the transmitter, "A search warrant? That cuts to the quick."

As the two females discussed their strategy I surveyed the Detective's desirable figure and noted that she scanned my office. Except for Mabel and myself, the premises was empty. The Detective handed me the phone and I said, "Willow, I still have that ring in my possession. Perhaps we could—"

The line went dead.

I said, "Good afternoon, Detective Spaulding. Is there anything I can do for you?"

She said, "Mr. Delmont, we have reason to believe that Helmut Kaufmann recently left his home and headed directly to your office. I am here to arrest him and book him for the cold-blooded murder of his brother, Ludwig Kaufmann." She continued to glance around the empty office as the tell-tale signs of frustration washed over her comely face. "I don't know how you did it, but it seems that my prime suspect has vanished."

"Detective Spaulding, please call me, Pinky. May I address you as Henrietta?"

"No you may not! It's Detective Spaulding to you."

I stretched to my maximum height of five-foot-five and three-quarters-inches—placed my nose under Henrietta's lovely chin—and using my sermon-on-the-mount tone, I demanded, "Detective Spaulding, as an officer of the court, I would never prevent a Carson City Police Detective from performing her duty. However, you need to be aware that Helmut Kaufmann is my client, and as such, if and when you do arrest him, you cannot interrogate him outside my presence. Do I make myself clear?"

I thrust my right hand toward her again, in a gesture of friendship. The Detective's eyes widened and I was surprised to see her slip her hand inside her tailored jacket—to reach for her weapon. She commanded, "Drop your hand to your side and do not make any quick moves." A tiny shudder raced across her well-proportioned shoulders. "Or I will be forced to place you under arrest for assaulting a police officer."

I lowered my arm, stepped away and turned my head, as if to indicate the way to the nearest exit. "After you, my dear."

Henrietta pulled her hand from her weapon. "Mr. Delmont, to be sure we are on the same page, I am not now, nor will I ever be 'your dear'. Now, as soon as I leave this legal morass you call your office, my next stop will be to see the District Attorney where I will seek her advice concerning an obstruction of justice charge against you. Ms. Stone is very adept on that aspect of the law, and I understand that she has a world of knowledge concerning you, and your clever ways of circumventing justice. Once I complete my meeting with the DA, I will begin my quest to track down and arrest your murdering client!"

Chapter Three

Bear—Carson City, Nevada

I heard Pinky tell me to hightail it to Tahoe without Flo, but he didn't have to live with her. As my truck pulled out of Pinky's parking lot, I grabbed my cell and hit Flo's number.

"Where are you?"

"Babe, I'll be at the gas station around the corner from our place in three minutes. Throw some clothes and your bathing suit in a bag and meet me there."

"What's going on?"

"Can't say any more than it's a rush assignment for you know who."

"Not good enough and what do you . . . my bathing suit? Okay, I'll be there."

A couple of minutes later, with Flo and Helmut squished on the front seat, I pulled out of the gas station as a cop car, with red lights flashing and siren wailing, shot past us heading in the direction of our apartment.

Flo frowned, "Was that cop car heading to our place?"

"I'd put money on it. Flo, meet Helmut. Helmut, meet Flo. We'll be a little cramped for the ride up the hill but once we get to Pinky's condo, you—"

Flo squealed, "Are you talking about Pinky's place by the lake?"

"Yup."

Flo said, "How long?"

"Don't know. We will pick up some expense money in the condo."

"How much?"

"Five g's."

Flo glanced at Helmut and her smile disappeared. "Who's this guy?"

"I told you, Helmut."

"Damn it, Helmut means as much to me as the Easter Bunny. Who in the hell is Helmut?"

"Oh. Me and Helmut lived in Elko and went to high school together."

"And twenty years later, Helmut just happens to be riding in your truck, and now we're all driving west on Highway 50 to Pinky's condo at Lake Tahoe. Damn it, this sounds like some kind of a Pinky deal, and that usually means all of us are in jeopardy of ending up in jail. Bear, spill it or I'm getting out at the next rest stop."

There weren't any rest stops between here and Pinky's condo, but I told my babe that Pinky told me to take Helmut to his condo 'cause I knew if I left out anything, and she found out, I'd not only be sleeping alone, Flo wouldn't even let me watch her when she takes a shower.

Flo said, "So because Pinky told you to take him to Tahoe, I can assume your buddy is running from the law. Helmut, what did you do?"

"The police think I murdered my brother."

Bear said, "And swiped a dime worth a couple of million."

"A couple of million what?"

Helmut said, "Dollars."

Flo said, "You're putting me on."

I said, "Nope."

Helmut said, "My brother, Ludwig, is . . . was a professional numismatist."

Flo said, "That tells me he was a collector who buys and sells coins. How did he die?"

I said, "A slug through the head. Babe, we are coming into South Lake Tahoe. Keep an eye out for cop cars. I don't know if they are looking for Helmut, or me, but just look around."

"And what are you going to do if I spot one? Are you going to make a run through the blockade set up next to Harvey's Hotel? Or are we about to die in a hail of bullets like Bonnie and Clyde. Jesus, Bear, you know better than to put me into a situation where we are overtly breaking the law."

"Sorry. There wasn't time to do anything else."

As my pickup crossed the state line, I said, "Helmut, you can breath a little easier. If Willow tracks you down to California, there ain't nothing that says she won't try to execute you, but—"

Flo said, "I think you mean extradite Helmut, not execute him. By the way, Helmut, did you shoot your brother?"

"No! He was my best friend."

Flo said, "So why do the cops think you did the dirty deed?"

"Babe, it's complicated. Helmut found the body. He stepped in a pool of blood. He picked up the murder weapon."

"And we're risking arrest because he told you he didn't murder his brother? Pull over and let me out. I'll call a friend and she'll give me a ride back to Carson City."

"Babe, calm down. I'm doing this 'cause Pinky told me to. Remember? You can't go home or the boss will fire both of us." I drove the truck into the parking space for Pinky's condo and pulled on the brake. "Besides, look at that blue sky, and the bright sun. I'll take care of Pinky and Helmut. Get your bathing suit on, head out to the beach, and soak up some rays."

Flo jumped out, grabbed her bag, and said, "Whatever."

Chapter Four

Pinky—Carson City, Nevada

The intercom buzzed and Mabel said, "It's Willow on your line."

I lifted the handset. "Willow, my love. I can pick up two rib-eye steaks that will pair perfectly with a 1987 cabernet I have—"

"Can it, Pinky. We can't find Helmut. We can't find Bear or Flo, and Detective Spaulding and I can't quite figure out how to tie you to their being gone. Speaking of Detective Spaulding, she recently joined the Carson City force. She came from Sausalito because her widowed mother, who lives in Carson City, became too ill to live alone. Henrietta felt it was time to assist her mother. I tell you this so you will understand Henrietta's situation and perhaps you can cut her a little slack during your future encounters."

"Of course. I will direct Mabel to send her mother a get-well-soon card. Now, back to those steaks—

"No steaks. No dinners. No nothing between us but work until the Ludwig Kaufmann case is closed. Now, I don't know where you found the time but according to Henrietta, you are now representing Helmut Kaufmann. Am I correct?"

"You are."

"Then you should hurry over to my office. Honoring my prosecutorial commitment of full

29

disclosure, and the fact that we once had true feelings for each other, I will present all the evidence we have against your client. The moment I am finished, I am positive you will make me a laughable plea bargain—an offer no District Attorney in his, or her, right mind would consider much less accept. Are you still listening to me?"

"I am, but—"

"Pinky, be quiet for a change. Can you hear the drum roll and the trumpets playing in the background? You know what I am talking about— the celebratory anthem that always proceeds monumental news? Counselor, I have in front of me the story of your legal demise and it will be disseminated throughout Northern Nevada once the Kaufmann trial is over. My dear ex-husband, if you insist on defending Helmut Kaufmann during his first-degree murder trial, then I can guarantee that your one hundred percent acquittal record will come to an abrupt end!"

After having just been accused of a criminal act by my favorite ex-wife, I struggled to maintain my composure. "Willow, you think your facts are bullet proof. However, in previous trials your evidence always ended up looking like pieces of Chantilly Lace."

Willow said, "I knew you were stubborn but what about the fact that Helmut's business was about to go bankrupt? And that Helmut had contacted an east coast coin dealer to find out the auction value of the 1894 S dime? Or the fact that—"

"Those damning facts, as you call them, could all have reasonable explanations. From my viewpoint, they—"

"Pinky, where is Helmut? Every hour that passes puts you, and your right to practice law in Nevada, in jeopardy. If Helmut turns himself in, I can guarantee that there will be no investigation concerning an obstruction of justice case against you. However, as we speak, I have on my desk a request from Detective Spaulding for a search warrant of your house, your office, and other properties you own to seek the proof that you conspired to assist the escape of the suspected murderer, Helmut Kaufmann. Then she will question your entire staff: Mabel, then Bear and Flo when we find them."

My stomach tightened the moment Willow mentioned Mabel's name. Bear and Flo had been around this block more than once, but Mabel? I knew if Detective Spaulding took Mabel downtown, placed her in an interrogation room, and asked her if Helmut had ever been in my office, she would crack faster than Humpty-Dumpty. I said, "My dear, if by the wildest chance, Helmut Kaufmann contacted me, I promise that—"

"Not good enough. I'm positive you have him stuck away in one of your hide-a-ways. The Sheriff checked out both of your condos near Glenbrook Bay and came up empty handed. As we speak, I have a member of my staff reviewing all the real estate records for Lake Tahoe, on both sides of the Nevada and California state line."

It took all my years of court room stoicism to choke back the rise of stomach bile in my esophagus. Willow had just informed me that sooner or later, a member of her staff would discover that I owned a beach-front condo on the California side of the border. I said, "As you know, Bear is in my employ. I will contact him, ask him to begin a search for this man, Helmut Kaufmann, and if and when Bear is successful, he will turn Kaufmann over to you."

"Still not good enough. When we find the condo, and Bear, and Kaufmann, your conviction for obstruction of justice will be a slam-dunk!"

I found myself in an indefensible position, and taking into consideration that line from The Man of La Mancha, 'Whether a rock hits a pitcher, or the pitcher hits a rock, it's not going to be good for the pitcher', I was the pitcher and could see that it was now time for a strategic retreat. "I will contact Bear, and see if—"

"No more, 'I'll call Bear'. I want that fugitive in custody now!"

This situation was deteriorating from a strategic retreat to an out-and-out rout. "Hold on, Willow." I pulled out my cell and hit Bear's number.

"Hi, Boss. What do you need?"

Knowing that Willow was listening in on every word I said, "My boy, control your incessant prattle and listen. Your turn to speak will come soon enough. Now hold on."

"Willow, do I have your word that if I can come up with a way to convince Helmut Kaufmann to turn himself in, that our previous discussion concerning obstruction of justice will vanish quicker than a morning fog?"

"I agree."

The muscles that had constricted my stomach,

thus forcing the acid reflux into my throat, slowly relaxed. I moved my cell closer to my mouth. "Bear, bring your guest to Willow's office at once. The whole process should take you no more than an hour so I will meet you there in fifty-five minutes to facilitate any concerns your guest might have."

"Boss, if you're talking about you-know-who turning himself in, that'll cause him a shit-pot full of problems."

"Damn it, I did not call to listen to your blather. You have your task to complete, but do not inform your guest as to the eventual outcome of your journey back to Carson City."

Bear growled, "Pinky, this is the most chicken shit plan you've ever come up with."

"That is not your concern. Now get to work."

"Okay, but I don't want to be there when they slap the cuffs on him."

Chapter Five

Bear—South Lake Tahoe, California

As I stuffed my cell into my pocket, Flo walked in, her super body all wet and shiny with that suntan oil, "Who was on the phone? The legal shrimp-king of Northern Nevada?"

"Yup."

Flo got real close and took my face with both her hands. "I don't like your expression. What the hell is going on?"

Before I could answer Flo, Helmut walked in from the lake and stood behind her. He said, "What's up?"

I gave Flo my don't-you-say-a-word stare, and said, "Nothing much. How's the beach by the lake working out?"

"Bear, Flo, simple words cannot express my gratitude. The condo and the beach are outstanding. I'm not in jail, and—"

I said, "What do you think happened to that dime worth a couple of million?"

Helmut said, "I don't know. God knows I could use the money."

Flo glanced at me and said, "Helmut, we all could use some extra money, but two million is a bit much, don't you think?"

"Not in my case. My business, Kaufmann Development, has been going through hard times."

I said, "How hard is hard?"

Helmut looked at me and shook his head. "Bear, I think explaining everything would go beyond your ability to comprehend the subtle nuances of the world of commerce."

Flo said, "Try me, buster. I've run more than one successful business."

Helmut hesitated.

I said, "Cough it up or you'll be back in Carson City before Flo changes out of her bathing suit."

Helmut shrugged his shoulders, "My business, Kaufmann Development, constructed strip malls throughout Nevada. Those were the heady days with money rolling in faster than I could bank it—until the economy collapsed a few years ago."

Flo said, "I'll bet you financed each strip mall with a mortgage, sold the mortgage, and then used those funds to finance your next, larger project, right?"

Helmut nodded. "Correct."

Flo said, "Sort of like check kiting, but legal."

Helmut glared at Flo. "Let's say I agree to disagree with your check kiting definition."

Flo shook her head. "Buster, you call it what you want, but if your business plan was so damn good, how come you ended up underwater?"

Helmut sighed, "I thought I had the perfect business plan, until the money market dried up and I couldn't find a buyer for my one-point-seven million dollar mortgage. Stuck with an empty strip mall, and drowning under monthly payments I couldn't make, I contacted my brother and asked him for help."

Flo said, "You're not the Lone Ranger. The financial hurricane that hit in 2008 caused more than one business to collapse."

I said, "Hey, even a dumb-shit like me knows a bunch of joints went belly-up. Why do you think what happened to you was any different?"

"Sorry, I did not mean to leave you with that impression."

"Okay. Then what happened?"

"Ludwig, my dear brother, offered to help me out, no, that's not correct, he offered to loan me the funds I needed to pay off the mortgage."

Flo said, "And the missing dime, the one worth a couple of million, was going to be your ticket back to solvency?"

"That is correct. Flo, you do understand the world of business."

I said, "Helmut, listen to me. You needed the bucks. Your brother had a dime worth a lot. You go to your brother's house. Your brother ends up dead. Do you understand why the cops think you did the dirty deed?"

Helmut said, "I know it looks bad, but I didn't kill my brother."

Flo said, "Okay, forget the murder. What about the dime? Did you take it?"

"No! I'm a numismatist, just like my brother, but in my case I'm an amateur collector. He made his living buying and selling coins from collectors in every state of the union. Most importantly, he was known as a man of high integrity, a collector who would give everyone an honest appraisal concerning the true value of a coin, unlike Carlo Bonato, or that female who goes by the name, Madam May-ling Soong. Both of them were known to have unsavory reputations in the tightly-knit, and sometimes shady world of coin collecting."

Flo said, "Cut to the chase, Helmut."

"Last week, a few days before my brother was murdered, the Nevada Coin Collectors Show closed in Reno. Everyone who was anyone in the world of coin collecting was in Northern Nevada for the show. My brother had a booth where he bought and sold coins. I was there with my brother and know for a fact that Bonato, and Madam Soong, were at the coin show. More importantly, they both questioned Ludwig, in great detail, about his very rare dime."

Flo said, "Their motive sounds a little thin, but it's better than nothing. Now, Helmut, look me straight in the eye and tell me that you didn't have anything to do with the disappearance of your brother's million plus dime."

Flo stood nose to nose with Helmut while he told her what he told me. Then Flo said, "I believe you. Now, go back to the beach. I have to talk to Bear in private."

The minute he cleared the condo Flo got real close and grabbed my face with both her hands again. "I asked you this before Helmut interrupted us. What the hell is going on? I still don't know why we're standing in the living room of Pinky's Lake Tahoe condo?"

"The cops were about to arrest Helmut so Pinky told me to drive him up here, and then a couple of minutes ago he called and told me to drive Helmut back to Carson City and hand him over to Willow."

Flo's face got all scrunched up. "But we're both sure he's innocent."

"Yup! Babe, I know dudes sometimes stretch the truth, especially when they're talking about shooting their brother in the head, but I'm damn positive Helmut didn't kill his brother."

Before Flo could say anything, my cell buzzed. I checked the screen and it was Pinky. I looked at Flo. "Shit, it's the boss again. We can't turn an innocent man over to the cops for a murder he didn't commit. What am I going to tell him?"

Chapter Six

Pinky—Carson City, Nevada

"Tempus fugit, my boy. Can I expect Helmut to walk into Willow's office momentarily?"

"Don't think so. We ran into a snag. Helmut and Flo were sunning on the beach. Flo came inside to go to the can, and when she went back to the beach Helmut was long gone."

"What do you mean he is gone? That man is a fugitive from the law. He is wanted in Nevada for the first-degree murder of his brother and I promised Willow that he would turn himself in within the hour."

"I know all that, but how can I turn the dude over to Willow if I don't know where he is?"

"Hold on!"

I glanced at Willow. Her eyes were cold, as if we had never met before. She shook her head and said, "Don't bother to make up a cock-and-bull story. I got all the information I needed from listening to your half of the conversation. Pinky, my office will immediately make a request of a judge to issue a warrant for your arrest concerning an obstruction of justice charge. It is now four o'clock, and if by some miracle, you can come up with Helmut Kaufmann, and bring him to me before five, the warrant will be quashed. However, if Helmut Kaufmann, at the stroke of five, remains a fugitive, you are looking at jail time and a revocation of your right to practice law in this state."

Seldom am I caught off guard, but frankly I was stunned by Willow's vicious vitriol. My God, she was my favorite ex-wife and the woman was treating me as if I were a common criminal. "My dear, I take your accusations as a personal attack on my motives, honesty, and ethical conduct. I am doing my best to track down the aforementioned fugitive, and I will call upon my vast legal resources to fight your obstruction of justice charge. Perhaps your trumped up accusation would stand up in a third world country, but, as you well know, we live in the United States of America, which has a constitution, and a Bill of Rights that guarantees all of its citizens the right to a fair trial of their peers. You, my dear, lack the evidence that will prove, beyond a shadow of doubt, that I obstructed anything in any way, shape, or form. In fact, while you stood at my side, you heard me tell my chief investigator to bring the fugitive to your office tout de suite."

"Pinky, don't make me take you to court."

I directed my voice to my cell phone. "Bear, did you hear what Willow just said to me?"

"Yup!"

"So are you going to do what I told you to do?"

"Boss, as soon as we find the dude, I'll toss him in the truck and shoot down Highway 50 to Willow's office."

"Thank you, my boy. Now, I am going to put my cell phone on speaker and ask you to repeat your exact words to the Carson County District Attorney."

40

While Willow listened to Bear babble on, I considered my personal predicament. While I would never admit it to her face, Willow did have a potential case for obstruction of justice against me. The accusation was not a slam dunk, but I did not feel one hundred percent comfortable that I would escape with an acquittal either. I decided it was time for me to propose a détente.

I caught Willow's attention and said, "Please allow me to talk with Bear when you are finished."

She nodded and a moment later she handed me the phone. I stepped into the hall and said, "Bear, you put Helmut in your truck, and have him walking into Willow's office in less than an hour, or you will spend the rest of your days dicing onions at your mother's restaurant at the Star Hotel in Elko. Have I made myself clear?"

He did not respond. Then I heard Bear arguing with someone and Flo came on the line. "What did you just say to my man?"

"I said deliver Helmut inside an hour to Willow or find yourself another line of work! And do not construe my last statement as an idle threat. Helmut Kaufmann turns himself over to Willow in less than sixty minutes or your lover-boy returns to the job of tending bar and moping up vomit, two tasks he can handle."

Chapter Seven

Bear—Lake Tahoe, California

After I told Willow I'd toss Helmut in my truck, shoot down Highway 50, and hand him over to the cops, Pinky came back on the line and said, "Thank you, my boy. I think that should satisfy an overzealous prosecutor." The line went dead, and like I said, there are lots of times when I don't have a clue what the hell is going on when I talk to the boss.

Flo said, "I'm still waiting to find out why you and I are standing in Pinky's condo?"

"Pinky told me to. Now he wants me to go back to Carson City and give Helmut up to Willow."

"Why would that shrimp . . . forget it. Wait a minute. We both think that Helmut is innocent of murdering his brother. Why are we turning him over to Willow?"

"You're right! If we do that the cops will stop looking for the real killer."

"So we agree that we're between a rock and a hard spot."

"Yup! We both work for Pinky, and he pays us damn good money for doing damn near nothing. Babe, as long as we want to keep bringing in the big bucks for not doing much, we've got to take Helmut back to Carson City."

"If Pinky told you to hit Helmut in the head with a baseball bat would you do that?"

"Shit no, at least I don't think so!"

"But you're willing to turn him over to Willow, who'll punch his express ticket to the State pen, where a guy will strap him on a gurney and shoot some poison into his arm?"

"Okay, so we can't turn him over to Willow, but what can we do and still keep our jobs?"

Flo walked to the window where the sun sparkled off her pretty hair. I could stare at her hair, looking like that for a long time, but I've got to admit that eventually my eyes finally settled on her pair to die for.

Finally she noticed where my eyes were looking, "Bear, get your mind out of the gutter and concentrate on the problem at hand. Wait a minute, I can check out the names Helmut gave us on the internet."

Flo turned on the computer and her fingers flashed across the keyboard. This babe's got the brains to match her boobs. In fact, she's the only person in Carson City who can beat Pinky in a game of checkers by topping each one of his nasty moves with a move that's even nastier.

After a couple of minutes, she turned and smiled. "I think I've got the answer, but first, did Pinky give you some expense money?"

"Yup. I already told you about five G's hidden in a not-too-hard-to-find hiding place."

"Right. We'll drive Helmut to Carson City at once, and along the way, pick him up a toothbrush so he can keep his teeth clean while he's in jail awaiting trial."

"What do you mean? We're going to turn him over to Willow?"

"Somebody has to discover which of those two suspects actually murdered Ludwig Kaufmann. The web site told me that Bonato has a coin shop in Wilmington, North Carolina, and Madam Soong runs a similar operation in Kailua, Hawaii. Now all we have to do is go to Hawaii, and—"

"Hold on, Babe. If anyone is going to end up in Hawaii it'll be Pinky. "

"Fine. I guess we both deserve a vacation on the coast of North Carolina."

Things were happening too fast for me to keep up. "But Babe, we don't know if Bonato, or Soong killed—"

"Put a sock in it and let me finish explaining my plan."

"Okay. What's next?"

"After we take Helmut back to Carson City and give him up to Willow, we can go to Pinky's office and pick up a ten thousand advance on expenses."

"Ten grand? I don't think Pinky will go—"

"As I said, let me finish. I'll explain to Pinky about Bonato and Soong, and how one of the two has to be the murderer."

"But we don't know —"

"For the last time, be quiet. Give me the five G's and I'll put the money in my purse while you call Pinky. Tell him that we'll have Helmut in Willow's office in an hour."

"Wow, that'll make him happy."

Flo said, "On second thought, I'll call him with the good news." She hit the speaker button and after a couple of seconds we both heard Pinky answer. "Hello."

"Pinky, it's Flo."

"Where are you?"

"We haven't left the condo yet."

"What!"

"Pinky, sometimes you're such an ass, and after all the effort I've done on your behalf to get you to the Kona Coast of Hawaii."

"What did you just say?"

"The Kona Coast of the big island. We've interrogated Helmut. The man's innocent, in case you're interested, and he gave us two prime suspects. One, a beautiful Asian female who goes by the name of May-ling Soong. Madam Soong runs a coin shop in Kailua, and according to Helmut, she has a very unsavory reputation in the coin collecting world."

Pinky said, "And who is the other suspect?"

"A man named Carlo Bonato. He is also a coin dealer with an equally repugnant reputation. Bonato lives in Wilmington, North Carolina. Of course, if you want to pursue the man in the land of humidity, gators, and grits, and leave the lovely Madam Soong to us—"

"You do what you have to do to get Helmut into Willow's office in forty-five minutes and I will send the both of you to the low country of North Carolina."

"We'll require a ten thousand dollar advance for our expenses."

"Damn it!"

"Pinky, no ten grand, no Helmut."

"Fine. I will contact Mabel and tell her to give you a cash advance of $10,000. However, if Helmut is not standing in Willow's office, inside of forty-two

45

minutes, the advance money, and your boyfriend's cushy job, along with yours, will be history."

My babe's voice dripped honey, "See you-all in thirty minutes, and if you even think of reneging on the ten grand advance, I will swear to Willow, under oath, that you told Bear to take Helmut across the state line to California."

Flo killed the call and said, "That should do it. Willow gets her man, Pinky gets to chase a good looking woman around Hawaii, and we get a nice vacation on the coast of North Carolina."

I said, "Babe, you never can tell. Maybe Pinky will change his mind and go to North Carolina."

"That will happen just after pigs learn to fly. No, that pint-size attorney will go to the Kona Coast and we'll fly to North Carolina."

"Will North Carolina work out for you?"

"Hey, it beats the hell out of suffering through the stifling heat of Needles for nearly a month!"

"But Babe, I still don't feel good about turning Helmut over to Willow when we're sure he's innocent."

"I don't know what else to do. Besides, you know Pinky. We'll convince him that either Madam Soong, or Bonato, murdered Ludwig. Hell, Pinky doesn't give a damn which one shot poor old Ludwig, as long as it's not his client."

"Babe, besides having a great body, you've got brains."

"I'm happy to hear that you finally recognize that fact, but I would appreciate if in the future, when you admire my brain, you'll lift your eyes off my boobs and stare into my big blue eyes."

"Oh my God, your eyes ARE blue!"

46

Chapter Eight

Pinky—Carson City, Nevada

Memories of walking hand-in-hand, with Willow, on Hapuna beach flooded my thoughts. We were on our honeymoon and we acted as if we were in our teens. She pushed me into the surf. I dragged her in with me and we fell into the warm ocean. How we laughed. We were in love and . . .

My subconscious picked up the faint sound of a phone ringing. I glanced at my watch. I had three hours before my flight to the Kona Coast, just enough time to grab a drink at the airport before my plane took . . .

The ringing continued—an indication that my office phone was not being answered swept away my happy memories of Hawaii.

I buzzed Mabel.

No answer.

I buzzed her a second time.

And again no response.

I stormed out of my office and Mabel's desk was empty. In fact, I was the only person in the outer office. I grabbed the phone and snapped, "Hello!"

"Mr. Delmont, Louis Loomer here—the owner of Rapid Replacement. I understand that you have an immediate need for someone to answer your phones and take messages, and a second requirement for a candidate to manage your office affairs on a permanent basis."

What was he talking about? I glanced down and spotted an envelope in the middle of Mabel's desk. "Loomer, I have another call. I will get back to you in a few moments."

"Mr. Delmont, I pray you do not procrastinate. Competent legal secretaries are rarer than hens' teeth these days and it's only because of the excellent business relationship we have built over the years that I feel obligated to help you to fill your immediate needs. I was about to send my top legal secretary to one of your competitors when—"

Fighting back the anger that was attempting to take over my voice, I said, "Loomer, I told you I would call you back." And I slammed the receiver down.

I slumped into Mabel's chair and opened the envelope.

Pinky,

I was very grateful that you gave me a second chance when you hired me back some months ago.

At that time, I told you that I would never challenge your authority again and I kept my promise until your ruffian investigator, Mr. Zabarte, came to me and demanded a $10,000 advance so that he, and his 'live-in' paramour, could spend a month vacationing in North Carolina.

We both know that at one time, Mr. Zabarte was a murderer whose next address was sure to be the State Penitentiary, until you used your courtroom skills to get the man an acquittal. Since you managed his release from prison only God knows what he has done to other law abiding citizens.

And that brazen woman who lives in sin with Mr. Zabarte forces me to daily call upon what's left of my Christian charity. As you requested, I gave the money to the two, but reminded them both that all expenditures will require a receipt of the expense or that money will come out of their pockets. I know that you did not authorize me to make such a statement and I accept that what I told Mr. Zabarte could be considered by you as a challenge to your authority.

However, my error was a minor digression compared to your bald-faced lie concerning the whereabouts of Mr. Kaufmann to the Carson City Detective, Henrietta Spaulding along with the possibility that you might expect me to give false testimony concerning your illegal activities with Mr. Kaufmann.

Under those circumstances, I contacted Mr. Loomer and told him that I would be abandoning my post and that you would require immediate assistance.

Please send my final check to my sister, Myrtle Potts, in Billings Montana. Her address is in my personnel file.

With this letter I tender my immediate and final resignation.
Sincerely,
Mabel Potts

My grandfather always told me, "Pincus, you can't trust anyone, and that includes me," then he would chuckle, as if to indicate that I really could trust him. But Mabel's actions reminded me of my grandfather's sage advice. I never should have given that woman a second chance. I grabbed the phone and keyed in the number for Rapid Replacement.

"Rapid Replacement. You need 'em—we get 'em. Louis Loomer, here."

"Louis, as you insinuated during your previous call, I do need someone immediately, and also a permanent legal secretary. I'm looking for a female, twenty-five to thirty-five who can take dictation, run my office computer system, and, finally, show up on time every day, and who speaks only when spoken to."

"Ah . . . Mr. Delmont, some of your requirements are a little harsh, if not illegal. Perhaps this is the reason you have so much trouble keeping—"

"Mr. Loomis, I am a lawyer, and as such, my clients seek advice and counsel. I require an employee who understands and adheres to the attorney/client privilege—an employee who does what she is told to do without argument or complaint—an employee who will show initiative, and understand that initiative is what I expect from her—an employee who keeps her personal ideas and complaints to herself. Was that specific enough for you?"

"Yes. I will have a clerk to answer the phones in your office in five minutes. As far as a permanent legal secretary, that could take an hour."

"Not good enough. Presently, I represent a client who is accused of a capital crime and I must leave my office in less than an hour for an extended period of time."

"How long a period are you talking about?"

"I could be gone for a month."

I heard Loomis sigh. "Mr. Delmont, you are in luck. At this very moment, I am talking to a candidate that I feel will fit your narrow criteria. Her name is Pamela Carson. She recently left an identical position with a well respected San Francisco law firm."

I said, "Why did the woman leave a good position with a top San Francisco firm and move to Carson City?"

"Just a moment . . . Ms. Carson, would you excuse us for a moment? Thank you . . . Mr. Delmont, according to Ms. Carson, she left San Francisco due to a deteriorating personal relationship. I have in my hand a glowing recommendation from her previous employer."

There are times when you have to trust your gut and with my flight leaving Reno shortly, this was one of those moments. "Send her over. I will check her out, and if she passes muster, I will give her a crash course on my office protocol."

"Thank you, Mr. Delmont."

"Call me Pinky."

"Thank you, Pinky. I will cancel your request for a clerk to answer phones, and Ms. Carson will be by your side in five minutes. I will bill you for our latest transaction and I need to warn you that there will be an additional surcharge for the rush situation concerning the placement of Ms. Carson."

"Louis, I understand that emergency situations call for emergency surcharges."

51

A few moments later Pamela Carson walked
into my office and I knew this was going to work.
She was around five feet, very attractive, light
blonde hair, and had those azure blue eyes that
every woman would kill for.

She walked directly to Mabel's desk and
glanced around with a knowing look.

I thrust my hand in her direction and said, "I
am J. Pincus Delmont, known to everyone in
Carson City as Pinky."

She took my hand and smiled. "I'm Pamela
Carson, known to my friends, and that includes my
employer, as Pam. I've worked in the legal world
for five years and there's not much I haven't seen,
or heard. Pinky, that's my way of telling you that I
am the right person for your vacant position."

Pam was knowledgeable concerning the
computerized scheduling system that my practice
uses for my daily calendar. She had previously
worked with the courts to juggle court calendars. In
short, the woman seemed to be the answer to my
problem.

I said, "Pam, I will contact my banker and
each week, while I am in Hawaii, he will deposit
one hundred dollars into the office petty cash
account. While I am gone, you may receive calls, or
emails, from my investigator, Bear Zabarte, or his
female companion. At present, they are both in
North Carolina and under no circumstance should
either one be trusted."

"Pinky, I may be talking myself out of a job,
but I have to ask the obvious question— why would
you employee investigators you do not trust?"

I smiled. "My dear, your job is safe.

Occasionally those two create more problems than they resolve, but overall, they get the job done and in the final analysis, that is more important. The old adage, "keep your friends close, but keep your enemies closer" is a perfect example of why I continue to employ Bear and Florence. Now this is very important. Those two have been given a ten thousand dollar advance for their expenses, more than enough cash to complete their investigative task."

"Ten thousand dollars? My God, are they going to be there for a couple of months?"

"No, and the exorbitance of that advance is the single reason I fired the woman who used to occupy the chair where you now sit. If Bear or Flo calls for more money, respond to their request with an emphatic no! One final point on the subject of my investigators. When you deal with Bear remember that he is blessed with an attribute he defines as positive—street smarts—but from my viewpoint the man's IQ is slightly below that of a three-toed sloth. On the other hand, Florence is a cunning and manipulative femme fatale so be on your guard at all times. If either one bothers you, call me and I will take care of the problem."

I checked my watch and saw that I had less than an hour and a half before my plane took off. I picked up my suitcase and gave my final instructions.

"Pam, you can reach me at the Sheraton Kona Resort at Keauhou Bay. I will be housed there for a few days, or my stay could be extended based on unknown factors. As such, I will need you to keep on top of my court dates and reschedule when needed. Do I make my self clear?"

"I understand so don't worry. Pinky, I've got your back. I know you are going to the Kona Coast due to business requirements, but be sure to take a few moments each day to enjoy the beach, the warm, gentle breeze, and the incomparable sunsets."

"I will take heed of your advice. And if anything comes up that you feel you can not handle, please feel free to call me."

"I will do that, but only if everything else fails." Pam opened her purse, pulled out a crisp ten dollar bill, and handed the note to me. "Have your first Mai Tai on me. Aloha!"

I grabbed my suitcase and rushed to my car, but as I set the bag in the trunk, I realized that I had forgotten my briefcase.

I ran back to my office, opened the front door, and noticed that Pam was talking on the phone. Her back was to me but I heard her say in a forceful voice, "Look, you are not the only person in this world capable of finding things. I tracked you down because you charged your stay at a Carson City motel on our joint credit card the day before you closed the account. Darling, in 1697 William Congreve wrote: 'Hell has no fury like a woman scorned.' Since then, more than three hundred years have passed, but Congreve's simple declaration still hits the mark. Meet with me at the law office of J. Pincus Delmont, or . . . "

When a passing car honked its horn, Pam turned and saw me standing in the doorway. She lowered her voice to a whisper but I still picked up her closing remark. "Face it. I'm here in Carson

City and I'm not going away . . . Don't threaten me. Threats can be a two-way street."

She set the phone down and made a valiant attempt at a smile. "Pinky, I thought you had a plane to catch."

"I do, but I forgot my briefcase."

Pam grabbed my attaché, walked to the door, and handed it to me.

"Here it is. Sorry about that personal call. Just trying to clear up a simple disagreement with my San Francisco landlord over a thousand-dollar cleaning deposit."

"I understand." After a perfunctory nod in her direction, I turned and made sure my expression did not waver until I reached my car.

As I drove to the airport I considered the limited alternatives I had at my disposal.

One: Return to my office and immediately fire Pam Carson for lying to my face. However, that action would leave my law practice unattended while I was in Hawaii.

Two: Do nothing and hope that Pam's personal problems resolve themselves.

Three: Before I boarded my plane, call Willow, explain what I had overheard from Pam's call, and ask her to keep an eye on things while I was gone.

Obviously, for my legal practice, and my mental welfare, the call to Willow was my only viable possibility.

While I shuffled through the security lines at the airport I pondered my recent lack of success concerning the women I had hired through the Rapid Replacement Company and I knew I had to do something concerning the shoddy Louis Loomer operation.

Suddenly, I recalled the previous week and my last interaction with Florence, when she showed me how to use my new iPhone 4S.

Flo said, "Pinky, your new iPhone is like your old one but the 4S has Siri."

"Who?"

"Not who. Siri is a part of your iPhone. It's almost like you have a tiny secretary living inside the case."

"Stop talking to me like I am a child and demonstrate what you are blathering about!"

Flo proceeded to lift the iPhone to her ear and she said, "Siri."

A voice came from my iPhone. "How may I assist you?"

Then Flo said, "Call Pinky's office."

In a moment, my office phone rang. I picked up the handset and heard Flo say, "That's a demonstration. Now do you understand?"

Oh my God! Flo didn't push any buttons. She just commanded, 'Call Pinky's office.' I am an attorney by profession, and as such, any waste of my valuable time keeping abreast of the latest technological advancements was not a good use of my day, but Siri seemed like magic.

"Pinky, Siri is like having a secretary, or a personal assistant in your pocket. All you have to do is lift the phone to your ear and tell Siri what you want her to do."

Now, a week later, and with some trepidation, I pulled out my iPhone, and said, "Siri." After I heard a couple of beeps, I said, "Remind me when I return to my office to fire the Rapid Replacement company."

I listened to Siri's voice repeat my reminder request. For the moment I was pleased with my new found success until I recalled that it was Bear's witch who taught me how to use the new technology.

A voice over the loudspeaker informed me that first class passengers were starting to board. Emboldened with my first use of my pocket personal assistant, I lifted the iPhone to my ear and said, "Siri." I heard her response and than I said, "Call Willow."

A moment later, Willow answered. "Pinky, now that Helmut Kaufmann is in jail, are you calling to beg my forgiveness?"

"How did you know it was me calling?"

"Caller ID."

"Oh! Yes I am calling for your forgiveness and a minuscule favor."

"With you there is no such thing as a small favor. Go ahead and ask, but I warn you, I'm still mad so don't get your hopes up."

"Mabel just resigned. She received a telegram that her sister Myrtle, the one who lives in Billings, Montana, is very ill. In fact, her sister might not live through the month. As much as I needed Mabel, the charity in my heart would not allow me to say no, so I have now been placed, through no fault of my own, into a—"

"What is that booming voice in the background? Where are you calling from?"

"I am at the Reno airport and that voice is telling me that I must board my plane at once. Willow, I hired a replacement for Mabel, a woman named Pam Carson. She is experienced and should be able to cover my practice while I am gone. However, I overheard her arguing with someone on the phone, about following her to Carson City, and then she threatened that person. When Pam realized that I may have monitored some of her conversation, she lied to me as to the content. The favor I ask is for you to drop by every couple of days and check to be sure that my new employee has not done anything untoward."

"Hold on, you're leaving an untested, and possibly suspicious woman to run your office? Where are you going? Why is this trip more important than your practice? Pinky, answer me or—"

"Sorry my dear, a flight attendant just told me to turn my cell phone off. I'll call you tomorrow." The flight attendant part wasn't true, but Willow could not know that and I did not feel like explaining to her that I was going to the Kona Coast where she and I had spent our honeymoon. I handed my boarding pass to the attendant, walked down the jet way, and found my first class seat. A comely stewardess approached and asked, "Mr. Delmont, would you care for a drink before we take off?"

"Please call me Pinky. Yes, I could use a libation. A gin and tonic, and make that a double."

"Whatever you say, Pinky."

As she left, I lifted my phone to my ear, heard the two beeps that indicated Siri was waiting for my latest instruction. I said, "Siri, in eight hours remind me to send Willow a five-pound box of chocolate-covered Macadamia nuts."

58

Chapter Nine

Bear—Southport, North Carolina

We could've—no damn it—we should've moved into a cheap motel in Wilmington—but no, Miss high and mighty told me to drive our rental car south—to the dumb—no, Flo called it quaint— whatever the hell that means—to the town of Southport.

Southport ain't a really bad place, in fact it's on the ocean, with fisherman and fishing boats, and lots of restaurants with fresh fish, but once in a while I want to eat a big juicy hamburger, with ketchup, two slabs of meat, and mustard dribbling down my chin—not the fresh catch of the day, every day, day after day!

And every restaurant in North Carolina serves hush puppies with every meal. After a couple of days, I'd had my fill of those little balls of fried dough made out of smashed corn.

And another thing! In the summer it can get hot in Carson City, but like Needles, it's a dry heat. I never tumbled to that dry heat crap until we got to North Carolina. Now I know the difference between a dry and a wet heat. Trust me, when it's 90 degrees with 98 percent humidity, all anybody has to do is stand there and they'll start sweating like a pig. And the air's so thick that you can damn near chew it.

But that's what I think. Flo tells me that it's

not really so bad, but I notice she finds an excuse to duck into every air conditioned store she can find.

Sort of like, "Oh Bear, this is a cute place. They could have a bathing suit I might want to buy."

Or, "I like the look of this shop. They might have the perfect soap dish to fit our bathroom decor."

Or—ouch!

Flo pulled her elbow out of my side and said, "What were you mumbling about?"

"Nothing. Have you finished shopping yet? It's hot, and my Red Sox are playing a game on TV, and —"

"Let's walk down the block into that nice restaurant. We ate there a couple of days ago and I just loved their fish and chips."

"But they served those damned hush puppies along with the french fries and that's just wrong."

"Go get us a table by the bar so you can watch the game. All you have to do is ask the bartender to put your damn baseball game on the TV. Now go away and let me shop in peace."

"Hey, downing a cool one and watching a ball game on TV beats standing in the sun, sweating like—"

"Stop complaining. Pinky sent us on an extended vacation. Sit back and enjoy!"

"Babe, we're not on a vacation. Pinky's ten G's is to do an investigation of the Botano dude and he'll expect something for his money. The least we can do is walk into Botano's coin shop and talk to him. It'll only take me a few minutes to figure out if he is a lowlife or an okay guy. How are we going to do that if we don't go to Wilmington?"

"Okay. After I check out this shop. It looks like there's a cute gift section inside."

For a second the sun caught Flo's face and she looked the same as the first time we met in LA. "Babe, was it three, or four years ago when we met? Remember? You cooked me that kick-ass breakfast after we did it and then you jumped into my car and we drove to Bakersfield."

Flo smiled like she was remembering that morning. "Go get a beer and stop trying to distract me. We'll go to Botano's place after I've checked out every soap dish in this shop."

If I knew Flo, and I did know this broad, she wouldn't go to Wilmington until she was good and ready and not a second sooner. Hold on, there was one way I knew to light a fire under her. "Babe, don't shop too long. According to the laws here in North Carolina, a dude shouldn't drive a car after he's downed more than eight brews."

As Flo walked into the store, she snapped, "I'll be with you in ten minutes, and don't you dare drink more than two beers, or you'll spend the night sleeping with the mosquitos."

A night fighting bugs slowed me down and I was halfway through my second cold one when she walked in and said, "Okay, buster, I'm ready to go to Wilmington, but you're in for a big surprise."

The Red Sox second baseman swung and poked a high fly ball to left field. "I can hardly wait."

"Get your eyes off that stupid baseball game and look at me."

The ball hit above the scoreboard and bounced

over the head of the dumb left fielder. Two runs scored and my Sox were now up by six runs. I turned. Flo was standing a couple of inches away and when I dragged my eyes off the TV screen I was staring directly at her beautiful boobs. "Babe, you're standing too close. I can't look into your baby-blue eyes without straining my neck."

"A likely story. The lady at that last shop asked me where I was going next. I told her Wilmington. She told me we should catch the state-run ferry about a mile from here. The ride is cheap. You get to see some great scenery, and it cuts twenty miles off the drive."

I tried to sneak a peek at the ballgame but Flo's boobs kept getting in my way. I said, "So what's your surprise?"

"That's it, damn it. We get to ride on the ferry. If we leave right now, we should be able to catch the next one."

I could see that I was going on a stupid boat ride instead of watching the last three innings of a great ballgame. I grumbled and downed the rest of my beer.

We walked back to the car. I had parked it under a tree but the inside of the rental was hotter than a pizza oven! We had to wait for a couple of minutes for the damn seats to cool down before we could sit on them. I turned the air on to high and we sat there with cool air blowing in our faces, but by the time I'd pulled out of the parking spot, even after all that time sitting in front of the car's AC, my shirt was soaked with sweat.

A few minutes later I pulled behind a line of cars and followed them onto the deck of the ferry.

I was trying to figure out if I should turn off the air when Flo said, "I have to pee."

Jesus, she has to pee more often than the whole Red Sox baseball team. "Babe, there's a sign over the door on my left that says restrooms."

She shook her head. "When I was seventeen, I tried to use the bathroom on a fishing boat once. You don't—"

"They're called 'heads' on a ship."

"I don't give a damn what they're called onboard a ship. Anyway, I walked through the bathroom door and found myself inside a tiny room about the size of a phone booth. The water sitting on the bottom of the toilet was sloshing back and forth as the ship was rocking. I latched the door, and immediately felt the onset of mal de mer."

"Mal de what?"

"I almost tossed my cookies."

"Oh

"You can't imagine my panic when I couldn't get the door unlatched."

"Did you barf all over everything?"

"No, I made it outside just in time to lean over the rail, but since that day, just the thought of entering a bathroom on anything that floats starts my stomach roiling."

"Can you hold it for thirty minutes?"

"I don't have to. There was a powder room inside the building where I purchased the ticket and that building is built on solid ground, not water."

I looked around the ferry. The little boat was filling up with cars and people. "You sure you can pee and get back on board before we leave the dock?"

Flo opened the car door and said, "I can if you'll stop asking me all these stupid questions."

She sprinted off the ferry and into the ticket building.

By this time I had a weird feeling things were starting to turn bad. My car was surrounded by other cars so there was no way I could back up before the ferry left the dock. I heard a couple of toots on the whistle above my head.

I glanced at the building and no Flo.

A dude on the dock threw a big rope with a loop on one end to another dude who stood on deck.

Still no Flo.

The whistle gave three hard toots and the ferry pulled away from the dock.

That's when Flo shot out of the building. Everybody on board saw her as she sprinted to the dock. They could all see that she wasn't going to make it, but they rooted for her anyway. I grabbed my cell phone, ran to the back end of the ferry and waved my cell phone. Flo stopped running when she saw she was not going to make it. Then she saw me standing on the ferry and pulled out her cell phone. I called her number. "Babe, sit tight. I'll talk with the head guy steering this tug, find out the fastest way to drive back to Southport, and I'll call you as soon as I figure out how long it'll take me."

She was blubbering. "Bear, I feel like such a fool. All those people on board saw me running to catch the ferry and I didn't make it."

When we first met, Flo cried a lot, like she was afraid of somebody, or something. But in the last couple of years, she hadn't cried once, at least not in front of me. "Babe, I promise I'll pound anyone I see laughing at you. You did the same thing I would have done if I had to decide between pissing in my pants, barfing, or missing a dumb ferry boat. Get out of the heat. Go back into the building, sit down and have a cool one. I'll call you as soon as I get some new skinny."

After my call to Flo, the ferry rounded a bend and the dock was gone from sight. I sat down and the shop lady was right. The ferry ride was a real surprise. The boat chugged past pretty birds and a cool-looking shoreline all the way to Wilmington.

Before we docked, I pulled out my cell phone and called Pinky's office. "Law Offices of J. Pincus Delmont."

Hey, that isn't Mabel. "Hey, who is this? Where's Mabel? And why are you answering Pinky's phones?"

"I'm going to make a quick assumption that I am talking to Bear Zabarte. If I am correct, just say yes, or you can grunt an acknowledgement."

Shit, Pinky went out and hired another ball-buster. "Yup, this is Bear, and who are—"

"My name is Pam Carson. Mabel Potts is on her way to Billings, Montana. I am answering Pinky's phones because I am his new legal secretary. Now that we've gone past those pleasantries, I do hope you are not calling Pinky for more funds. He gave me explicit instructions to deny any requests from you, or Florence, your investigative partner."

"Pinky told you what?" I growled.

"Temper, temper, Mr. Zabarte. It's nothing personal. Pinky informed me that you and Florence have been advanced ten thousand dollars for expenses."

Now, I know the next thing I said was dumb, but with Flo missing the ferry, and this new broad Pam ragging at me, my brain wasn't working at its best. "You just said ten thousand. Does that mean that Pinky doesn't know about the five G's we picked up when we were at his condo next to Lake Tahoe?"

"Not to my knowledge, but I'll be sure to report that information to him when he calls in later today."

"Shit!"

"Please Mr. Zabarte, no hissy fits. Now, do you have anything else to pass on to the big boss?"

"Babe, have you actually met Pinky?"

"My name is Pam, not Babe, and yes I have met Pinky."

"Pam, either you're blind, or bonkers, 'cause no one with half a brain would call Pinky big, except maybe Willow 'cause she knows him better than anyone else in Carson City."

"I take it that your last insult concerning your employer means that you have nothing further to report?"

"Well, almost nothing. We're in North Carolina. We've got a place to stay in Southport, and we've rented a car, and all the restaurants here serve fried fish, and you get hush puppies with every meal, but a cold brew or some cheap California red helps make up for the rest of it."

"Is that it?"

"I almost forgot. Tomorrow we'll go to Wilmington so I can nose around Botano's coin

66

shop."

"Nose around?"

"Look Babe—"

"I told you before my name is Pam."

"Right, it's Pam. Okay, Pam, you hide behind your desk and do your picky little job. Leave the dangerous investigative stuff to me and Flo. Got it?"

"Got it. Now here's a summary of your call."

"Damn, Mabel never did a summary of anything."

"I'm not Mabel. Now, this is what I will report to Pinky when he calls. After two days in North Carolina, you and Florence have managed to rent a car and a motel room—you have also determined that your nutritional needs are barely being met with fried fish and hush puppies. And finally, on your third day in the state, you will begin to do your investigative work by 'nosing around' the Botano coin shop in Wilmington. Did I miss anything?"

"One more thing, Babe."

"For the last time, my name is Pam."

"So what happens if I call you Babe again?"

"The moment I recognize it is you calling, I will terminate the call."

"Does terminate mean what I think it means?"

"Yes. I will not talk to you and I will hang up the phone. Considering that I answer all incoming phone calls to this office, that means you will never again be able to talk to Pinky via the phone."

Shit, why did Mabel have to go to Montana? "Okay, Pam, you got me. Hold on, you missed one thing on your summary—the part where I wash

67

down the fried fish and hush puppies with a couple of brews, and Flo chokes down those fried balls of corn mush with glasses of red wine."

"Got it. Thank you Bear. Pinky told me to expect the unusual when you called, but I do believe he understated the murkiness of your communicative abilities. Goodbye, and please pass on my sympathies to Florence. After one conversation with you, I have a funny feeling that she will need all the help she can find."

"Pam? You should call her Flo."

"But Pinky calls her Florence."

"We don't have the time to go through all the things that shrimp calls my babe. Just like you told me to call you Pam, and not Babe, call Flo by her real name, Flo, and we'll get along just fine."

"Loud and clear, Bear. From now on it's Flo."

Chapter Ten

Bear—Southport, North Carolina

It took me more than an hour to drive back to the Southport ferry terminal and Flo was pissed at me for taking so long. Shit, nobody told me that the ferry left me off on a road that I had to drive north for thirty minutes before I got to the highway to head back south so I could drive to Southport to pick up Flo at the ferry terminal. She pouted with her nasty look while I drove back to our motel, but after a couple of glasses of her crappy red wine, both Flo and the outside temperature cooled down enough so we could go out to dinner. I ordered the shrimp and grits and it was damn good. Flo got her fish and chips, and the waitress brought us a big basket of hush puppies in case we hadn't had enough of those fried balls of corn mush.

The next day, me and Flo started out to go to Wilmington and when I asked her if she wanted to take the ferry from Southport, she flashed her nastiest glare so I used the highway all the way.

On the outskirts of the downtown area, we drove down a street lined with really old, but well-kept houses.

Suddenly Flo yelled, "Slow down, damn it. I want to look at these beautiful houses."

I had to admit the old joints were pretty cool, but Flo seemed to forget that there were cars behind us. "Babe, I can't go any slower unless I want the truck behind us to start making love to our rental."

"Okay, then we'll walk. Find a place to park so I can stroll up and down the streets at my leisure."

"Jesus, it was eighty-five when we left the motel and even with the air on high, I'm sweating so much that I'll have to stop for a brew pretty soon just to keep me from becoming disagrated from the heat."

"Did you mean to say desiccated from the heat?"

"That's what I said."

Flo shook her head. "Doesn't make any difference. We're not going to stop for a brew due to disagration or desiccation. Now find a place to park under some shade and you can wait for me in the car."

I could see that I had no chance of ducking into a pub for a brew. And then, a half block away, behind the trunk of a giant tree, I spotted the store-front of the Botano Coin Shop, across the street from a funky-looking bar and an empty parking place by the curb.

I raced a pick-up to the empty spot, won, and ignored the middle-finger-salute the dude flashed me as he drove by in his bright red truck. "Babe, now you can look at all the houses you want to and afterwards we can do some nosing around Botano's joint."

Flo said, "It's too damn hot to wander around. We'll hit Botano's place. While you've been wasting your time watching baseball on TV, I've been reading up on coin collecting so let me do the talking. After we've finished with Mr. Botano, and if it becomes a bit cooler, I'll walk around and look at those marvelous homes."

"Or I could grab a cool one at the bar across the street."

Flo frowned and pushed me toward the coin shop.

I opened the door and heard a little bell ring.

The joint was small. There was not much more to it than a counter, a cash register, and about fifty fake gold coins displayed under the glass counter top. At least I was pretty sure the coins were fake 'cause it would be too easy for a dude to break the glass, grab the coins, and be gone before anybody could call the cops.

A short guy, maybe an inch taller than Pinky, was sitting behind the counter. A few hunks of hair combed over the top kept him from being called bald, and he had two gold teeth that showed when he opened his mouth. He set down a little spyglass kinda thing and a coin. "Good afternoon. May I help you?"

Flo muscled past me. The dude's eyes landed on her chest and got real wide. She said, "Good afternoon. My driver and I were enjoying your lovely southern mansions when I noticed your coin shop. Are you Mr. Botano?"

His eyes never left Flo's rack. "I am. Again, how may I assist you?"

"Mr. Botano, I have a question."

"Please, call me Carlo."

"Carlo, my late husband, Eric Johnson, collected coins." Flo stopped, took out a hankie from her purse and dabbed at her eyes. "Eric didn't collect in a big way mind you, he concentrated on a

71

small group of coins he admired."

Botano gave me the fish eye, like he was trying to figure out just where I fit into Flo's story. "And you want to find out the value of your late husband's collection."

Flo gave a nervous giggle. "How did you know that?"

"I am a professional numismatist. Buying and selling coins is my business. Can you give me a little more detail concerning your late husband's collection?"

Flo looked peaceful, like she was watching her late husband sitting on a cloud in heaven. "Eric had a love affair with what he called Morgan silver dollars. He told me they were minted near the end of the nineteenth century and—"

Botano interrupted. "Between 1878 to 1904 to be exact. The Morgan was revived for a short while in 1921, but—"

"I remember now. My husband told all his friends that he had only two loves in his life—little old me, and his Morgan silver dollars, but that I was his number one love."

Botano opened his hands, like he was waiting for Flo to dump a bunch of coins on his counter. "Did you bring the collection with you?"

"No! They reside in a safe deposit box. Eric told me I should be careful."

"And your late husband was correct."

Flo batted her eyelashes. "I would love to call you by your given name, Carlo, as long as I haven't violated southern propriety by addressing you that way?"

"Not at all, Mrs. Johnson. As my dear mother

used to say, 'Call me anything but don't call me late for dinner.'"

Flo giggled. "How very clever. Carlo, in my purse I have a list of the number of coins and the years. On his death bed, my dear husband told me his silver dollar collection might be worth as much as thirty thousand dollars. I loved my husband with all my heart but truth be told, Eric was not an astute businessman. Could it be possible that he overstated the value of his coin collection—his final legacy to me?"

"It's possible. But the year, and the condition of each coin is the most important aspect of its value."

"I believe Eric told me all of his coins were uncirculated, no, I believe he called them proofs. Is that bad?"

"As I stated, the condition of the coins and the year they were minted are most important."

Flo leaned closer, so close that her boobs were dusting his counter top. "Carlo, I need the money to pay off the mortgage on my home and thirty-five thousand would do that. Now that my husband is gone, I'm all alone. I had hoped that the coin collection would provide me with a home, free and clear of debt. I know you're busy so I will leave the list with you and return tomorrow for your estimate."

Botano glanced at me again, like he wasn't completely falling for Flo's 'I'm all alone' line. "Mrs. Johnson, leave your list and I'm positive that I can provide you with a rough estimate of the collection's value by tomorrow. Would 3:00 in the afternoon work for you?"

"Carlo, you have been most courteous." She turned and poked me in the arm. "Bentley, did you get that? Three tomorrow afternoon. And we must not be late."

Bentley, where in hell did she come up with that name?

Flo poked me again. "Please acknowledge what I just told you."

I stood up straight, threw my shoulders back, and snapped, "Yes, ma'am. One o'clock tomorrow afternoon."

"Carlo, as you can see it's very difficult to get reliable help these days. Bentley, I said three."

"Yes, Ma'am. Three in the afternoon."

"Carlo, when I entered I noticed that you were looking at a coin through a loupe."

"My dear, what you saw is a Hastings Triplet Loupe. A loupe made especially for coin collectors. Would you care to look at a coin through my loupe?"

"I would love to."

I didn't have a clue where Flo was going with this loopy thing.

Flo stared at the coin for a couple of seconds. "Carlo, I like the feel of this loupe. Do you sell them? If so, how much are they?"

"My dear, I have plenty. Please, accept my Hastings Triplet Loupe as a gift to the loveliest customer I have had in my shop this year."

"I thank you. Now, could you recommend a book that would provide me with a better understanding concerning the art of collecting rare coins?"

"My dear, you should go no further than the 2014 Whitman Red Book, Large Print. I recommend the large print edition because that edition produces larger photos of the coins."

"And where might I purchase a copy of that book?"

"I could loan you my copy for the evening."

"How gallant of you."

The dude reached under the counter and handed Flo a red book and one of those loopy things.

Flo smiled at the gold-toothed dude. "Carlo, I will return your book tomorrow." She put her fingers to her lips and blew the dude a kiss. "Until we meet again."

Flo spun around and cruised out the door like she was the Queen of England.

As soon as the shop door closed Flo mumbled, "Don't say a word until we are in the car."

Once the car door closed, I said, "Okay, what the hell is going on?"

"I baited the hook."

"What bait? What hook? And what about—"

"Slow down and I'll try to explain. In 1878, the United States began to produce the Morgan silver dollar at five different mints, but not all coins were produced at all mints during the twenty-six years of production. Coins were struck at Philadelphia which had no mint marks and they are called plain. Coins struck at New Orleans have an O mint mark, and San Francisco an S, Denver a D, and Carson City a CC. Everything worked fine until 1895. That year there were the planned amount of coins struck in New Orleans and San Francisco, but for some unknown reason, Philadelphia only made 880 Proof specimens. According to my research there are various estimates as to how many of the proofs remain today but it is generally accepted there are seventy to eighty. But that's not the best part of this story. It turns out that of the 12,000 regular, or business silver dollars that were supposedly produced at the Philadelphia Mint, not one 1895 plain, non-proof silver dollar has ever been found."

"That doesn't make any sense, and I still don't understand what this has got to do with baiting the hook."

"Some collectors believe that the twelve thousand 1895 plain silver dollars were struck, but were melted down for some unrecorded reason. Others postulate that they were lost at sea while the majority think that they were never made. But today none of that makes any difference. The important part is that one Morgan silver dollar, an 1895 plain proof, recently sold at auction for $125,000! Now, I included one 1895 plain proof in the list of coins my poor departed husband left me. If tomorrow afternoon, Carlo tells me that my late husband's coin collection of twenty-six Morgan silver dollars, years 1878 to 1904, is worth in the neighborhood of $35,000, not the actual value of $150,000, then Carlo Botano is at least an unethical bastard who is ready and willing to take advantage of a defenseless widow, if not a murdering bastard capable of shooting a cripple in his wheelchair while pocketing a two-million-dollar dime."

"Okay, but what about the loopy thing? And the book?"

"I figured that sooner or later one of us would need a loupe to verify the two million dollar dime, so I conned Carlo out of his."

"And the book?"

"Just something to read in my spare time so I can learn more about coins and coin collectors."

Shit, if I was looking for something to read, I'd steal a good mystery, not a stupid book about coins. But what the hell, my babe does a pot full of things I don't get.

Chapter Eleven

Pinky—Kona Coast, Hawaii

Flying first-class offered a multitude of benefits for the traveler—such as inexhaustible gins and tonic—a decent steak with a reasonable cabernet—wide, comfortable seats—but most of all, the first-class passenger had the unique opportunity to get up-close and personal with the first-class flight attendant. In my case she was an attractive, thirtyish blond, named Josephine, or Josie to her new best friend.

An hour out of Kona, Josie stopped by my seat and whispered, "Pinky, where are you staying?"

"At the Sheraton Kona Resort at Keauhou Bay."

"What a coincidence! That's the hotel where the crew stays during layovers. Are you renting a car?"

"Yes."

"Could I catch a ride with you to the hotel? Normally I'd ride the shuttle provided for the crew, but—"

"My dear, providing your transportation to the hotel would be my pleasure." I handed her my luggage ticket. "If you would be so kind as to have a luggage attendant bring my suitcase while I pick up my rental car I will meet you by the arrivals curb."

After signing the requisite paperwork at the

rental office, I eased behind the wheel of a brand new Mercedes CLS550 and was encouraged to find Josie, and a baggage attendant standing with her at the curb.

I popped the Mercedes' trunk latch, jumped out of the car, and opened the passenger side door. "My dear," I said, "I have turned the air conditioning on high so we should be cooled off by the time we exit the airport."

Josie batted her eyes. "Pinky, you're my hero. You think of everything."

I handed the baggage attendant a ten, on the faint hope that he'd remember me when I departed Kona. I fully understood, however, that a male attorney, no matter how successful, could never compete with the memory of an attractive flight attendant.

After a short drive we reached the Sheraton Hotel and checked in.

Josie said, "Pinky, how about we meet at the bar by the pool in fifteen minutes?"

"Make that thirty minutes. I have a few matters to take care of concerning life and death before I can let go of the cares of the real world."

Josie giggled. "I just love the way you lawyers talk. See you soon."

As I watched the elevator close on my newest best friend, a beep from my phone caught my ear. and as reminded, I walked to a shop in the lobby where I selected the largest box of chocolate-covered macadamia nuts available and shipped my purchase to Willow.

After a cursory inspection of my suite, I unpacked and considered my tête à tête amoureux with Josie. I knew our assignation in paradise would not last more than a few days, but what a wonderful way to start my Kona Coast investigation. I lifted the phone and pressed the button for room service. "This is Mr. Delmont in suite five. I want a chilled bottle of your best Champagne and a dozen oysters, no make that two dozen on the half-shell, delivered to my suite at eleven tonight . . . yes, the time I gave you is correct, eleven o'clock tonight."

After I donned my bathing suit, I checked the phone directory and discovered that Madam Soong's coin shop was located a few miles north in Kailua. I tore out the page from the directory, folded it, and placed it in my wallet. Investigative work completed for the day, I slipped my room key-card into the inside pocket of my swim trunks and took the elevator down to meet my date by the pool.

Josie looked fabulous in her bikini, and she was waiting for me at a barside table by the pool, but so were four other females. She waved and called, "Pinky, over here! Grab a chair and join us. There's always room for one more."

As I nodded to the other females, my plan of enjoying a drink or two by the pool, dinner, followed by a night with the luscious Josie began to fade. I forced a smile. "Josie, you have the advantage as I have not been formally introduced to your lovely friends."

Josie said, "See! I wasn't kidding. This guy's a real gentleman. Okay, from left to right—Dawn—Regina—Liz, and Lady Di. Sometimes Liz calls the five of us the Sky Goddesses. Now that we're all friends, let's order another drink."

I said, "Only if you will allow me to purchase the round."

The female identified as Lady Di said, "When Josie told us your name was Pinky, I didn't know what to expect. But frankly, I don't care if your name is Attila the Hun as long as you keep buying the drinks."

The rest of the group nodded so I called to the barmaid. "Another round for the table and because I am a drink behind the group, a double gin and tonic for myself."

Regina said, "Is this your first time on the Kona Coast?"

I sat back and immersed myself in the warm, fragrant, tropical air. "No. I was here a few years ago."

Josie said, "On legal business or pleasure?"

The barmaid served the drinks. I signed the tab and said, "I was here with a woman."

Dawn said, "Sounds interesting."

"Actually, she was my wife."

Josie frowned. "Hold on, are you married?"

"No. I am happily divorced. The woman's name is Willow Stone and she remains the favorite of all my ex-wives."

Regina frowned. "Jesus, how many times have you been married?"

"That my dear, is none of your business."

Josie said, "Regina, I agree with Pinky. That's like asking when was the last time you did a mile-high with the pilot."

Liz laughed. "Right on, Josie! Pinky, what type of law do you practice?"

I was halfway through my second drink and

81

the bright sun had warmed my back. The tension that had built up during the day—Mabel leaving—discovering my new girl Pam could not be trusted—the long flight over the Pacific, all faded in the combination of tropical breezes and gin. "Most of my clients are persons accused of murder."

Liz said, "Wow! I'll bet that's exciting. Do you get any of them off?"

"Let me see." I paused to give the impression that the number was not lingering on the tip of my tongue. "A few months ago I successfully defended my twenty-fourth client accused of murder."

Lady Di said, "And how many ended up at the end of a rope because you screwed up?"

I waved to the barmaid. "Another round for my friends." I turned my head and stared directly into the emerald eyes of Lady Di. "If you just asked me how many of my clients were executed for their alleged crimes, the simple answer is none. Zero. Zilch. I am twenty-four out of twenty-four acquittals."

The barmaid set more glasses onto the table and again I signed for the round.

Josie said, "Let's change the subject. Where are we going for dinner?"

As I worked my way through my third drink, the tight muscles in the back of my neck had relaxed and the air temperature was perfect. While listening to the girls make various suggestions, I finished the rest of my gin and tonic and their babble began to fade. I set my glass down and for a split-second, gave in to the demands of my heavy eyelids.

Willow and I are walking hand-in-hand along a pristine beach carpeted with soft, white sand. The ambient temperature is flawless. The sun, a brilliant fire-ball, paints the clouds a pink-orange-purple pastel as humanity's personal star takes its nightly swim into the Pacific. Four days into our honeymoon, Willow says, "The last few days on the Kona Coast have given us a peek at what our lives could be." Willow kisses me gently. "Pinky, we are standing in paradise. We're both happy. In fact, you haven't said a disparaging word for days. I cannot see any reason for us to ever leave here."

I look into her hazel eyes. "I agree, up to the point of practicality. But you know how hard I have worked to build up my law practice in Carson City and you have to consider my unprecedented streak of acquittals."

Willow pulls her hand away. "There are times when you can be such an egotistical bastard—no, cancel my last observation, you're an egotistical bastard ninety-five percent of the time. Every once in a while, your good side peeks out, the side of you I loved enough to marry, but that side of you never lasts for long."

She starts to cry, turns and before she walks in the direction of our hotel, she says "As soon as I get back to our room I'm going to pack my bags. With any luck, we can get out of this paradise trap tomorrow morning and you can return to Carson City so you can figure out a new way to increase your damn acquittals."

After a few moments of contemplation, I follow her but by the time I reach our hotel room, as promised, Willow's suitcase is packed.

After a silent, lonely night, we check out of our hotel. During the long flight home I spend the next five hours trying to understand if our honeymoon, and perhaps our marriage, was over because I refused to ignore my clients whose very existence depended on my legal expertise.

"Mr. Delmont . . . Mr. Delmont, wake up."

My eyes snapped open and I looked around. The chairs circling my table were empty along with every other chair in the pool area.

The barmaid thrust a sheet of paper at me. "Mr. Delmont, the lady with the short blonde hair left you this message."

My brain was in a slightly befuddled state. I snatched the folded paper out of the barmaid's hand, and again I glanced around the pool area as if to verify that Josie and the four sky goddesses were gone.

The ice in my empty glass had melted, but the cold water beckoned to me. I took a large gulp and opened the note.

Pinky:
You fell asleep. Don't feel bad. My mother's brother, good old Uncle Harry, takes a nap every afternoon and he snores a lot louder than you do. I'm used to guys like you. Anyway, the five of us got hungry. We caught a ride into Kailua so we could grab some grub.
I leave the Sheraton at eight tomorrow morning on the airport shuttle. My flight takes off at eleven so it's possible we'll never see each other again, unless I end up working the first-class section during your

84

flight back to the mainland.

Thanks for the ride from the airport and the drinks.

Aloha,

Josie

P. S. All the girls wanted to thank you for the drinks, especially Liz. She thinks you're sort of cute and she told me if you're still here when she returns to the Sheraton four days from now, she'll give you a call.

Chagrined, I handed my empty glass to the barmaid, and returned to my room. I called Josie's room and got no answer. Then I called room service and ordered a filet mignon, medium rare, and a bottle of their best cabernet.

Much later, satisfied that the cabernet had acted as a balm to sooth my battered ego, I heard a light tap at my door.

Josie?

I glanced at the remains of my dinner and rolled the cart into an empty closet. I took a quick glance at myself in a mirror to be sure I was presentable and opened the door.

My heart sank. The knock had not come from Josie, but from a man standing behind a rolling cart. "Mr. Delmont. Your order of champagne and oysters."

I glanced at my watch. It was eleven o'clock and I had completely forgotten! I collected myself. "Yes." I glanced over my shoulder and paused, as if to make sure my paramour was either fully clothed, or out of sight. "Please, bring in our late night repast. The night is young and there is nothing like a glass of the bubbly and a few oysters to make everything right again. Do you agree?"

"As you wish, Mr. Delmont."

The waiter handed me the bill. I added a substantial tip, signed it, and handed it back.

For a brief moment the waiter's eyes lingered on the closed door to my bedroom and a faint, knowing smile crossed his lips. "Have a good evening, Mr. Delmont."

"Thank you, we will."

I closed the door and walked into my bedroom. After placing my keys, iPhone, and wallet on the night stand I noticed the torn phone directory page neatly tucked in my wallet. I pulled out the page, unfolded it, and placed the page next to my wallet. I had come to the end of a long day but those hours were yet another example of what I would do to provide my client a safe harbor.

Chapter Twelve

Pinky—Kona Coast, Hawaii

A mechanical chirrup, a din not unlike a bird on steroids, forced its way into a pleasant dream that filled my subconscious. By the third or forth chirp I lay there, half awake and half asleep. Finally the clamor punctured through my reverie and I realized my cell phone was attempting to awaken me.

I extended the fingers of my right hand, searched the night stand, and found my iPhone.

"Hello?"

"Boss, how's island life hanging?"

I glanced out the sliding glass doors at the dark horizon above the breaking waves, and then noticed the top edge of the sky had taken on a pale glow. "You ignoramus! Do you have any idea what time it is?" I sat up, swung my legs over the edge of the bed and gingerly placed my feet onto the floor. "Damn it, answer my question. What time is it?"

"Me and Flo are waiting to eat lunch. Why?"

"Because when it is lunch time in North Carolina it is six in the morning on the Kona Coast, you cretin."

"Boss, does cretin mean the same as that ingnormussus name you called me a minute ago?"

"Yes! Cretin, ignoramus, dolt, fool—"

"Hey, stop calling me dumb! So how's Hawaii?"

I walked out of my bedroom and nearly ran

into the rolling cart with the oysters and champagne. The malodorous aroma of senescent shellfish assaulted my nostrils and my stomach did a flip. I quickly moved through the sliding door onto my lanai and took a deep breath of fresh sea air.

Once my stomach had settled, I said, "My boy, Hawaii is perfect. I must admit I had planned on sleeping a bit later, but now that you have interrupted my slumber . . . Hold on. My original question remains unanswered. Why did you wake me?"

"Boss, I called the office and a nasty broad named Pam Carson answered. She told me that Mabel's gone for good and that me and Flo are stuck with her. Then she told me that we've been advanced ten thousand clams and that's more than enough money and we'd better not ask for anymore. Then she wanted to know what me and Flo were doing. Then she summarized, or something like that, and . . . shit, I almost forgot, me and Flo took the five G's you had stashed at your Lake Tahoe condo 'cause we didn't want to leave that much cash lying around. You never know what might happen—a dude could break in—a fire—shit, anything! But that's not why I called. What's up with this Pam broad?"

"Calm down. Mabel had to leave to take care of her sister. Pam Carson is Mabel's replacement. Concerning the five thousand cash you took from my property, I will subtract that amount, plus ten percent interest for an advanced payment, from your next month's salary."

"Don't worry, you'll get your cash back. Hell,

that's why I told you, so you'd know why the five
G's are missing from the condo."

Even in my befuddled mental condition I now
understood that Bear's early phone call was meant
to precede Pam's call accusing the two of theft.

I said, "Are you making any headway with the
East Coast coin dealer?"

"Flo's set up a great scam."

"I am not the least bit interested in her scam.
Did that man murder Ludwig Kaufmann?"

Bear said, "If you're asking me if Botano's the
one who popped a slug into Ludwig's forehead I
don't have a clue, but by tomorrow we'll know if the
dude is a crook. Not bad for a couple of day's work.
How's it going with the Chinese broad? What's your
scam?"

"Scam?"

"Jesus, what's your plan?"

In reality I had no plan but I was not going to
inform that fatuous clown of my failings. "I plan on
stopping by Madam Soong's place of business to
inform her that I am in the market to buy a rare
dime. I am positive—"

Flo's voice cut me off. "A rare dime! Why don't
you just walk in and tell her you're a cop looking for
the person that murdered Ludwig Kaufmann?"

The witch had been eavesdropping. "Florence,
I believe that every state in the union has a law
that prohibits surreptitiously listening in on a
conversation."

She said, "That won't fix the problem that
you're going to walk into Madam Soong's business
with all the subtlety of a bull in a china shop. Now
shut up and listen to me. You need to tell Madam

Soong that you are an attorney in charge of investing for a client who, at present, has hundreds of millions placed in diamonds, platinum, frozen pork bellies, real estate trusts, oil shale fracking, and now, to continue his portfolio diversification, your client wants you to put a minimum of ten million dollars in rare coins."

My mind raced through her proposal and as much as I wanted to tell her that she was wrong, her brief scenario had some merit. In the past I had found her input lacked significance, but this time her scheme had possibilities.

I said, "So Madam Soong would think I am seeking extremely rare coins without directly informing her that I am looking for Ludwig's stolen dime."

"You've got it, Sparky. Now you'll have to excuse me because the waitress just served me an outstanding plate of shrimp and grits. Good bye."

Bear said, "And Boss, my burger and fried onion rings just showed up. Good luck with the Chinese broad."

I turned my phone off. Returned to my bedroom, closed the drapes, and crawled back into bed.

Two hours later I woke to the sounds of the crashing surf. A warm breeze gently moved the air as I called room service and requested a Denver omelet, whole-wheat toast, a large pot of coffee, and copies of the *New York Times* and the *Wall Street Journal*.

My repast ordered, I returned to the rolling cart with the champagne and oysters. I dumped the oysters into the toilet, flushed, and then placed the unopened champagne in the refrigerator under the wet bar.

I then pulled the second rolling cart out of the closet, the one with the remains of my steak dinner and cabernet, and pushed both carts into the hall.

Morning housekeeping duties completed, I again walked out onto my private lanai, sat down and watched the azure ocean waves as they broke over the black lava. The setting was ideal for my call to Madam Soong.

I pulled out the phone directory page and keyed in the number for her shop, The Coin Gallery.

On the third ring a female voice answered, "Madam Soong. How may I help you?"

I informed her I was an attorney with a client who wanted to invest at least ten million dollars in rare coins.

She said, "May I have your name?"

"Padriag Joseph Murphy, but my client's name must remain anonymous."

"Of course, Mr. . . . ah . . . Murphy. Today I am busy with clients until four o'clock. Will that be convenient for you?"

Her hesitation concerning the name I offered informed me that she suspected Padriag Joseph Murphy was a non de plume. I considered her suggestion. The afternoon appointment would allow me more time to relax by the pool. "Yes. Today at four will work for me."

"Mr. Murphy, are you familiar with the location of my place of business?"

"I am."

"One final question. I am an insignificant

numismatist on the Kona Coast of Hawaii. Why did you call me? Did a mutual friend, or a business associate, recommend me?"

"Madam Soong, I do not feel comfortable giving out those names over the phone."

"Excellent. I look forward to a business relationship that both rewards us and promotes continued longevity. Good bye."

As I hit the red END button on my iPhone I heard a knock at my suite door. I opened the entry and a waiter pushed in a rolling cart with my omelet, toast, coffee, and newspapers.

I said, "Please take everything out to the lanai. A man would be insane to pass up a morning this grand."

"As you wish, Mr. Delmont."

For a time I acted as if I was the Great Gatsby, casually nibbling my breakfast, sipping coffee, and reading the world news while the ocean waves crashed a hundred feet from my private lanai. My reverie was broken when my room phone rang.

"Hello?"

"Pinky? It's Liz. Remember? We had a few drinks by the pool last night before dinner? I'm one of the five Sky Goddesses?"

"I recall, but I thought you had a flight to . . . I don't remember."

"San Francisco and points east, but I called in sick."

"I am sorry to hear that. Is there—"

"Pinky, wake up and smell the coffee. I'm not really sick. Are you free today?"

"My dear, at the moment I have nothing

scheduled for two days. Your wish is my command."

"Josie was right about the way you talk. Can you meet me by the pool in an hour?"

Chapter Thirteen

Bear—Wilmington, North Carolina

Me and Flo parked under the same tree that I used the day before.As we got out of the car, she said, "Bear, remember your part. You are playing my hired driver named Bentley. As such, you need to stay in the background, unobtrusive, and don't forget what we talked about last night. Botano needs to think you might be doing more for me than just driving my car."

"I get you, Babe. Speaking of yesterday—did I drive your car the way you wanted? Last night, did you get enough of whatever Bentley might be doing to you?"

"From this moment on, you address me as Mrs. Johnson; do you have that straight?"

"Yup."

"Do not answer yup! Say yes, Mrs. Johnson."

"Yes, Mrs. Johnson."

"Thank you. Now that we've cleared that up, Bentley, for your future edification, unobtrusive is an adjective that means not conspicuous or attracting attention, and the word unobtrusive has nothing to do with sex."

"Gotcha, Babe . . .whoops, Mrs. Johnson. One question before we go into the coin joint. You and I know you don't own any old silver dollars, so what the hell are you going to do when he asks to see your collection? And, I don't mean what you've got up front."

"It's my brother's fault."

"Uh! I didn't know you had a brother."

"And neither does Botano. From now on just follow my lead."

"Yes, Mrs. Johnson, and I promise that I'll be a good Bentley. Hey, why did you give me that stupid name?"

"First, I am pleased that you remembered that I am Eric Johnson's grieving widow. Second, the name Bentley gives you stature. I gave the title of my driver a lot of thought. Bentley is the make of one of the world's most desirable vehicles, a nearly perfect car, but a shade below a Rolls Royce, and Bear, that definition describes you perfectly."

"Yes, madam." What the hell does a Rolls Royce got to do with anything?

Flo flashed me her sort-of-friendly stink eye as I opened the door to Botano's joint. The dude was sitting behind his counter, holding a little glass thing in his hand, and staring at a coin.

He set the glass thing down, jumped up, and said, "Ah, Mrs. Johnson."

"Carlo! Good to see you. I trust I am not interrupting you in any way?"

"My dear lady, there is no way that you could interrupt my day." The dude shot me a quick look. "And I trust you had a pleasant evening?"

Flo batted her lashes. "Yes, nearly perfect."

I said, "Mr. Botano, what do you call that little glass thing you've got in your hand?"

He dragged his eyes off Flo's boobs and flashed me a pissed-off glare. "It's called a jeweler's loupe.

The loupe allows me to identify details, such as mint marks, or dates on coins. Now, Mrs. Johnson, by any chance did you bring your late husband's coin collection?"

Flo looked like she was about to turn on the tears. Her lower lip quivered as she said, "Carlo, before I go any further I need to know if my late husband's coin collection will cover my mortgage?"

"My best guess is thirty-seven thousand dollars, but I will be able to give you a closer estimation of their true value once I inspect the condition of the coins in your possession."

Only thirty-seven grand? Flo's right, this bastard would steal money from a begger with one leg!

Flo shook her head. "I am sorry, but last evening, a few moments before I retired for the night, I received a phone call from my older brother. Do you have any siblings?"

"No. I was an only child and raised by an aunt and uncle after my parents were killed in a . . . let us call it a motor vehicle accident outside of Gela."

"Gela?"

"Yes. It is a small town in southern Sicily. Anyway, back to your story concerning your older brother."

"Carlo, as far back as I can recall my older brother, Dan, has acted as a surrogate father to me. Once our parents passed on, my brother felt as if he was my guardian."

Botano said, "Go on."

"I do not see any way to soften Dan's concerns. He feels it would be unwise of me to turn my silver dollar collection over to a man I just met."

Botano jerked his head back. "Mrs. Johnson, a lesser person than I would take umbrage at your brother's insinuation. I am a nationally respected numismatist with clients all over the world. I find it hard to believe that your brother feels he can besmirch my reputation in such a cavalier manner."

I'll be damned! The dude just did that 'protest-too-much' crap that Flo told me to watch out for. Shit, if I was Flo's brother I would have told her the same thing. Besides, I didn't know Flo had an older brother named Dan. Maybe he's just part of her scam.

Flo said, "Carlo, please do not take my brother's concerns personally."

"Mrs. Johnson, your brother has left me no alternative. I am sorry but under the circumstances I see no future in continuing this conversation. Good day."

Botano turned and had his hand on the door knob to his back office when Flo said, "I think it's time we cut to the chase. Bear, lock the front door, flip the sign over to closed, and get close to our host. Carlo, my name isn't Johnson. I don't have an older brother. I don't possess a collection of valuable silver dollars, and if I did, I sure as hell wouldn't sell them to an unscrupulous bastard like you. Last night I spent a couple of hours on the internet and discovered some interesting facts about you. Your parents didn't die in a car accident. They were murdered when their car was blown up, victims of the war between the two criminal organizations known as the Stidda and the Mafia in the mid 1980's. With your less than savory background, I've asked my partner, the man standing next to you, to be ready for anything. He's as strong as an ox, and I fear not always controllable, so even if you do have mob connections, please, for your personal safety, do not make any moves that might upset him. Just nod if you understand everything I just said."

Botano's mouth started to open, like he was going to say something, but I growled and he thought better of it and nodded.

"Excellent! Now, I have a few questions. A couple of weeks ago you attended a coin show in Reno. Nod your head if that is correct."

The dude nodded, and then he said, "If you two think you can intimidate—"

"I thought I told you to keep quiet. The next time you open your mouth I'll leave it up to Bear to decide the punishment he will levy. Okay, back to my questions. While you were at the Reno Coin Show, you stopped by Ludwig Kaufmann's booth. Am I correct? Please nod."

As he nodded I saw him glance to his right. Before he could move, I grabbed both arms, lifted him over the counter, stood him next to Flo and said, "Was that some kind of an alarm?"

He nodded.

"Okay, Babe, he's ready for your next question."

Flo said, "Were you aware that Kaufmann possessed a 1894-S dime, one of twenty-four struck at the San Francisco Mint?"

He nodded.

"Good. Now we come to the final few questions. First, were you aware that Ludwig

Kaufmann was murdered soon after the coin show closed?"

"Yes, I received an email on—"

I grabbed Botano's shirt collar and lifted him off the floor. "Dude, the lady told you to nod your head. I don't like slow learners."

His face was turning bright red as he shook his noggin up and down so I set him back on the floor.

Flo said, "Thank you, Bear. Carlo, did you shoot Ludwig?"

He shook his head.

"Did you steal his two-million-dollar dime?"

Botano pointed to his lips.

Flo said, "Go ahead and talk but I need to warn you that Bear has a built-in bullshit monitor and if he thinks you're lying, there's a good chance you won't see the sun rise tomorrow morning."

"A coin dealer in Chicago emailed me that Kaufmann had been shot but I didn't kill him. Shooting people is not part of my modus operandi. I make a damn good living buying low from ignorant customers and selling high to even dumber collectors."

I lifted him up again. "Sort of like what you were going to do to Flo when you thought she was a dumb widow with a pile of silver dollars."

Flo said, "Carlo, so far you've avoided the final question. Did you steal the two-million-dollar dime?"

"Hell no."

I tightened my grip on his collar. "So who did?" Then I set him back down. I didn't want the dude to go belly-up on me.

Botano coughed a couple of times, then he said, "Give me a second to breathe, and I'll tell you how things work in the world of coin collecting." After a quick snort and a hack, he said, "The word was out that a collector was looking to add a 1894-S dime to their collection. Everybody knows that there are at least ten of those coins floating around so it's not like a rare painting. I mean there's only one Mona Lisa so if someone clipped that canvas out of the Louvre, the thief would be hard pressed to sell it. But if you own a ten-cent coin, struck in San Francisco in 1894, no one would know if the 1894-S dime you have in your collection was bought legitimately, or obtained under less than legit circumstances."

I said, "Flo, help me out here. I don't get it."

"There's no way for anyone to know if the dime was bought from a coin thief."

Botano said, "That's correct. Now—"

I said, "Hold on buster. What about a bill of sale from a dealer?"

He said, "Ah, provenance. Many coin transactions take place privately, with no questions asked and no publicity. Think about it. How comfortable would you be if everyone knew that you'd just purchased a dime worth two million?"

I said, "So you're telling us that all a collector has to do is pass the word to the street that he wants to buy a 1894-S dime, and then he sits back and waits for someone to knock on his door with the coin?"

Botano smiled, "Exactly."

I said, "Except in this case my old high school bud ended up with a bullet in his brain."

Botano said, "As I said, murder is unusual. Generally, coin deals like this don't end up—"

The bastard was starting to piss me off. "Dude, a few seconds ago you told us the word got out that a collector was looking for a 1894 S dime. Besides yourself, who else got the word?"

"Truthfully, I'm not sure. One hears rumors every day, and—"

I grabbed his collar and gave it a squeeze. "We're looking for a name."

He said, "There are so many people in the business that—"

I twisted harder and the dude's face turned purple. "I said give me a name, damn it!"

He wheezed, "Madam Soong."

I let go of his collar. "That's more like it."

Flo said, "Botano, just how dumb do you think we are?"

"Huh?"

"How do we know that a woman named Madam Soong exists? Bear, grab his collar and this time don't stop when his face turns—"

He cried, "Please don't hurt me! I know Madam Soong shot the guy in Reno and took the dime because I drove her to the house in my rental car. She told me she had a cash buyer in China who was ready to pay her two and a half million. She had tried to buy the coin the day before at the show, but the guy, I think his name was Ludwig, didn't have the coin with him. Soong doesn't drive. She asked me to take her to the guy's home so she could complete the transaction. I didn't know the crazy woman was going to kill him!"

I said, "I know that there was a video camera

monitoring the front door. How did the broad get in?"

"She told me that Ludwig gave her a key to the servants' entrance. All I know is that she didn't go in the front way because I was parked across the street."

"How long was she gone?"

"Five, maybe six minutes."

Flo said, "Botano, you didn't drive Soong to that house for free. What was your take on this deal?"

His eyes darted back and forth between me and Flo. "She gave me ten grand to drive her to the house."

Flo said, "What do you think, Bear? Do we have enough evidence to arrest him and take him back to Carson City as an accessory to murder?"

Botano cried, "Oh my God, you're cops! Please, when I drove Soong to Ludwig's house I didn't know she was going to kill him! Like I told you, that sort of thing is not the way I work."

Flo said, "But murder fits the modus operandi of Madam Soong?"

Botano looked like he was going to cry. "Please don't arrest me. Soong killed him. "

Flo said, "Shut up and listen to me. How about a deal? You promise us that you won't call Soong to warn her we're onto her and we'll tell our boss in Carson City that you had skipped town."

Botano said, "Does your deal mean that I won't be arrested?"

Flo looked at me and nodded. I said, "Hey, whatever she says is good for me."

Botano said, "Alright. I promise."

I looked at Flo. She nodded again, so I said, "Dude, we have one more thing to clear up before we leave. Anyone with this much dough lying around must have a video system that records everything that goes on. You've got two choices. I could find the system, rip the damn thing out, and leave you and this joint a complete wreck. Or, you could remember that you said things that you don't want anyone to know so we can call our visit today a push—like when you and the blackjack dealer both have twenty. Nobody wins, but nobody loses either."

Flo said, "Look, we can't have our little visit recorded. Give it to Bear or I can't be responsible for what he does."

The dude started to blubber like a little girl. "Thank you for not tearing up my establishment. I just spent twenty-five hundred installing the video system. Don't worry, once the two of you leave my shop I will erase the recording and our little discussion today never happened."

I grabbed his collar. "Just how dumb do you think I am? Dude, I don't trust you, got it? Stop screwing around and take me to the recording system."

He walked me through the back door into a tiny office. On a shelf above a desk sat a recorder and a video screen that showed Flo standing by the front door.

"Okay, now give me the tape, or disk, of everything that thing recorded."

He pushed a couple of buttons, a few lights flashed on and off and then a little drawer slid out. He handed me a DVD and said, "That's it. This is what the system recorded over the past thirty-six hours. I change the DVD every four days."

I stuck the disk into my back pocket. "Dude, I'll check this out when I get back to our motel room. If this DVD doesn't show me and Flo and you, your ass is glass and I'll be the sledgehammer looking for something to smash."

"Trust me, that disk is the one you want."

The dude led me back to the shop where Flo waited by the counter.

When she turned to leave, her boobs brushed against Botano's arm, like she was giving the bastard a little thrill for all his trouble.

I pushed her toward the door and said, "Carlo, we're going to track down the Soong broad, but if we find out you've been lying to us about your part in Ludwig's murder, me and Flo'll catch the first plane back to Wilmington, find you, and I'll pound your ass. One final warning. If you break your promise and call Soong, to warn her that we're coming, I'll do more than kick your ass. Babe, what'll we do if he calls Soong?"

"You'll cut him up and feed him to the alligators!"

Botano was crying like a baby as we walked out the door.

When we reached our rental car, I said, "Babe, I'm afraid Pinky could be in deep-shit."

"I know. The shrimp is about to get up close and personal with a murderer and as usual, he's totally clueless. As soon as we get things cleared up here, we need to call and warn him."

"Right." I said that to keep Flo happy, but as close as I could figure, calling the boss wasn't going to do a lot of good. Hawaii was about ten hours away and Pinky doesn't think real good when he stares down the dark end of a murderer's pistol.

Chapter Fourteen

Pinky—Kona Coast, Hawaii

As my mind constructed a mental picture of Liz, my cell phone began to buzz. "Liz, excuse me for a moment. I have to take another call."

I set the room phone down and walked toward the lanai. "Hello."

"Boss, we got some good news and some bad news. Which one do you want—"

"I need to call you back. I am involved in some delicate negotiations concerning my—"

A female voice interrupted. "Pinky, Bear's got his cell on speaker so we can both talk and listen. Carlo Botano just informed us that Soong murdered Ludwig Kaufmann. If that woman would shoot a crippled man in a wheelchair, she wouldn't think twice about pumping a couple bullets into a worthless lawyer."

I said, "Florence, your concern over my health is commendable. Now hold your tongue and let me talk to my real investigator."

"I'm here, Boss. What do you want to talk about?"

That was when I completed the mental image of Liz and she was everything a man could ask for. Suddenly I recalled that Liz was holding on my room phone. "Bear, hold on while I take care of a pressing matter."

"Boss, I never heard anybody call taking a wiz

a pressing matter."

I do not have time for this, Liz is waiting. "You dolt, I am not talking about urinating. I was . . . Never mind, hold on."

I set the cell down on a table by the glass door and rushed back to the room phone. "Liz?"

"I was about to hang up. What are you doing?"

"Somehow I have managed to surround myself with a confederacy of recalcitrant cretins."

"Does that include me?"

"No, no, no! I was not talking about you. I was describing the people on my other phone. My dear, shall we meet by the pool in thirty minutes."

"Forget it. You're too busy working."

"Liz?" The line went dead. I slammed the receiver down and returned to my cell phone.

While holding the cell at my side, I stared at the pounding surf in a futile attempt to calm myself down. "Bear?"

"Right here, Boss."

"Why are you so sure that Soong shot Ludwig?"

Florence said, "He just told you that! Carlo Botano, the man we were sent to North Carolina to check out, told us he drove Soong to Ludwig's home. Then she walked into the house, shot him, and took the dime."

"Did you call Willow to request extradition for Carlo Botano as an accessory to murder?"

"We didn't think he fit the criteria as an accessory. Botano claimed he didn't know that Soong was going to shoot Ludwig. But that's not why we called you. Our real concern was to warn you that any meeting with Soong could be lethal."

"Florence, I find it difficult to believe that you, of all people, are concerned with my health."

"Boss, Flo's giving you the straight skinny. We both thought you needed to—"

"My good man, I did not fly to Hawaii to lie on the beach or drink rum punches. I came here to investigate Madam Soong. We all knew that she was a potential murderer, and—"

"Put a sock in it," Flo's tone tightened with anger. "That was when Soong was a potential murderer. Now she's been fingered as the one who pulled the trigger. Pinky, it's time—"

My room phone rang. "Hold on. I have another call." I set the cell down and ran to the couch. Perhaps Liz had reconsidered and was waiting for me by the pool. I grabbed the receiver. "Yes?"

"Pinky? It's Pam."

It was Pam, not Liz. I said, "Good morning," My greeting was perfunctory because so far this morning had been anything but good.

"Pinky, I'm sorry. I told you that I would only call if things got out of hand. I have two items. First, the arraignment of Helmut Kaufmann will be held in Judge Stephens' court tomorrow morning at ten."

"Damn! Willow had promised me that she would hold off the arraignment until next week. What was the other item?"

"Pinky, I love my job, but I have to quit."

"What!"

"I should explain. I came to Carson City following the love of my life when she became a detective on the police force. I had hoped that the people of Nevada would look upon our relationship

108

with—"

Now this was all making sense. "Pam, is the name of your partner Detective Henrietta, ah, I apologize, but I do not recall her last name."

"It's Spaulding. How did you know that?"

"She was the newest detective in town and then you showed up. Also, I overheard your conversation in my office before I left for the airport, when you stated that you had tracked your partner down and felt like a woman scorned."

"Wow! You're good."

"I still do not understand why you feel the need to quit."

"Henny and I were enjoying a glass of wine last night when she mentioned the Kaufmann case. That's when it hit me. When we lived in San Francisco, we did the same jobs as we are doing now, Henny was a detective, and I worked with a law firm. However, the San Francisco system of justice is huge compared to Carson City. Until last night, she and I had never run into a conflict of interest concerning a client who was being represented by my legal firm. I'm here one week and bang, I can't sip a glass of wine with my partner without feeling like we are walking through a minefield."

"My dear woman, I am pleased to see that you quickly recognized your conflict problem. Now, I hope you can just as rapidly comprehend my situation. I cannot function without a competent person sitting in your chair. That person can be you as long as you refrain from discussing business when you are with your partner."

"I appreciate your vote of confidence, but I'm

still quitting. Now, I have a question for you and please be totally honest: Did my sexuality, my preference for a female partner, ever bother you?"

Pam's quitting? She cannot leave my office uncovered. "Pam, would you reconsider your decision if I offered you a thousand dollar bonus?"

"I'm sorry but my mind's made up."

"Can you stay on the job until I return?"

"I can do that. I'll wait until you get back for the arraignment and then I'll say my goodbyes. Now, back to my sexuality question."

"My dear, who you choose to sleep with is none of my concern. Now, please hold on for a moment. I have another call to tend to."

I ran to my cell. "Bear, Florence, what exactly did Botano say to you?"

Bear said, "It went something like this—when I drove Soong to Ludwig's house I didn't know she was going to kill him—Boss, it was so cool. Flo had him shaking in his boots. That's why he confessed."

"Outstanding! What else did you two do today?"

Florence said, "Pinky, you and I are making real progress today. You called me Florence for the first time and included me as one of your investigators. Thank you for that. After we conclude this case you and I will sit down and negotiate my salary."

Damn it, that witch never stops looking for an opening. "Over my dead body."

"Don't tempt me," She said. "Now, where do we go from here?"

"I just talked with Pam and she informed me that I have to return to Carson City because Willow

110

reneged on her promise. Helmut's arraignment is tomorrow morning at ten. Contact Pam and tell her to arrange for your flights to Kona to investigate the Soong woman. That way—"

Florence said, "Hold on. I thought you went to Kona a couple of days ago to do that—to hear Soong's side of the story."

I said, "Florence, as the leader of the Delmont legal consortium, I, and I alone, determine the direction of all investigations. As your employer, I demand you limit your advice until your input has been requested. Have I made myself clear?"

"You are such a pompous—"

I interrupted. "Stay on the line. I will return in a moment."

I returned to the couch and picked up the receiver. "Pam, Florence will be calling you momentarily to arrange their transportation to the Kona Coast. Along with their tickets you will provide them with an additional five thousand dollars for expenses. I will return on the next flight in time to arrive at my office tomorrow morning at nine, an hour before the arraignment. Finally, contact Henry, the guard at the jail. He and I are old business associates. Among Henry's duties are to make sure all my clients look presentable in court. To ensure that Helmut's toiletry needs are met, take three hundred dollars out of petty cash and give the money to Henry."

"Got it. Sorry I have to quit on such short notice and thanks for being so open-minded."

I sighed. It was good to know I had a woman running my office that I could trust even if it was only until tomorrow morning. I hung up the room phone and returned to the cell. "Bear, I have returned. Now, I want—"

Florence said, "Pinky, did you even try to contact Madam Soong?"

"I talked with her on the phone and set up an appointment to meet with her this afternoon. However, as I previously stated, Willow moved Helmut Kaufmann's arraignment up to ten tomorrow morning and as his attorney, I have to return to—"

"So once we arrive we're starting from scratch. Hold on, Bear wants to ask me something."

"My good woman, I still have to pack my bags and—"

"Bear wants to know if you met any cute flight attendants during your trip?"

"I do not understand what that has to do with—"

Bear said, "Pinky, give me a simple yes or no."

"If you must know, I did. However, Josie and I spent very little time—"

Florence said, "If I know men, and I do know men, you spent all your time in Kona chasing Josie around your hotel room. Was your little flight attendent worth the extra money it's going to cost you because Bear and I will be flying to Kona?"

Actually, I never touched Josie, but there were times when a man had to do what a man had to do. "Yes, my moments with Josie, however brief, will be worth every penny."

"Is she there now?"

"Who?"

"Josie."

"She is not here."

"And when did she leave?"

"About an hour ago."

Bear said, "So she spent all night? Boss, I'm proud of you. I hear when a dude gets to your age, it's not as easy to—"

Florence cut in. "That's enough man talk. Pinky, I was looking forward to a few days off to do a little shopping and to lie around our pool. Now, without any break, we have to fly half way around the world to cover up your failure. Don't worry, once we arrive in Kona, Bear and I will get to work as soon as we check into our hotel and unpack our bags. But all of these extra days of work will not come cheap. And that brings me to an important item that I've wanted to discuss with you. However, our endless days of non-stop toil has limited me to these impersonal phone calls. Pinky, tomorrow is the first day of the month, and from that moment on, I'll be calling you boss, just like my man does."

"What? I do not understand."

"And don't forget to tell Pam to add me to the payroll."

"But you are not a salaried member of my staff!"

"I'd better be as of next month!"

"But I do not pay you a monthly stipend!"

"Look, if you want your investigative team to pursue Madam Soong, my salary of thirty-five hundred per month starts tomorrow morning!"

Chapter Fifteen

Bear—Southport, North Carolina

Our cell was still on speaker and Flo was smiling, like she's got the little fart by the short hairs.

Pinky said, "Florence?"

"Yes?"

"I will contact Pam and instruct her to put you on the payroll."

"At thirty-five hundred a month?"

"Correct."

"Excellent. I've been looking at a new living room suite at the Reno IKEA store for weeks. Now, as my large bed-partner would say, let's cut to the chase. If by any chance Soong has flown the coop, don't worry, we'll track her down where ever she goes. We both have up-to-date passports and if I need more assistance, I still have my contact at the State Department."

Pinky said, "Where do you think she'll run if spooked?"

She said, "I don't know, but she's Asian so somewhere in Asia is my best guess. But as I said, my guy in DC owes me a couple of favors so I'm positive he can cut through any red tape."

Pinky said, "Fine. I will call Pam so she can make all the arrangements. Did I mention to you that today is Pam's last full day on the job?"

I said, "Nope, but if you get in a pickle you can

always call Lu."

I heard Pinky suck air past his teeth like he was thinking about getting pissed off. "Are you talking about the same Lu who once worked for me?"

"Yup."

"Why should I call her?"

"Because she and Flo are buddies. Hell, they go out to lunch once or twice a week and she knows your office like the back of her hand."

Pinky said, "Regular lunches? Florence, do you break bread with Lu on a frequent basis?"

"Yes, Pinky, regular lunches are generally construed to mean meeting on a frequent basis."

"Did this happen before, or after, she left me?"

"Both. Lu and I are good friends and at least once a month Bear joins us at The Nugget's all-you-can eat—"

Pinky interrupted. "That woman ran my office like a fine Swiss watch and I never understood why she left me."

Flo flashed her stink eye at the cell phone. "Pinky, the two reasons she gave me were that you have the morals of an alley cat, and the abysmal way you treated your ex-wife, Willow."

Pinky said, "Is there any way she could be convinced to come back?"

Flo sighed, "I could ask her."

"Please do. By tomorrow afternoon my ship will be rudderless. Now I have to pack. Goodbye."

I said, "Hey Boss, before you go, describe that Josie broad. Was she built like a brick—"

Flo dug her elbow into my ribs. "Don't you dare say another word. And Pinky, we both thank you for our new living room set."

Flo dumped the call and smiled.

"Babe, I'm confused. Why the big push to bring Lu back?"

"I'll bet our new living room suite that if Soong did run, she'd head to China. That means we could be going to China to track her down."

"Okay, but—"

"You know, China. It's that great big country across the Pacific Ocean."

I said, "I heard that there was a shit-pot full of people living in China on one of those Discovery TV shows. I think the dude said there were more people in China than the good old US of A, but he can't be right."

"The announcer was correct. In fact, around a billion more than in the U. S."

"A billion? Come on, Flo. I know you think I'm dumb, but I graduated from Elko High School so I'm not stupid. A billion more people?"

"Plus or minus a couple of million. Last year, the population of the capitol city Beijing was about twenty-one million."

"Babe, how in the hell are we going to find one Chinese broad in a country with more than a billion Chinese people?"

"That's why I'm pushing Pinky to bring back Lu. I think she can help us find Soong."

"I sure hope so. By the way, do those Chinese dudes speak English?"

"I'm afraid not. There are more languages spoken in China than menu items in a Chinese restaurant."

"Shit."

"And one more thing. They don't use the same alphabet we do. They make little pictures out of lines that sort of look like things, but people like us can't figure out what those things are."

"Jesus, I hope she's still in Kona 'cause we've got a better chance of spotting a black dog inside a coal mine than finding that broad in China."

"I didn't say it would be easy. That's why we'll need Lu's help."

Chapter Sixteen

Bear—Southport, North Carolina

While I packed up, Flo called her buddy in Washington. I could hear only one side of the conversation and listening to Flo, I could tell things weren't going her way. But that dude in Washington knew Flo, and what she could do to a guy if she didn't get what she wanted, so I was pretty sure he'd come up with something.

Flo said, "But Sam, if we do end up going to China we can't wait two weeks for a visa. It's a matter of life and death."

She listened for a minute and then shook her head. "I understand that China issues the visa's but can you guys in the State Department work around that? Great! Now, where can we pick up the visa's? No, San Francisco won't work. How about Hawaii?"

Flo listened and then smiled. "Honolulu could work and by that time I'll be ready for a day on the beach at Waikiki."

Flo nodded. "Okay. You'll have the visas ready for us to pick up in Honolulu forty-eight hours from now. Thanks Sam. I knew I could count on you . . . Yes, I'll be sure to stop by the next time I'm in DC. Bye now."

"Babe, where's Honolulu?"

"Hawaii. On the island of Oahu—the home of Diamond Head, Waikiki Beach, and surf boards."

"I thought we were going to Kona. Pinky's dumb, but he'll never fall for a vacation at . . . Wait a minute. Is Honolulu the place I saw on TV where those island broads dance with grass skirts and bare boobs?"

"Not any more."

"Babe, what happens if we find Soong and don't go to China?"

"Nothing. My buddy cancels the visas and we take Soong back with us to Carson City."

"But I'll miss going to Honolulu to see all those topless babes."

Flo pulled off her sweat shirt and posed like that Venus statue I'd seen with no arms. "Bear, you can search the world but you'll never find any better than what you're seeing right now. If we do stop by Waikiki beach, while you're searching for the girls, I'll be scouring the area for one of those bronzed beach boys with muscles on top of muscles."

"Babe, two can play at that game." I pulled off my tee shirt. "You can walk all over that Waikiki beach and you ain't never going to find a better six-pack than this."

She stared at me for a second, and then said, "Okay. I'll drop the beach boys as long as you forget the topless Hawaiian girls."

"Right."

I was about to jump her bod, but before I could move Flo threw her sweatshirt back on. "Bear, no time for that right now. Grab a pencil and write this down because I only want to go through this once. Call Pam and tell her we need two business class tickets on the first flight out of Wilmington to

119

Kona, and reserve us a five-star hotel suite for two nights."

"Hold on. A suite for two nights? I thought you said we were going to Soong's place to nose around—"

"Next, in case we need to use the Chinese visas, we'll need a flight from Kona to Oahu. Tell Pam while we're in Honolulu we'll require a first class hotel for one night on Waikiki beach. We can always cancel the hotel."

"A hotel at Waikiki beach? But what happened to—"

"Clam up and keep writing. After I call Lu, and convince her to go back to work for Pinky, she'll need to go into the office and talk with Pam to get up to speed. Got that?"

"Jesus, are you sure Pinky'll go for Lu coming back?"

"Right now he's more concerned about chasing a flight attendant around his hotel room. By the time the shrimp gets back to Carson City and figures out she's running his office, we'll be back home."

"I don't know, Babe. Pinky can be pretty nasty when he gets pissed."

"I can't worry because Pinky's a piss-ant. The man's only concern is to clear his client from this murder charge, and to accomplish that task we have to bring him Madam Soong."

"What if she's gone when we get to Kona?"

"Then Pinky will need Lu more than ever. If Soong heads to Beijing, the logical place to land in China, Lu can set up our contacts in Beijing."

"The Boss won't like any of this."

'Hey, if his Jockeys get all twisted up, so be it! Now get cracking and call Pam."

"Babe, I screwed up."

"What did you do?"

I handed her the paper where I was supposed to write everything down. Flo looked at it and yelled "What the hell! All you wrote down was call Pam!"

I said, "I know. But you rattled off all that crap so fast I couldn't keep up."

I could see that Flo was kinda of pissed at me, but she said, "Okay. I'll take care of Pam. You call Lu."

"What am I supposed to say to her? And talk slow."

"Try this. Lu, this is Bear. Flo told me to tell you that she needs you back working for Pinky!"

Chapter Seventeen

Pinky—Carson City, Nevada

As I packed my bag, I considered stopping by
the pool to inform Liz of my sudden change in
plans. However, upon further reflection, I recalled
that Liz was not the most desirable of the five Sky
Goddesses and as such, not worthy of any extra
effort on my part.

My room phone rang.

"Pinky?" It was Pam.

"How soon should I leave for the airport?"

"You have a little less than two hours so I'd
leave at once. You are booked on a flight to Reno at
2:30 pm but there's a stopover in Los Angeles, and
then on to San Francisco. That means you'll arrive
in Reno after midnight."

"What? My good woman, I have to be in court
at ten tomorrow morning."

"Hey, I'm damned good at what I do, but I
can't change reality. Your actual flight time will be
a little more than six hours. Once you add in the
fact that there's a three-hour time difference
between Carson City and Hawaii plus the layovers,
a little after midnight is the best I could do. I could
have a car pick you—"

"Forget the car. My vehicle is waiting for me in
a secure lot in Reno. I will call Willow. I am
positive that if I explain my situation perhaps I can
persuade her to move tomorrow's arraignment to

the afternoon."

Pam said, "I already tried that. After I reserved your seat on the plane, I could see that your time was going to be tight. I'm sorry to report that Willow wouldn't budge from her scheduled time of ten o'clock."

"Pam, after years of marital bliss, I am positive I hold more sway over Willow's decisions than you do. Now hang up. I have a call to make."

"Don't forget you have to be on that plane in a couple of hours. Bye."

That woman had just spoken to me as if I were a child. I made a mental note to discuss this undesirable flaw with her as soon as I returned from the arraignment. Then I recalled that Pam was counting down her last hours as my secretary so discussing her shortcomings would be a waste of my time. I made a mental note to call Rapid Replacement after the arraignment to seek a new majordomo for my office.

I picked up my room phone and dialed Willow's personal office number. "Ah, Willow my love. It has been too long since we last—"

"Can it, Pinky. My staff is assembling in my office for our weekly meeting so make this brief."

"My dear, I have been informed that for some unknown reason, you have moved up the Kaufmann arraignment to ten o'clock tomorrow morning. My love, as you well know, I am presently on the Kona Coast of—"

"It was the judge, not me, who moved the arraignment up a week. It seems his wife was promised a vacation, and this judge, unlike the spouse I was once married to, loves his wife. My meeting is about to start. See you bright and early tomorrow morning."

I slammed the phone down and stood there for a moment. My anger began to rise, as if I were an active volcano. However, before the lava began to spill over, my phone rang.

"Pinky, it's Liz. I apologize for the cold way I ended our conversation. Will you forgive me?"

I glanced at my watch. It showed thirty minutes past twelve. I was positive that if I left the hotel by 1:15, I would have more than enough time to get through the security check and board my flight on time.

With a touch of panic in her voice, Liz said, "Pinky, are you there?"

"I am. My dear, I have had a major change in my plans. Due to circumstances beyond my control, my stay here has been cut short. I only have forty-five minutes of free time before I must leave this glorious land of orchids and Mai Tais."

"So we won't have enough time for a walk on the beach?"

"Or a dip in the pool. But, my dear, I have a bottle of chilled champagne in my refeigerator and we could spend few moments together."

"Normally I wouldn't do this on the first date, but you are so cute, and God knows when we'll get together again. What's your room number?"

"Suite Five."

"Oh my God, that's one of those fab suites with the big lanai that overlooks the water. I'll be knocking on your door in five minutes."

"Don't take any longer, my sweet. When two lovers have only a few moments, every second apart becomes an eternity."

"Wow! It's just like Josie said, you really know how to sweet talk a girl."

"I'm not all talk. Now hang up. I must leave for the airport in forty-one, no forty minutes."

"Get ready, I'm running out the door."

As I waited for Liz to arrive, I decided that she was my exclusive opportunity to turn this horrible day around. From her first distressing call, to the endless blather of Bear and Florence, followed by Pam's quitting, and Willow's treachery, this was the moment for me to receive what I rightfully deserved—a few glorious minutes of euphoria. Once restored to my normally positive self, I would be ready to throw down the gauntlet to those who aspired to see me, the number-one defense attorney in Northern Nevada, toppled from his pedestal.

Chapter Eighteen

Bear—Kona Coast, Hawaii

I don't know how Flo, or that broad Pam did it, but they worked some travel voodoo and when we checked into our Kona hotel, there was a message from Lu to call her at Pinky's office.

Flo said, "Let's take a few minutes to jump in the pool and then we'll go to work."

"Sounds great to me."

While I unpacked, I watched Flo throw on her swimsuit, a mind blowing show that made being trapped in an airplane for a day and a half seem almost worth it. I dropped my drawers, and before I pulled on my swim trunks, I started to wonder if me and Flo had enough time to fool around.

"Bear, I can see what you're thinking but we've got work to do. We'll have plenty of time for that after the sun sets."

I looked down. Whoops! Sometimes she knows what I want almost faster than I can figure it out.

We got on the elevator and while it went down, I started thinking. Me and Flo were in Hawaii, on the way to the pool, like we were on a paid vacation. That's when I knew we were in deep doo-doo. As soon as Pinky figured out how much money we're spending the shit was going to hit the fan.

I said, "Babe, God help us when Pinky tumbles to the fact that he paid for business class tickets for me and you and he's forking out a bucket of cash for this fancy hotel. Did you forget? The Boss doesn't like to spend money on anybody but him!"

"Calm down. He owes us because he screwed us out of a trip to Hawaii a couple of years back. And don't forget, we're here to finish the job that pip-squeak was supposed to do. Relax, once we get to the pool, I'll call Lu."

"And don't forget, later on tonight, there's all sorts of stuff we can do in our room."

"Right! Now stick with me while we talk to Lu."

Flo grabbed my cell and pushed Pinky's number and the speaker button.

"Law office of J. Pincus Delmont."

"Lu, it's Flo and Bear. We got your message. What's up?"

"I'm back, but I told Pinky I would leave for good if he ever acted like he did the last time."

Flo said, "Good for you. After we take a quick dip in the pool we're heading to Madam Soong's coin shop."

Lu said, "Flo, when we talked yesterday, you left me with the impression that you might need more out of me than just coming back to run Pinky's office."

"That's true. If we discover that Madam Soong has vanished, and I'm betting on that, I think she'll head for China. If that happens, we'll need you to contact your uncle in Beijing to see if he can offer us any help tracking down Soong."

"I'll call my uncle as soon as you hang up."

"Thanks, Lu. I'll call you as we get more information."

Flo stuck my phone under a towel and we both

jumped in the pool. After paddling around for ten minutes. I said, "Are you ready to go?"

She nodded so I grabbed my phone and we went back upstairs. After we got dressed, I drove us to Soong's joint.

The place was small. It wasn't much bigger than Botano's dump but those two crooks weren't selling washing machines so their buildings didn't need to be too big.

Flo peered out the window and said, "I can see a note has been taped to the front door."

"Babe, you check it out. I'll wait in the car."

"So who made you king for the day?"

Damn, she can be a pain. "Look! It's too hot for me out there. I've got the air up as high as it will go and look at my arm pits? I'm sweating like a pig. By the way, while you check out what that note says, I'll pull back under the shade of those palms—to keep the car cool. And take your time. Write down anything that you think we might need to know."

Flo gave me that look, like she wasn't sure what was going on, but she was pretty sure it was being done to her. Finally she said, "Okay, but don't go too far. It's hot out there for me, too."

She jumped out and while she walked across the street I backed the rental into the shady palm jungle.

It took Flo a couple of seconds to reach the front door. She read the note and then pulled out a pencil and note pad from her purse. My babe was ready for anything, even taking notes.

She finished writing, turned and almost cleared the porch when a Rent-a-Cop car raced around the corner and cut off her escape. A big bastard jumped out of his car and yelled, "Stop right there, lady! What were you doing snooping around Madam Soong's shop?"

Now, I couldn't see Flo's face 'cause that fat Rent-A-Cop blocked my view, but I was pretty sure that she was really pissed 'cause she screamed, "Get out of my way, you jerk! I came here to buy some coins from Madam Soong and discovered her shop was closed. Then I noticed a note on the door. I read the note and the next thing I know a stupid, fake cop starts yelling at me. Move your fat butt out of my way or I'll call a real cop and tell him to arrest your sorry ass for assaulting a woman."

"Sorry. Madam Soong hired me to keep an eye on her place while she's gone. I guess I shouldn't have come on so strong, but Madam Soong told me to be on the lookout for anything. She's got a lot of valuable coins in that place."

"Apology accepted. Now, if you will excuse me, I have to call a cab."

The Rent-A-Cop's eyes finally connected to his brain and the poor bastard tumbled that he was talking to a babe with the greatest pair of knockers in the world. His lips worked like he was a fish out of water, and then he said, "Where are you going? I could drop you off."

"No thank you. When I was a young girl, my mother taught me to never get into the car of a strange man." Flo pulled out her cell phone and the Rent-A-Cop jumped into his car and drove away.

Once the cop car rounded the corner, Flo stormed up to the rental, jumped in and said, "I'll give you five seconds to tell me that you didn't set me up for that stupid cop. Five, four, three—"

"Okay, but listen to me before you restart the countdown. The first time we walked into Botano's joint I noticed his building had motion sensor alarms. I guessed that Soong's place would have the same stuff, so I sent you across the street to check out the note on the door and bingo, the private cop shows up. I didn't want to scare you but if we're going to nose around Soong's shop, I had to figure out a few things first. Okay?"

"You could have told me."

"I was afraid if you knew, you wouldn't do it, or you might get pissed off at me. Babe, you were perfect. 'Cause of you, I'll bet that Rent-A-Dude had to drive home to change his pants!"

Flo flashed me a crinkly smile. "You dodged a bullet this time, but don't ever do that to me again. Promise?"

"Yup, I promise." I really didn't know if I'd never do that to Flo again but I'm not stupid. "Babe, 'cause of your cool scouting job this afternoon, we should be able to get inside that joint without a hitch once it gets dark."

Flo slugged my arm so damn hard it almost hurt. "Are you setting me up again?"

"Nope. Tonight we'll head straight to the back entrance, check it out for motion sensors and if they only covered the front, we'll get in the back way."

"You do what you want, but count me out."

I said, "What did the note say?"

"Not much. Soong closed her shop for a couple of days so she can go shopping in Honolulu."

I drove back to our hotel and we spent the rest of the afternoon lying on the beach. After it got dark, the hotel had set up a spot where we could watch the manta rays swoop through the water below the cliff. Those babies were big, like ten feet across, and were shaped like a little stealth bomber you see on TV during the Rose Bowl on New Year's day. I knew this was a cool place, with the manta rays swimming through the waves, but we had a coin shop to break into. "Babe, let's go."

Twenty minutes later me and Flo were parked around the corner from Madam Soong's empty shop.

As I killed the engine, Flo said, "Like I told you this afternoon, I'm not putting myself through that again. If you want to get arrested, be my guest. But you're on your own, buster."

"Okay, but after I nose around, and get in the building, and if I need your brains, like there's a computer or something, you'll come in and help me, right?"

Flo didn't answer, but I figured she was still pissed off from this afternoon. I got out of the car and once I got to the shop I made my way along the side of the building while I checked out the roof line for more motion sensors. The rest of the joint looked clean. I've never been able to figure people out. They get all worried about crooks breaking in but then they go the cheap route—buy a fifty buck home alarm kit at the local hardware store, hang a couple of motion sensors near the front entrance, and a door sensor on the back door, plug the system in, and head off on vacation thinking all their goodies are safe and sound.

The trouble is that all those chintzy systems depend on a little 12 volt battery back-up, and in every system I've ever run into, the back-up battery was dead five minutes after it got installed. I crossed my fingers and threw the main power switch to kill the alarm system. Then I sat back to give the Rent-A-Cop a couple of minutes to respond just in case I'd run across the one back-up battery that still had some juice. Five minutes later I jimmied the back door and waited again. After a few minutes, I restored the power, turned on a light in the back room, and called Flo's cell.

"Bear, did something go wrong?"

"Nothing's wrong, Babe, but this Soong broad has a computer so I'll need your help. By the way, I've killed the alarm system so you can walk through the front door. Just close the door behind you so the rent-a-cop won't know you're here."

While I nosed around Flo checked out the computer.

The next thing I heard was a noise coming from a little printer.

Flo grabbed the paper from the printer. "Botano lied to us about his involvement in Ludwig's murder. Then the bastard emailed Soong telling her that the Carson City cops were on to them. I printed the email and forwarded it to Pinky."

She waved the printout. "This is a nice piece of evidence for Willow."

"Yup, except we got it after I broke in and you know Willow, she's really picky about things like that."

"Pinky can still give it to her. If nothing else, the email shows there are two people involved in Ludwig Kaufmann's murder."

Flo went back to the computer to do her thing while I kept nosing around the building. The only thing I found that looked out of place was a crumpled-up note in the trash can and Soong's passport. The little paper had a string of numbers written in pencil that didn't make any sense to me. At least we had the email Flo found, and Soong's passport, so once Flo told me she was done with the computer, I turned off the light and locked the doors. While I drove back to the hotel, Flo said, "We should have slapped some handcuffs on Botano and dragged his sorry ass back to Carson City."

"But once the dude figured out that we weren't cops, all he had to do was yell kidnapping and we'd be the ones in the cuffs."

While we rode the elevator up to our room, I gave Flo a little kiss on her nose.

She shook her head. "We still have a few more minutes of work."

"Okay, Babe. Whatever you say."

I opened our room door and after Flo walked in, she turned and said, "First thing tomorrow I'll call Pinky to make sure he understands Botano's email to Soong." She started to unbutton her shirt. "And Willow needs to see that email. In fact, I can fax a copy to—"

"Babe, if Pinky wants to tell Willow all that crap that's up to him. You know how the cops are. Once they got a guy for the crime, they don't like to keep looking for more suspects. Besides, I'm pretty sure that Botano's not waiting around Wilmington for someone to show up and arrest him."

As I dropped my drawers Flo said, "Hold on. What happened to that note you found with the numbers?"

I looked at her. She was standing naked in the moonlight. "Babe, I've got a lot more stuff on my mind then a stupid piece of paper."

"Hold that thought and get back to my question. Get that note and give it to me."

"That's exactly what I'm about to do."

"I can see that. But first, give me the note. I want to look at it."

Damn it! I grabbed my pants, fished out the paper, and handed it to her.

Flo sat down and her eyes looked back and forth across the note. "Bear, I think this could be a telephone number!"

I started to move closer. "Let me see."

"Stay where you are. We're still working the case and until we figure this out there will be no fun and games. Here, you take a look and tell me what you think."

I sighed. "Okay. I looked down and stared at 011861055598878261. Zero, one, one, eight . . . shit, there was a pot-full of numbers and I didn't have a clue what they meant. "I don't get it. Do you think it's some kind of a code?"

"It's not a code, it's a telephone number. The first three numbers, 011, that's the code for international calling. Hand me the phonebook."

"Come on, Babe. You're sitting there, naked, and you want me to hand you a phone book? Give me a break."

"Never mind. I'll get it." Flo walked to the desk, pulled out the phone book, and flipped a couple of pages. Then she said, "I'm right! It says here that 86 is the code for China and that 10 is the code for Beijing. Hold on. There are ten digits after the Beijing code. That's interesting. We have seven digits in our telephone numbers in America."

"Babe, didn't you tell me that China had a potfull of people?"

"I did. In fact, China has more than four times the population of our country. That's it! With more than a billion people, and with all those cell phones, China would require more than seven digits for their telephone system. Bear, thanks for figuring that out."

"You're welcome."

Flo said, "Bear, Soong is going to China and that's the phone number of a contact, or her hotel."

I hated to keep talking but she forgot something important. "Babe, how can Soong fly to China without her passport?"

Flo said, "Soong could have more than one identity."

"And more than one passport. Babe, this is going to be tough. We're going to be looking for an Asian broad, in Beijing, a city with more than twenty million people, and we don't know what name the broad's using."

Flo grabbed the phone by the bed. "Concierge please." She tapped her fingers on the end table for a second. "Hello. When does the next flight leave for Honolulu? Excellent. Book me two seats. Thank you."

"Were flying to Honolulu?"

"We are."

"When?"

"In two and a half hours."

"But Babe, you promised me that we'd—"

Flo said, "We will, but we'll have to hurry. One more item before things get out of control. I'm going to send an email to Pinky right now. He needs to know that we're following Soong to China."

"Come on, Babe, Pinky's got a pot-full of crap on his mind right now. You can send him the email from Honolulu."

She ignored me, opened her laptop and typed away like I was talking to the wall, instead of the best looking naked broad in the world.

A few minutes later, Flo hit the send button and smiled. "Okay, I declare work's over for the day, but before you do anything, hand me that note with the phone number. I think that will come in handy when we get to China."

I handed her the scrap of paper. "So my idea of putting you out there as bait for the Rent-A-Cop turned out to be pretty good. Right?"

Flo said, "Don't push your luck big fella. If you ever set me up like that again, you will spend a lot of nights sleeping by yourself!"

Chapter Nineteen

Pinky—Carson City, Nevada

After an exhausting few days of attempting to relax on the Kona Coast, the land that many people erroneously call paradise on earth, I arrived back in Northern Nevada, and to my profession of extracting innocent men and women from the clutches of overly zealous law enforcement. The Kaufmann arraignment lay before me—a huge mountain to scale. All decisions concerning the case flowed from me—the only person I trusted to control the helm of my legal ship as its prow cut through the stormy seas.

Before I boarded the plane at the Kona airport, I had called Pam and told her to place all pertinent data concerning the arraignment on my desk so I would be able to review the significant details relating to the murder of Ludwig Kaufmann the moment I arrived at my office.

Due to my unplanned exit from Kona, it took me three flights, and nearly eleven hours of travel to eventually reached home. I crawled into bed and enjoyed a short, but tranquil slumber. Everyone claims they enjoy traveling, but one's bed, their own personal cocoon, is the only true answer to a restful night.

At seven the next morning, still a touch travel worn, I stopped and picked up a large coffee to go on the way to my office. Not my normal habit as I prefer freshly brewed, but I was sure that my weary brain would appreciate a caffeine jump-start at this early hour. Sixty minutes later, with only half the coffee consumed due to its vile nature, I heard a soft knock on my office door. "Yes?"

A female voice said, "Pinky, it's Pam. I have fresh coffee brewing. May we come in?"

We? The door opened and Pam and Lu stood in the doorway. It was heartwarming to have employees so loyal that I could trust them to anticipate my every need.

"Please enter."

Pam and Lu walked in and stopped at my desk.

Lu had not changed. A stunningly beautiful asian female with dark eyes, coal-black hair, and flawless features.

On the other hand, Pam looked nervous, as if she were a school girl anticipating a rebuke from the Head Master. What was she worried about?

I said, "As soon as the brewing process has run its course, please bring me a fresh cup. I cannot wait to replace the black, acidic liquid that is masquerading as coffee in the cup on my desk. Lu before you go, I appreciate your commitment to my law practice. That is all."

Lu made her exit but Pam hesitated for a moment before she turned toward the door.

"Stand where you are, Pam," I commanded. "Your hesitation has raised my internal alarm. Why does your facial expression imply that I just caught you with your hand in the petty cash drawer?"

She couldn't control the fear that flashed

across her face.

I jumped from my chair and planted both hands on my desk. "Now what is going on?"

She backed away and said, "I'm sure you would have approved, but I have a feeling that I should have checked with you before I booked Business Class seats for Bear and Flo to Kona."

Business Class for my investigators? I would have been no less shocked if Pam's shoe had just crushed a burning cigarette on the irreplaceable Persian carpet that lay beneath my feet. I struggled to control my rising anger. "Did you just tell me that you wasted my hard-earned money on Business Class airline tickets for Bear and Florence?"

"I did."

In a flash of temper I slammed my fist on the top of my desk and the half-full cup of warm coffee tumbled onto my priceless mahogany desktop.

Lu rushed in as Pam pulled a handkerchief out of her pocket and captured the leading edge of the brown liquid just before the wave fell onto the aforementioned carpet below.

Lu exclaimed, "Pam caught the results of your anger in time to save your fancy rug. Pinky, if you cannot find a way to control your temper, both Pam and I will walk out that door and your office will be left empty."

My God! This is what happens when jet lag rears its ugly head. I sat down, opened my drawer and tossed a handful of dry tissues onto the shrinking brown pool. "Pam, please close the door and sit down."

She glanced at Lu, and then followed my

direction.

I said, "Lu, please sit down."

Before I could say a word, my phone rang.

I picked up the receiver. "Hello?"

"Pinky, I wasn't sure you'd return in time for the arraignment."

It was Willow.

I snapped my fingers and motioned for the two women to exit my office. Once the door closed, I said, "Willow, my love. The giant hole in my heart continues to grow since we last spoke. Will you be free for lunch after the Kaufmann arraignment?"

My door popped open and Lu, followed by Pam rushed in. She thrust a paper at me and mouthed, "Read it!"

"Willow, please hold your response to my invitation for a moment. I have a small emergency in my office that I must attend to."

I hit the hold button and Lu said, "Pinky, you need to read this email from Flo before you say any more to Willow."

I snatched the paper from her.

Pinky:

The information I gleaned off Madam Soong's computer indicates that Botano and Soong were both involved in the Kaufmann murder. By the time you read this Bear and I will be on our way to China in pursuit of Soong and the two million dollar dime. We think you should convince Willow that she needs to broaden her investigation and track down Carlo Botano as we are positive he's an accessory, if not a co-conspirator, to the murder of Kaufmann. Last time we saw the guy he was in

Wilmington, North Carolina.

Flo

- S. Don't get all pissed off about the Business Class seats to China I just booked. And we appreciate your bringing Lu back to the team. We desperately need her help to set up our contacts in China. Without her input, flying to Beijing would be a waste of our time and your money. Just thank your lucky stars that Lu likes me because I can guarantee you that she wouldn't let you lick the sweat from her arm pits if you were dying of thirst.

I set the paper down and pushed the hold button. "Willow, my investigative team just informed me that a man named Carlo Botano should be considered a viable suspect concerning the Kaufmann murder."

"Give it a rest, Pinky. I know you hate to lose, but as we speak, the killer of Ludwig Kaufmann, your client, happens to be sitting in the Carson County jail. By the way, Manuel Vaca, my number one ADA will be handling the arraignment. If you have any information concerning other suspects in the Kaufmann murder, turn it over to him, or to the police. I'm positive they will take your information and respond accordingly. Finally, concerning lunch, my answer is an emphatic no! In fact, we need to maintain a reasonable separation between the two of us until this Kaufmann trial is over."

"My love, you cannot mean—" I heard a click and knew that Willow had hung up on me.

I looked up. Pam and Lu were still standing

there.

I said, "Pam, take a copy of this email and give it to Henrietta Spaulding. Pretend it is an accidental leak from my office."

"I don't think I could do that."

Lu said, "I agree with Pam. My decision to return and run your office depends on your ethical behavior and 'accidental leaks' are not included in my definition of proper ethics."

Before I could respond, my iPhone alarm sounded, indicating I had ten minutes before the Kaufmann arraignment began.

"Lu, I must leave at once. I will return in approximately ninety minutes once the arraignment proceedings are completed. At that time I trust Pam will have turned over the email to Detective Henrietta Spaulding. Regardless of your opinion of my ethics, a creditable murder suspect, Carlo Botano, freely wanders around Wilmington, North Carolina."

Pam said, "Pinky, I don't think that Henny's boss will spend the money to fly her to North Carolina on an email from one of your investigators."

I considered for a moment the absolute need to obfuscate the issue concerning my client's position as the only suspect in Kaufmann's death. I knew that once I fostered the creditable theory that Carlo Botano, and Madam Soong, were co-conspirators in the murder, that concept would create enough doubt to slow down a trial, if not gain the release of my client. "Pam, to allay your concerns, and to prove my conviction that Botano was involved in the Kaufmann murder, as your last act as my employee, book me on a flight to Wilmington, North Carolina. I have an innocent client wasting away in jail and his very life depends on me proving him innocent of the Kaufmann murder. At present, Bear and Flo, my crack investigative team are flying to China to track down the other suspect. My dear, if this email does not convince the police to follow the lead, then it is left up to me—"

Pam said, "Okay. I'll make your reservation. Henny's meeting me for lunch and I'll give her the email. Once she hears that you are willing to put your money and your time on the line, I'm sure she'll convince her boss she needs to go with you."

"Excellent. Now, are all my employees satisfied?"

They smiled.

"Excellent. Lu, from now on my office policy will be to book all flights for the members of my investigative team in Coach Class, and you are required to check with me prior to any upgrades."

Lu nodded. "As long as you understand that it's too late to change the round trip Business Class tickets Flo booked for their flight to China."

I froze my expression to one of calm and forced back the urge to once again pound my closed fist on the desk. "I understand, but from this moment on, no upgrades beyond Coach Class without my prior approval."

Pam said, "Pinky, what class of ticket do you want me to book for your flight today?"

"First Class. In the case of my travel, you will book first class hotels, airfare, and car rentals. Always First Class!" I gritted my teeth and said, "Are you both clear on that?"

143

Lu said, "Loud and clear."

Pam left my office.

I glanced at the stack of call back messages on my desk. "Lu, a moment please. I see that I missed a call from George Sterling reminding me that I have to make an extended visit to his residence to verify his continued sobriety. I am not sure if you recall George is a pro bono client and the court requires me to monitor his progress on a regular basis. George's physical health comes first and I fear that my afternoon with him will force me to change my travel plans. Ask Pam to cancel my airline reservation to Wilmington. Her friend, Detective Spaulding, will have to fly to Wilmington to arrest Carlo Botano without me by her side."

Lu stared at me, as if she could spot something in my eyes that would disprove the veracity of my story.

"You do recall George Sterling?"

"I'm not sure."

I handed her the message Pam had taken the prior day.

She read the note and nodded.

"I trust Pam, and Detective Spaulding, will understand my dilemma. I have to go to George's apartment or be held in contempt of court for neglecting my legal duties."

Chapter Twenty

Bear—Kona and Honolulu, Hawaii; Tokyo, Japan; and Beijing, China

Some vacation on Kona! All I really saw were some pictures at the airport that showed the beach and the cool volcano park where red-hot lava runs like water into the ocean. Lu had called Flo with all the scoop that we needed for our trip to China, including our contact in Beijing, an old uncle of hers named Joe. Hell, I even called the dude on the phone. Guess what? Joe talked real English, not real fast, and not real good, but he said real English words, just like you and me. I think that Flo must have been feeding me a line of crap that the Chinese talked French, or something like French, and that they wrote funny pictures instead of using letters like the rest of the world does.

Right on time, we left Kona and flew to Honolulu. I had Soong's passport in my carry-on and Flo had her loopy thing along with that coin book in her suitcase. The first thing after our plane landed we took a cab to a big government building downtown, and just like that dude in Washington had promised, me and Flo picked up our Chinese visas.

Flo said, "We have thirty minutes before we need to go to the airport. I'll ask the cab driver to stop by a Waikiki beach so you can see that the cute Hawaiian girls are all wearing tops."

Damn it, Flo was right about the broads, but it was still fun to watch some people jump on a surfboard and fall off. Every once in a while a lucky dude would stay up and ride the wave all the way to the beach. Shit, I couldn't figure out how they did it 'cause standing up on one of those ironing board things, slipping and sliding around the water looked tougher than grabbing a greased pig at the Elko County Fair. Two hours later we walked onto an Air China plane and sat down in Business Class. Before the wheels left the ground, one of those broads wearing a uniform handed me my first brew.

After a pot-full of good American beers, three Batman movies, and some grub, we landed in Tokyo. We got off the plane and walked through the airport to switch planes. That's the first time I saw what Flo had told me about—that weird Chinese picture writing. I pointed to an ad on the wall that showed a big bunch of line pictures next to a bottle of Budweiser beer. "Babe, is that what you told me about? How sometimes the Chinese use squiggly line pictures instead of words?"

"That's it."

"But that broad on the plane, the one in the uniform, said that we were landing in Japan, not China."

Flo stared at me, like she wasn't sure if I was putting her on. "Both Japan and China use symbols instead of words."

"I still don't get it."

She said, "Okay, but I learned this a long time ago and I'm only going to say this once, so listen carefully. Chinese and Japanese symbols are

146

actually logograms and a logogram is a letter, symbol, or sign used to represent an entire word or a syllable of a word. The Chinese logograms are symbols called hanzi. The Japanese symbols are called kanji. Got it now?"

I really didn't have a clue what the hell she was talking on about but I took a wild guess and it turned out to be a lucky one. "Got it. Like all those lines on the Budweiser ad are some of those lo-go-go things, right?"

Flo smiled. "Bear, I'm proud of you. That simple concept took a couple of my spaced-out classmates half the semester to figure out. Of course, I think they were either drunk or hung over during all the lectures. Now what I'd like to know is how did you come up with the—"

A broad's voice over the loud speaker saved my butt when she told me and Flo they were boarding our plane for China and we'd better hustle.

Again, the beers were great, but Jesus it took forever to fly to where we were going. I don't have a clue how many miles we traveled, but thank God Flo had told Pam to get us Business Class seats.

After my third brew, I had to hit the john, and when I finished my business, I peeked through the curtain at the poor bastards jammed into the coach section. Shit, I didn't spot an empty seat all the way back to the tail end of the plane. It was sort of like I was looking down a big metal tunnel where someone had figured out how to stuff three-hundred losers into a space built for about two-hundred people.

And then there were the crying babies. It sounded like there were at least a dozen of them.

Don't get me wrong. I know babies have to cry, but nothing says that I have to listen to them, or sit next to them, or have anything to do with those puking, pissing, and pooping little rug rats.

Anyway, as I said before, thank God for Business Class. The seats were wide and almost as comfortable as my chair at home where I watch TV. And I had my choice of great movies, like the latest super hero, or James Bond, or . . . hell, the best flicks you can see.

The booze? It was like you'd just walked into a bar and found out that all the drinks were free during happy hour and happy hour lasted all day. No joke. If you're looking for an all-you-can-drink party—for free—get a Business Class seat and fly anywhere! I knocked off a half a dozen brews, and before she went to sleep, Flo downed three glasses of good red wine.

The food? Not as good as what we got at the Nugget's All-You-Can-Eat Tuesday night buffet, but for an airplane, rolling along at a million miles an hour, high up over the Pacific ocean, the spread they put in front of us wasn't all that bad.

And I can't forget those good-looking broads in uniform. Flo told me they used to be called stewardesses but now they want to be called flight attendants. Hell, they could call themselves coal miners as far as I was concerned as long as one of them kept handing me a cold brew every hour.

Pinky was always ragging at us about him being a sophisticated dude 'cause he was a world traveler, but after flying from Reno to North Carolina, and back to San Francisco, and then Hawaii, and now to China, Flo told me that I was

148

really getting the hang of traveling.

It took us another five hours, and few more brews, before we landed at Beijing. It was around ten in the morning when I looked out the window but I couldn't see anything—no buildings—no sunshine—no nothing but brown air that looked thick enough to eat. Then, just before the wheels hit the ground, I spotted a big building. I gave Flo a jab in the ribs."Babe, I can see something out there, but the air actually looks uglier than that bowl of old oatmeal you store in our refrigerator."

Flo leaned over me and a bolt of electricity shot through my lap when her boobs pushed against me.

"I save that oatmeal because I know I will eat it sooner or later." She looked out the window for a second. "You're right. The air looks terrible, but that's not surprising. Beijing has some of the worst air pollution in the world as measured by the number of particles per cubic meter of air, or the PM2.5 scale. For example, the air pollution in Salt Lake City was considered bad because the air there had reached 69 on the PM2.5 scale. The last I read, Beijing's air pollution had exceeded 500!"

"Wow! That means that Beijing's air is almost twice as bad as Salt Lake City!"

"Actually, more than seven times as bad, but who's counting."

"Babe, do you think Pinky didn't come here 'cause he didn't want to screw up his delicate lungs?"

"You never know with that little bastard. From what I've read, a bad air day is the norm in Beijing."

"What are the chances of us finding a good air day?"

"Don't know. I've never been here before."

After the plane landed we got off and walked through the biggest airport terminal I'd ever seen. And everywhere, there were people shoving and pushing, like they were all trying to find a hidden stash of c-notes. Getting to me and Flo's luggage was sort of like fighting our way back to my truck after the giant Carson City Fourth of July fireworks bash.

Finally, I found and grabbed our bags and was looking for a way out of this mess when Flo jabbed me in the ribs and pointed at a Chinese dude who was holding a sign with our names in big letters—MISTER BEAR—MADAM FLO.

The dude's gray hair made him look older than Pinky, but his face was as smooth as a baby's butt.

I pushed my way to the signs. The old dude nodded his head and said, "Mister Bear, Madam Flo, welcome to China. Lu's father was my older brother. My name is Jung Yong but my American name is Joe."

After all those brews on the plane, I really needed to take a piss. I mean really bad, so I said, "Hi Joe, can you aim me in the right direction so I can talk to a man about a horse."

"Excuse me?"

"You know—a can—a john—a bathroom where a guy can take a piss."

"Ah, a toilet! Yes. We have many toilets in the airport. All top class. Very American. Some of the finest in Beijing. Perhaps Madam Flo also needs to use the facility?"

"Yes, and as soon as possible."

"Follow me."

He pushed us through a flood of people and down a long corridor to a can. A few minutes later, and feeling like a new man, I found Joe standing outside the Ladies Room and said, "Thanks for that. My eyes were almost floating but you told me all top class, the finest can in Beijing. Fess up dude, is that porcelain palace the best you Chinese can do?"

"Porcelain palace? Sorry. I do not understand."

"You told us that crapper was clean. That joint wasn't any better than the one we had at the Old Globe Bar in Carson City after a full Friday night of barfing."

About that time Flo sprinted out of the women's john and she was holding her nose. She stopped and took a deep breath. "Joe, were you kidding us? If that's a top class toilet I shudder to think what the lower class ones smell like."

He smiled. "Madam Flo, I am pleased you liked the toilet. Very American—top class."

Flo turned to me and said, "It could be that top class means something different in China. Joe speaks pretty good English but I'm not sure he understands everything we say."

"Right, Babe."

"Mister Bear, Madam Flo, is this your first trip to Beijing?"

Flo said, "Yes it is. In fact, this is our first visit to your country. Tell me, Joe, is the air pollution always this bad in Beijing?"

The little guy shrugged his shoulders. "Air pollution? I do not understand your question concerning air pollution. The air is fine in Beijing. Please follow me."

Flo said, "Where are we going?"

"To my car. I have reserved you a room at a five-star hotel. Very American. Top Class! Tomorrow we will go to the Great Wall. The next day to The Forbidden City. Then I will take you to—"

Flo interrupted. "Joe, prior to our meeting today, we did not know each other, so I feel the need to lay our cards on the table."

"Cards?"

"In our country, Bear and I are the captains of our ship."

Shit, my babe was starting to sound like Pinky.

The little guy looked confused. "Captains?"

Flo said, "If our relationship is to remain on a collegial level we need to find Madam Soong, arrest her, and return to Carson City as soon as possible."

"Collegial?"

I reached over and grabbed the front of the little fart's shirt. "What she's saying is that we didn't come to China to look at a stupid wall."

"Stupid wall?"

The top button on Joe's shirt popped off and hit the marble floor so I let him go. "Like my Babe said, we're here to track down Madam Soong, the dime, and then go home."

Joe bent down and picked up his button. "I understand, but you don't realize how jet lag will effect you after a long east to west flight. You flew through nine time zones and your brains, even if they are top class American brains, will take a few days to catch up. I will drive you to the hotel, but tomorrow I promise that you will not feel like looking for Madam Soong. And speaking of Madam Soong, we need to talk about a big problem that—"

Flo said, "Joe, we'll talk later. Please get us to our hotel."

"My Babe's right. All we need is to sleep in a real bed."

The look on Joe's face told me he thought me and Flo were nuts, but he said, "As you wish."

He led us through the airport and the second we walked out the door of the terminal my eyes started to sting and my nose got all clogged up.

After we walked what seemed like a long way, he stopped next to a rusty, old, Volkswagen.

I said, "Is this it?"

He nodded.

"What year is the car?"

"I think 1978."

Flo said, "Jesus, more than thirty years old. Does it run?"

"Runs good."

I said, "Joe, is this your car?"

He shook his head. "No. The VW is my son's vehicle. My new Mercedes is in the shop to fix a broken headlight."

Flo looked in the back window. "Joe, judging by the newspapers, take-out boxes, and empty beer cans all over the back seat, I assume your son lives in his car."

The little dude looked startled by Flo's nastiness. "I am sorry, Mister Bear, and Madam Flo, but my son's car was the only vehicle available to me."

Flo said, "Joe, how about you drop the Madam and Mister formality. Just call us by our first names, Flo and Bear."

"Madam Flo, I will try. I will have difficulty doing what you request, but I will try."

While I brushed off the front seat trash, Joe stuck our suitcases under the front end trunk. Before Flo piled in, she pushed most of the junk to the other side of the car and then tapped my shoulder. "Bear, the back seat of this car smells almost as bad as the women's toilet at the airport."

I leaned forward and took a big whiff. "More like a garbage landfill up here."

I hadn't slept much during the flights with all the movies and beer, so I was as pooped as a pup who'd been chasing his tail for an hour. I put my head back and inside a second I was hanging at the edge of dreamland. Joe fired up the old VW. The engine noise brought me back for a second but then I started to drift into sleep. Suddenly the VW jumped a couple feet forward. My head snapped backward and crashed into the headrest. "Son-of-a-bitch!" I yelled. "What the hell just happened?"

"Sorry, Mister Bear. My Mercedes has an automatic."

I fought my way back from sleep and stared at Joe through my half-opened eyelids. "Do you know how to drive a manual transmission?"

"I'm not sure."

My brain snapped awake. "Joe, just give me the straight skinny."

"Straight skinny?"

"No bullshit—the truth."

"Okay, Mister Bear."

"Have you ever driven a car with a manual transmission?"

"Not before my son taught me."

"When did he do that?"

"Two hours ago."

All of a sudden, I wasn't sleepy. "No shit. Tighten your seatbelt, Babe."

After three more jumps, the VW shot out of the parking lot and toward an intersection. My stomach tightened when I figured out that the signal facing us was bright red and Joe seemed more concerned with shifting than braking. Then, out of the corner of my eye, I spotted a white car on the green-light side of the intersection, and that car was aimed directly at me. I ducked my head down. In those couple of seconds you get before you think you're going to die, like when your whole life is suppose to go by like a movie, I saw Pinky talking to Joe on the phone.

Pinky said to Joe, "I am about to fly to China but I have learned that you have smashed the front end of your Mercedes and the vehicle is in the shop. What car do you plan to use when you pick me up at the airport?"

Joe said, "My son's old VW."

Pinky said, "But the Volkswagen has a manual transmission and your Mercedes has an automatic. That means you will not know how to drive your son's vehicle and that could be potentially unsafe for me. Therefore, I will send Bear and Flo in my stead."

Shit! In my gut I knew that me and Flo going to China was Pinky's kind of trip. What I couldn't figure out was how did my chicken-shit boss know

155

that Joe's Mercedes would be in the shop and that me and Flo would die in a fiery accident instead of him?

Joe finally stopped screwing around with the gearshift, looked up, saw the red light and slammed the brake pedal to the floor. The VW's wheels locked and the tires screamed. Our car skidded to the left and the burned rubber smoke was so stinky that it overcame the landfill funk at my feet. I guessed that the white car missed us by the width of a layer of the old VW's rust.

While we sat there in the middle of the intersection, with cars flying by, I rolled the window down to clear out the burnt rubber smell.

I tried to say something but my mouth was as dry as the sand in the Northern Nevada desert. Finally, I got some spit back in my mouth and said, "Babe, you okay back there?"

"Just barely." She took a deep breath and said, "Joe, how long have you been driving?"

"Around a month. The Mercedes dealership taught me after I bought my car."

I glanced back at Flo. Her face was the color of a white fence post.

I said, "Joe, I know I told you that we were very tired, but forget what I said. Me and Flo are not in any hurry to get to the hotel, so please, slow down so we can get there in one piece."

The VW jumped ahead and almost ran into a giant truck overflowing with watermelons. Joe tried to shift down. I figured that his son had told him that a downshift would slow the VW, but all he did was make the gears grind. A second before we rear-ended the watermelon truck, I grabbed the wheel and steered to the right.

The truck with the watermelons swerved left and a dozen of the giant green monsters hit the pavement in front of us as the truck shot through an intersection against the red light. For some weird reason Joe decided he would stop at this red light and the VW slid to a halt on a layer of squished, bright red, melon.

"Smart idea, Mister Bear. You changed lanes. Do you drive a manual transmission vehicle in America?"

I didn't answer his question 'cause I was too busy scrambling around the front seat trying to find the seat belt I had ignored before.

Flo, looking like she was feeling better, leaned over the front seat and said, "Joe, did your driving instructor explain to you that regardless of the type of transmission, manual or automatic, you need to stop at a red light each time you reach an intersection?"

After chipping off a couple more teeth of his son's transmission, Joe said, "Madam Flo, thank you for reminding me. That rule was one of the many the Mercedes dealership taught me after I bought the car. Stop at red! Go on green! However, I am not used to driving to the airport. There are very few traffic lights on the streets in my part of the city."

The signal light changed to green. Joe managed to grind through three gears and then jerked the wheel to the left. The VW cut across three lanes of oncoming traffic and barreled into the driveway of the Excelsior Hotel.

"Mister Bear and Madam Flo, we have arrived

at the Excelsior Hotel. Five stars. Top class. Very American. Now you can relax and spend a few days recovering from jet lag."

Flo said, "Joe, we've already been through this. We need to start looking for Madam Soong at once. There's a man in Carson City accused of murdering his brother, and Madam Soong—"

"I am sorry but you will require rest to get your brains into top class order."

I said, "Joe, are you staying at the hotel with us?"

"No. I will sleep at my home in a different section of Beijing."

"Hold on, is there something wrong with this joint?"

"Joint?"

"The Excelsior Hotel, damn it!"

"No. As I said, the Excelsior is five star. Top class. Very American. Just too American for me. And as I tried to tell you back at the airport, you and Madam Flo might as well relax and go to the Great Wall, and the Forbidden City, because you will be wasting your time looking for a woman named Madam Soong anywhere in China."

Twenty plus hours trapped in an airplane, damn near killed in a rusty VW, and now the dude drops the next shoe. Looking for Madam Soong in China would be a waste of our time? This little shit was beginning to piss me off. "Joe, what the hell do you mean we'd be wasting our time?"

"The name that Lu gave me, Soong May-ling, is the same name of the woman who became Madam Chiang Kai Shek."

Flo said, "Of course! That's why Soong's using

158

another passport."

"Of course?" I turned toward Flo, "What do you mean, of course?"

"I mean Soong can't use the name of a Nationalist hero because Mao and the Communists won the civil war!"

I said, "What's all that Communist and Nationalist bullshit got to do with anything?"

Flo glared at me like she'd just figured out that I traveled all this way with my fly unzipped. "Bear, for decades a civil war raged in China, the country with the largest population on the planet. To call the Chinese conflict, and the eventual outcome, bullshit would exceed all my previously low estimations concerning your enormous lack of knowledge. But I know better so I'll explain the bullshit. There were two sides in the civil war, and the lady we are looking for has the same name as the wife of the losing side leader. Today, in Communist China, there can't be many Chinese parents who name their daughter Soong Mai-ling."

I said, "Okay, I get it now. Soong was named after the wife of the dude who lost the civil war."

Flo said, "I'm proud of you."

I said, "Not so fast, I've got one more question. Is the wife of the dude who lost the war still alive?"

Joe said, "No, Madam Shek died in 2003."

Flo said, "Can I go on now?"

I nodded.

Flo said, "Joe, now that we're all on the same page what hope do we have of finding Soong, or whatever she's calling herself these days?"

"Confucius say, 'He that would perfect his work must first sharpen his tools.'"

159

I said, "Sounds like something my Pop used to say. But who's this Confusion dude?"

Flo grabbed my arm and said, "Joe, you go sharpen your tools and . . . oh, I almost forgot something that could be important. We have a Beijing telephone number that should help us know where to start looking."

Flo gave the little dude the note with the telephone number. He took a quick glance and shrugged like it was worthless. But I picked up something in his eyes, like it might be important or something, before he stuffed the paper in his coat pocket. For Joe's sake, I was glad the little dude kept the note 'cause if he'd tossed the damn thing on the ground, Flo might have decked him on the spot.

I'm pretty sure that Flo didn't notice Joe's tumble on the phone number 'cause her eyes were half-closed. I felt the same way but I didn't want Joe to think I was a wimp. Flo gave one giant yawn and said, "Joe, I know one American woman that's about to fall asleep standing up. Give me a couple of days of real rest and I'll be ready to help you come up with a new plan."

Chapter Twenty-One

Pinky—Carson City

I stood over Lu's shoulder, and before she answered the phone, I said, "If it is a call from Bear, put him on speaker phone."

She nodded, pushed a button and said, "Law Office of J. Pincus Delmont."

Lu hit the speaker phone button in time to hear Flo say, "Lu? Glad to hear you answering Pinky's phone again."

Lu glanced at me. I smiled and gave her a nod, to indicate that she was free to express her feelings.

"I'm happy to be back. Pinky hired me back at twice my old salary, with three weeks paid vacation, fully paid-up health insurance, and two weeks free use of his Lake Tahoe condo."

Flo said, "Wow! Is he there?"

"I'm standing behind Lu. What can I do for you?"

Flo said, "Bear's in the john, and I can hardly wait to tell him that Lu's back in the fold. Come to think of it, why did Pam Carson leave?"

I said, "That is not something I am at liberty to discuss but it was a personal decision on her part."

Suddenly, Bear's voice boomed over the speaker. "I'm back and I heard the part about Pam. Come on, Boss, cut through the crap. What the hell really happened?"

I said, "In the future, I would appreciate the courtesy of being informed how many persons are a part of these informal conference calls."

Flo said, "Nice try, Pinky. You attempted to avoid Bear's question but it didn't work. What happened to Pam?"

I looked at Lu for a moment and was pleased that she had returned to the Delmont family. "Florence, I passed on to Pam your message concerning the viable murder suspect, Carlo Botano. I further informed her that according to our information, Botano was in Wilmington, North Carolina. She, in turn, contacted her partner, Detective Spaulding, and Spaulding agreed to pursue the matter."

There was a moment of silence over the phone. Then Bear said, "There's got to be more to this than that. That Pam broad seemed real happy the last time I talked to her. Come on, Boss, fess up."

I glanced down and noticed Lu was getting a bit on edge, as if she were preparing to leave. At that moment I recalled a line written by Shakespeare where Falstaff exclaimed, "The better part of valor is discretion." As Northern Nevada's most successful attorney, there had been moments when I had to back down, to reserve my pluck for another day, and this was one of those moments. I said, "Listen carefully because I am only going to say this once. Pam made up her mind to quit due to a personal conflict. After I received your email, I called Willow. For some unknown reason she was not impressed and refused to use her office to pursue Carlo Botano. I then talked with Pam and told her about the Kaufmann murder suspect who was thumbing his nose at the law in North Carolina. She was shocked that the District Attorney wouldn't act, so I encouraged her to contact her friend, Detective Spaulding, and suggested that Spaulding fly to Wilmington and return the miscreant to Carson City."

Bear said, "Like I said before, there's got to be more to this. Pam's gone. What else did you do or say?"

"There might have been some confusion concerning my flying with Detective Spaulding to Wilmington."

Flo said, "I get it now. You convinced Pam to send her partner. Then you told her to make a plane reservation for you on the same flight to prove to Pam, and Detective Spaulding, that you weren't trying to pull some sort of a scam to generate another murder suspect. Right?"

I said, "Florence, I take your insinuation that I would perpetrate a scam as a personal affront. There was no attempt on my part to—"

"Put a sock in it, Pinky," said Flo. "Did you tell Pam to make a plane reservation for you to fly to Wilmington?"

"Yes I did, but that had nothing to do with her decision to—"

"And Pam saw you as the unscrupulous bastard you are. Am I right?"

"Florence, as I stated earlier, I will stipulate that Pam left my employ due to a personal ethical conflict. The rest of what she told me is confidential."

Flo said, "Lu, are you still there?"

"Yes, I'm here."

Flo said, "Listen to me. I've known Pinky longer than you so I know not to trust him. But the email I sent him did identify a man, Carlo Botano, who should be arrested and charged with the murder of Helmut Kaufamnn. Bear and I are stuck in Beijing attempting to locate Madam Soong who we are positive was also involved in the Kaufmann murder. It sounds to me like Pinky has given you a great package, money, benefits, everything an employee could ask for but a decent man to work for. Please, for our sake, stay at that desk. As soon as we return, Bear will make sure Pinky gives you everything he has promised. Okay?"

I said, "Florence, if you are insinuating that—"

"Pinky, if you know what's good for you, shut up and give Lu a chance to answer me. Go ahead, Lu."

I was relieved to notice that Lu had relaxed as she said, "I'll do it, but not for Pinky, just for you and Bear." Her dark eyes lifted up and glared at me. "Pinky has to understand that the reason I left his employment was his total lack of character—his treatment toward women in general, and his ex-wife in particular. The future of my remaining at this position will be totally dependent on my definition of the proper conduct of J. Pincus Delmont."

I have been on this earth long enough to understand when I have been placed on the horns of a dilemma. This woman was demanding that she, and she alone, would determine if my daily conduct met her definition of morality.

"Come on, Pinky, say something," growled Bear. "Shit or get off the pot."

Flo said, "Pinky, do you accept Lu's terms, as defined and measured by her?"

Somehow that witch, and Lu, had conspired to position me between Scylla and Charybdis. Recalling the Odyssey saga, I could survive if I carefully sailed between the monster, Scylla and the living whirlpool, Charybdis. However, one mistake and all was lost. I determined that even the heroic Odysseus would understand that there were moments in every life when a strategic retreat trumped a humiliating defeat. After a rapid calculation that my practice would not last two days without someone of Lu's capability, I mumbled, "I do."

Then Flo said, "And Lu, do you take J. Pincus Delmont on your terms, and only your terms?"

"I do."

Bear said, "Come on, Flo, let's get this show on the road. I'm starving and we still haven't told Pinky why we had to call him."

"I hear you, but this is too good to pass up. Pinky and Lu, I now pronounce you employer and employee."

Chapter Twenty-Two

Bear—Beijing

"Florence," cried Pinky over the phone speaker. "Cease your inane babble and inform me what information was so important that you felt the need to interrupt my busy day."

My Babe said, "Look, when we left Hawaii we were under the impression that our target was an Asian woman who went by the name of May-ling Soong, or Soong May-ling as they say in China."

Pinky screamed, "I know all that! Remember, I was in Kona to investigate the same woman. I made an appointment to meet her and then she . . . hold on . . . did you just say *went* by the name of May-ling Soong?"

Flo chuckled, "I figured you'd slow down sooner or later. May-ling Soong was the maiden name of the woman who married Chiang Kai Shek."

We both heard Pinky groan.

"Boss, I didn't get it either. Soong's old man lost the Chinese civil war."

"I know that, you dolt. In fact, if our May-ling Soong was the original Madam Chiang Kai Shek, her return to China would be tantamount to Benedict Arnold's wife sneaking into Washington a few decades after the revolutionary war."

I said, "I don't get it. Joe told us Madam Chiang Kai Shek was dead."

Pinky said, "And you never will. Joe is correct. The real Madam Chiang Kai Shek died some years ago. The woman named Soong that you are attempting to track down was named after Madam Chiang Kai Shek, I assume to honor her memory."

"Ease up, Boss. What I didn't get was what the hell did a dude named Benedict Arnold have to do with China?"

Pinky sighed, "Florence, please help Bear achieve an intellectual awakening on the subject of Benedict Arnold."

Flo looked at me and smiled. "Sweetheart, you are a little confused, but no more than our exalted legal leader of Northern Nevada."

The phone speaker blasted, "Florence, I heard that! Now get serious and let us bring Lu up to date with the situation."

Lu said, "Don't bother. Flo and I already talked and I know all about May-ling Soong."

Pinky cried, "Lu, you have one minute to explain why I, your overseer, am the last one to know what is going on?"

I said, "Cool it, Boss. Now you know that Lu and Flo talk on the phone. Yelling at us won't find that broad or the stupid dime any faster. Shut it down and listen."

Pinky screamed, "Shut it down? Did you just tell me to shut it down? In my day, a minion would never consider talking to his superior in that manner. If the thrust of our conversation continues in this vein, I will put out the word that I am seeking a new investigator. I trust that—"

Flo said, "Pinky, you are not talking to minions, or slaves, or serfs. Bear and I are your only hope to recover that dime! Now shut up and listen! We're sure the woman with the dime is in Beijing and we're positive that she's using a different name. A couple of days ago I called my friend in the State Department, the one who fast-tracked our visas to China. I explained our unique situation and asked for his help. He told me he would see what he could do."

Pinky said, "And?"

"That's why we called. Ten minutes ago my friend emailed the answer."

"Explain yourself."

"He said that his friend in the Chinese Embassy issued twelve visas to American-born asian females on flights from Oahu to Beijing. His email included a list of twelve names."

Pinky said, "Florence, that State Department employee is risking jail to email confidential information to you."

I said, "Boss, do you want us to find the Chinese broad or give us a lesson on law?"

"An error on my part, my boy. Please continue, Florence. What happened next?"

"We checked the list and found two females that fit the age profile."

I jumped into the conversation. "Flo got Soong's age off the passport I pinched from her coin shop. The broad's thirty-five and if you can believe it, she's a knockout in her passport photo. Pinky, I know you've always got your line in the water trolling for chicks and you can take it from me, that Soong broad is a chick. With a capitol C."

Pinky said, "My good man, I am more concerned with the comfort of my client who remains incarcerated while awaiting his trial for the murder of his brother. By the way, do not show Soong's passport to anyone. It is against Federal law to steal someone's passport."

"Flo told me that! We figure that once we find the broad we think is Soong, we'll need to check her against the passport photo. Lu's uncle Joe took the phone number we found in Soong's coin shop. He told us that once he tracks that number down finding Soong should be a piece of cake, but—"

Flo interrupted, "Pinky, Beijing has a population of nearly twenty-one million so I wouldn't call finding her that easy. At least now you should understand the problems we've been dealing with and why we spent our first two days in Beijing doing reconnaissance."

"Babe, Joe called that word you just used sightseeing, right Joe?"

Joe said, "That is correct."

Pinky screamed, "Sightseeing? I never agreed to pay for you to wander about Beijing visiting tourist sites."

Flo said, "Calm down, Pinky. Jet lag is a horrendous problem. Joe told us it would take two to three days to get over it. He offered to drive us to the Great Wall and The Forbidden City while we cleared the cobwebs from our brains. Now, if you will stop interrupting, I will continue. The list my friend gave me included the names of two asian females that are age thirty-five, so now we can start looking for our mysterious woman in earnest."

Pinky said, "And more importantly, that tiny two-million dollar coin! Now, I am ready to move to the next item on the agenda. I have experienced an

169

uneasy feeling concerning the expenditures involved in this investigation. I asked Lu to review all the expenses that have been charged against Helmut's woefully limited retainer. Lu, the floor is yours."

Lu said, "Thank you. Bear, Flo, and hello Uncle Joe. I've completed the review of expenses so far, and made an estimate of future expenses. The total to date is thirty-five thousand. However, I could be on the low side with my estimated future expenses so perhaps forty-five thousand might be closer to—"

Pinky moaned, "Oh, my God! When you add in my practice overhead, this single case could financially wipe me out."

Flo said, "Come on, Pinky. Isn't your reaction over the top?"

"My good woman, need I remind you that I am the man who butters your daily bread. And do not forget Lu's excessive salary, the alimony of my ex-wives, and—"

"Hey, Grandma Zabarte used to tell me, 'Bear, you dropped the glass. There's no use crying over spilled milk.' So suck it up, Boss, and grow a pair. What can me and Flo do to fix this mess?"

Flo flashed me her stink-eye, stuck her finger to her lips, and said, "Lu, all this talking has left me sort of parched. I'm going to ask Joe if he can find me some hot tea."

I said, "Tea? Are you nuts?" Joe, rustle me up a cool one from the sink in the bathroom. I dumped some ice in there so the cans should be cold by now."

Flo gave me the double stink-eye look that told

me clam up or I'd never see her naked again.

Pinky yelled, "Florence, we still have many items to clear up."

Flo said, "We'll get to that once Joe returns with our tea."

Joe scratched his head and left the room. Flo said, "Pinky, as soon as Joe returns with my tea we can continue."

Pinky said, "We don't need Joe for me to tell you that you circumvented my explicit rules and flew, more than once, in Business Class. My God, the two of you have spent enough money to find a dozen asian females!"

"Jesus, Boss. Nosing around China ain't as easy as you think."

Pinky yelled, "And I need that dime! Helmut's running out of money and as the rightful heir to the Kaufmann estate, the two million dollar coin belongs to him."

"Hey, I'm just a dumb Basque, but even I know a dude can't pump a bullet into his brother's forehead and still inherit the big bucks."

Flo jumped in. "Bear's right. If he's convicted of murdering his brother he can't inherit the money. How are you going to get Helmut off?"

"I have two plans to be exact."

Flo said, "Just a minute. Pinky, Joe just showed up with my pot of hot tea. I'm ready to listen."

"Florence, you are the most exasperating female I have ever been forced to deal with."

"Pinky, I'm not in the mood to listen to your pompous blather today. Make your point or hang up!"

"Listen to my pompous what? My good woman, if—"

"Boss, you're beginning to piss Flo off. What's the plan?"

"Your mystery woman, Soong, is my obvious choice."

While my babe poured herself a cup of that hot, green, watery crap, I said, "I don't know, Boss, me and Flo have gone over this a dozen times. We'll find Soong, and the dime real soon. But the second that broad tumbles that we are going to hustle her back to Carson City, to face a murder-one charge, there's no way in hell that she'll get on a plane with us."

"My boy, I hate to admit this, but you have a point. And the extradition process from China could be problematical, if not impossible. Therefore, I am willing to switch to plan two, your Wilmington suspect, Carlo Botano. By now, Detective Spaulding of the Carson City Police Department should have placed Mr. Botano under arrest for the murder of Ludwig Kaufmann."

I said, "Oh shit!"

Pinky said, "My boy, explain yourself. What does your expletive mean?"

"Boss, I forgot to tell you that when me and Flo were in Wilmington, we might have said and done some stuff to Botano that we shouldn't have."

"Give me an example."

"He might think we were cops from Carson City. And I made him destroy the DVD that recorded our visit. And then I sort of pushed him around. And then I—"

Pinky said, "Oh shit!"

Chapter Twenty-Three

Pinky—Carson City.

After a moment to recover from Bear's devastating admission, I said, "I believe we have talked enough. Florence, Bear, we all have work to do. I will contact Willow and attempt to extricate the two of you from your overzealous, if not illegal, behavior in Wilmington."

Florence said, "Pinky, what kind of trouble are we looking at? Is impersonating a cop a felony?"

"I am not sure but I will find out. Each state determines the magnitude of the charge. For example, I know from a previous client's personal situation that in the state of New York, impersonating a law enforcement officer is a felony offense, punishable by up to three years in state prison. Now, get to work!"

I hung up and truthfully, my only concern was not the possibility that my investigators could be arrested for their criminal indiscretion, but that they may have fouled the nest to the point that any half-witted attorney in North Carolina could delay, if not quash, an extradition proceeding. I needed Carlo Botano here, in Carson City, and I needed him—

My office door popped open and Lu silently slipped in. "Pinky, there's a man in the waiting area and he demands to see you. I told him you were on the phone with a client and could not be disturbed."

"Excellent." We both knew that nearly all my valued clients appeared without an appointment due to the fact that murder was not normally a scheduled event. However, I asked, "Does he have an appointment?"

"No."

"Did he give you a name?"

"First name, Gotthold." She hesitated and then she whispered, "I don't think you want to hear this, but he told me his last name is Kaufmann. He claims that Helmut is his half-brother."

Another Kaufmann? A half-brother?

My stomach did a half gainer and for a fraction of a second I was fearful that I was going to lose its contents. Then, through the power of mind over matter, I forced myself to calm down and the vile vomitus slowly slid back down from whence it originated.

Throughout my professional career, I had learned to cope with the unexpected—the surprise statement from a witness—the unanticipated judge's ruling—but to discover that Helmut Kaufmann's pending inheritance, my newfound war chest for all his pending legal billings, could be threatened, shook me to the core.

I took a deep breath and rapidly evaluated my situation:

First, a cursory review of the extraordinary expenses that my investigators had blown attempting to clear Helmut Kaufmann's name had exceeded all expectations. And, more importantly, their excesses had pushed my once impregnable financial situation into an untenable position.

Next, as my client's singular hope, I would required a large, additional retainer to develop the defense he fully deserved and my definition of a large retainer would begin at five-hundred thousand and could eventually reach seven figures.

Finally, to meet my retainer requirement, Helmut Kaufmann, as the solitary heir to the Kaufmann estate, would need access to every dollar from his inheritance. That meant that the man in my outer office, Gotthold Kaufmann, the pretender to the throne, must be exposed as an impostor!

I smiled. "Give me a few moments and then send the gentleman in."

I spun my chair around and pulled out a bottle of brandy from my credenza. I quickly poured a splash into a glass and downed the golden liquid in a single swallow. The hot alcohol shocked my body and cleared my brain. I placed the glass and bottle back into the credenza as my office door opened.

"Mr. Delmont?"

Standing in the doorway was a man who looked to be ten to fifteen years younger than Helmut. He was more or less the same height and build, with a carbon copy nose and the identical green eyes of my client. Damn, based on physical appearance alone, proving him to be an impostor was not going to be an easy task. I stood, smiled, and gestured toward the chair in front of my desk. "Yes. J. Pincus Delmont. Please have a seat."

We both sat and I continued. "Now Mr . . ." I glanced at a note pad on my desk, as if I had written down his name before he entered. " . . . Mr. Kaufmann. I am due in court shortly, so I can allow you but a few moments of my valuable time. What

175

can I do for you?"

"I'm surprised you didn't recognize my last name. It's the same name as the man who shot and killed my half-brother."

"Ah yes, Kaufmann, I should have made the connection but I have so many clients that occasionally their names just merge into a visual cacophony of letters. Now, Tempus fugit. Please, let us move on."

"Okay. I'll cut to the chase. I'm your client's half-brother. Our father, Augustus Kaufmann ran a butcher shop in Elko. Every night, my mother, Berdina Zweibel, cleaned the butcher shop along with a couple dozen other stores in Elko. One night, old Augustus pulled my mother down behind the brine barrel and nine months later, I was born."

I said, "Excuse me one moment." I picked up my phone and pushed the intercom button. "Lu, please bring us two coffees." I set the phone down and said, "Please continue."

While Gotthold ranted over his 'father's' lack of parental duties such as missing all his birthday parties, Lu served the coffee. After watching the man take a few sips from his cup, I considered how lucky I was to live in the scientific age where a DNA test using the Polymerase chain reaction method would provide me with a complete DNA profile on the man in my office. The results would prove if he is a Zweibel, or a Kaufmann, but regardless of the results, I would know the true facts and that would give me a big edge in all future negotiations.

Also, until proven otherwise, I will treat Gotthold as a pretender to the Kaufmann estate and as such, he will be known as Gotthold Zweibel, the name of the impostor who is attempting to gain a financial reward by deceiving my client.

I glanced at my watch and said, "Mr. Zweibel, my time is up. I must leave at once. Please leave your phone number with my secretary and keep in touch."

I jumped up and sprinted out of my office before the stunned man could open his mouth. He did not know, but I was not headed to court. I was going directly to the county jail, for an overdue conversation with my client concerning his inheritance and how my judicious use of his money was the only path left to accomplish his eventual release.

Ten minutes later, while I was sitting alone in the attorney/client conference room, I called Lu. "Has he gone?"

"Yes, about five minutes ago. He told me you wanted him to leave his phone number and he did."

"Lu, go into my office and whatever you do, do not touch his coffee cup with your fingers. Use a pencil to lift his cup and place it, untouched, into a paper bag."

"We don't have any paper bags in the office."

I snapped, "Well run out and buy some, damn it." I immediately caught myself and exclaimed, "Lu, I am so sorry I lost my temper." I could not afford to lose her until I had time to pull myself out of this deep well of crisis.

She hesitated, then said, "Apology accepted."

"Thank you. Once you have the cup in the bag, call me. I will stop by the office to pick it up."

"Pinky, what's going on?"

"I believe there is extractable DNA on that cup which will be able to produce a DNA profile."

Lu said, "I don't understand."

"A DNA profile will prove if that man you brought into my office today is, or is not, the progeny of Augustus Kaufmann."

"I'm still confused."

"Lu, I will explain later. Henry just entered with my client."

I dropped my cell phone into my pocket as Henry, the guard, whispered in my ear, "Pinky, I'm down to the last bottle of you-know-what."

Frankly, Henry's habit of drinking the expensive Scotch I purchased was becoming tedious. However, I needed him as much as he needed his whiskey so I could see no reason to cease our quid pro quo equilibrium. I said, "Point taken. I will take care of your request immediately. Now, excuse yourself so I can converse with my client in private."

The moment the door closed, Helmut said, "Pinky, what's going on? I haven't seen you for days. Don't you understand? I'm locked up in jail and the only person you'll let me talk to is you. Over the past week my life has become—"

"Calm down and listen to me. Are you familiar with the name Berdina Zweibel? She worked for your father cleaning up his butcher shop each evening."

Helmut thought for a moment. "Yes, I recall her. She was very pretty. My father told me her name, Berdina, translated into glorious in English.

"Helmut, what are your childhood memories concerning your family life?"

178

He sat back and pondered my question for a moment. "Pinky, most of my early childhood is a bit murky. At school I was Ludwig's right-hand-man, but at home, mother shouldered the bulk of the effort required to care for my brother. My father never accepted Ludwig's disability so the daily task of taking care of his crippled son was left to my mother and myself."

"So in your opinion, your father and Ludwig were not close?"

"I'd call that an understatement. Even as a child I noticed that my father avoided all contact with my brother. For example, the butcher shop opened every morning at eight, six days a week, and closed at six. But my father would leave home around six each morning and he'd never get home before ten in the evening. He was gone before I finished breakfast and back home after I went to bed. Later, when I was older, I'd be doing homework when he came home and there was never an excuse offered to me, or my mother, for the late hour. But what does my father's relationship with Ludwig have to do with my present situation?"

"I will get to that in a moment. Now, an hour ago a man named Gotthold Zweibel walked into my office and claimed to be your half-brother. As your attorney, it is my duty to—"

"My God. I have a half-brother! Did he look like me?"

"Slow down, Helmut. As I was saying, it is my duty as your attorney to look into his claim. Trust me, this sort of thing happens all the time. I had a case last year where there was an extremely large inheritance to be dispersed and you would not believe the hundreds of so-called relatives who crawled out from under rocks to claim their share."

"What did you say his name was?"

"Zweibel. Gotthold Zweibel."

"Oh my God! My father used to say that if he ever had another son, he would name the boy Gotthold. In English that name means God strong."

I asked, "What does Ludwig mean?"

"Famous warrior."

"So you think that once your father struck out with Ludwig, he figured he make up his error with Gotthold?"

"Pinky, I can't really say what my father was thinking because he was so distant to everyone in the family."

"But occasionally close enough since he fathered two sons by your mother, his legally wedded wife."

Helmut perked up. "I just remembered. One Saturday, when I was thirteen, I was at the butcher shop and the cleaning lady came in with a little boy. The child was about three or four and I recall noticing that the little boy had green eyes, just like all the men in our family. I asked my father about the boy's eyes and he didn't say anything for a second. Then he smacked me on the side of my head, and told me to finish placing the uncured beef briskets into the brine barrel."

I said, "That is interesting. The man, Gotthold, claims your father impregnated his mother behind a similar brine barrel." Helmut's level of excitement concerning his possible half-brother visibly increased. I continued, "Do not worry, Helmut, I will conduct a—"

"Pinky, two quick questions. Does he have green eyes? And how old is he?"

"This is just an educated guess, but I would say the man is in his late twenties to early thirties. And his eyes were . . . Helmut, you do understand that if this man is your father's son, he would have unfettered access to half the money that you, and you alone, would inherit from your late brother's estate?"

"But the estate should exceed more than two million. Don't you understand? A million dollars would be a small price to pay to gain a brother."

I stood and paced around the small room for a moment while I considered my next move. Each of my clients who faced a first-degree murder charge progressed through a series of steps. First, the endless protestations that they are innocent, followed by the awaking that they could possibly spend the rest of their life in prison. Finally, came the realization that if they were found guilty, the state had the right and the legal duty to put them to death.

At this point in Helmut's progression, he seemed to be trapped between steps one and two, so it was time for me to shake the tree, so to speak. "Helmut, I do not believe that you have a true understanding of your present legal situation." I stood, walked to the door, and asked Henry to join us.

"Henry, how long have you been a guard at the county jail?"

"Gosh, Pinky. I guess a long time."

"And during those years, how many of my

clients, just those accused of first-degree murder, have you escorted between this room and their jail cell?"

"Golly." Henry pointed at Helmut. "Do you want me to include this one?"

"Yes, Henry. Include Helmut in your count."

"Twenty-four."

"Have you ever witnessed any executions during your career in law enforcement?"

"Gosh yes. I don't remember how many, but—"

"And Henry, how many of my clients took their final walk to the execution chamber?"

"Golly gee, not a one. So far you are twenty-three wins, no losses." Henry tapped Helmut's shoulder. "I didn't count this one yet but we'll know where he falls soon enough. Pinky, after his trial you'll end up with a score of twenty-three wins and one loss, or twenty-four wins and zip. I heard the sports book at the Gold Nugget has set odds so everybody in town has been laying bets. A bunch of the guys at the court house have pooled their money on the twenty-three to one side, but you know me—"

My cell phone buzzed. "Henry, I am going to step outside and take this call. While I am gone, I would like you to describe, in as graphic terms as you can, the final moments of those unfortunate souls who did not have J. Pincus Delmont as their attorney."

The moment I cleared the door, I lifted my cell and said, "Hello."

"Hi, Boss. how's it hanging?"

"Bear, I am in the middle of a conference with your old school chum, Helmut. For some reason, I have been unable to convince him of his dire situation, but that is my dilemma. How is the quest for Madam Soong and the missing coin progressing?"

"We didn't finish our report during the last call. I've got some good and bad news. Which one do you want to hear first? I bet Flo five bucks you'd want to hear the good first and she's backing the bad. Come on, Boss, who wins our bet?"

One more inane remark from a man who continues to prove that old adage, 'ignorance is bliss'. Bear and his woman have been wandering about China for some time. They do not speak or understand the language. They do not read or understand the signs written with the Chinese hanzi symbols. Yet Bear remains apathetic to his pitiful situation. I demanded, "Give me your report and hurry up."

"Okay, but does that mean our bets are off?"

"Damn it, give me the good news."

"Flo, I win the fin. Pinky wanted the good news first . . .hey . . . don't take my phone away . . . "

A female voice said, "Pinky, this is Flo. Do you really want the good news first or is Bear pulling my leg?"

"Florence, I have important work to complete with Helmut and do not have time for this sort of tomfoolery. Call me on my office line in thirty minutes and finish your report then."

"I'll do that but I'm adding the five bucks to my expense account."

I cried, "Stop right there. Florence, as I previously discussed, the expenses on this case have gone through the roof."

But I was talking to myself. She had already hung up.

Chapter Twenty-Four

Bear—Beijing

I grabbed my phone back. "So what did Pinky say?"

Flo shook her head. "We're supposed to call him back in a half-hour, but before we do that we'd better get our ducks lined up."

"Babe, what the hell do ducks have to do with talking with Pinky? And another thing, the last time we talked to Lu, she said something about Joe's squinchy stuff. What the hell was she talking about?"

"I mentioned to Lu that without Joe's help we'd be back in Carson City without Madam Soong, or the two-million dollar dime. And she said that her Uncle used his influence, or as they call it in China, guanxi."

"Babe, if we've got a minute, could you go over what Lu said about Joe's squinchy stuff."

"It's guanxi, but I guess it sounds a little like squinchy. What you have to do is say the word like this—gwan—then shee."

"I'm not talking about how to say the damn thing. I don't get what it's all about."

"Guanxi is one of the most powerful forces in Chinese culture. It's like doing a favor for someone, but stronger and more formidable."

"Sort of like the Carson City council where one council-dude scratches the other council-dude's

185

back?"

"More, much more. It's like you have a large amount of guanxi money in your checking account. You need a favor? Just write a guanxi check. But like a real checking account, once you've overdrawn your account, you're broke. Men like Joe must be careful to not write too many checks against their guanxi account."

"I get it now. If Joe writes too many squinchy checks, his account gets closed. But I still don't understand what all this squinchy crap has to do with us tracking down Madam Soong."

"Remember how Joe seemed to change after he dropped us off at the Excelsior Hotel?"

"Yup. He's sort of taken over the whole investigation. Like the time we all went to see the Great Wall."

"I'm not talking about the Great Wall. There he acted like a tour guide. I'm talking about when I felt he was leading us by the nose. A great example was when I gave him the names on the State Department list. Somehow, don't ask me how, this old guy who can't drive a stick shift VW gained access to the Chinese government's data base of tourists presently in the country. That allowed us to trim down the list to the one we're looking for."

"I remember that, but by the time we got to Soong's hotel here in Beijing she'd checked out."

"And then Joe used his guanxi to get that desk clerk to open up and tell us he'd made a hotel reservation for her in Lhasa, Tibet."

"Shit! that took Joe's squinchy along with four Benjamin's out of our expense money."

"First Joe used his guanxi to get us travel

permits to Lhasa. I really cannot comprehend how he pulled that one off because westerners are not allowed into Tibet on a whim. Then Joe took us to the concierge and requested three seats on a flight he wanted to take us from Beijing to Lhasa. I'm sure you recall that at first, the concierge told Joe the plane was booked up but Joe flashed his little card and suddenly we had three seats on that plane."

"I remember all right. Bingo, three seats were suddenly not-sold-out. But, Babe, I've got one more question about Joe's squinchy stuff. When I opened our joint checking account back home, I handed the bank clerk two grand in cash. Those were real U. S. bucks. How much Chinese cash did Joe have to put up to open his squinchy checking account?"

"Joe didn't use cash, he just did favors. Bear, to use the old Mafia term, Lu's uncle seems to be connected, big time."

"Okay. Enough of that squinchy crap. Are we ready to call Pinky?"

"Not quite. When I hung up, he was whining about expenses."

"Hey, I told you that those Business Class seats were bound to get us into trouble with him. Hell, money's all that dude thinks about. That's why I wanted to be the one to tell him the good news. Remember? I got stuck with the bad news last time. This time it's your turn."

"I know, and that's why we needed to discussed guanxi, so we'd be on the same page. Without Joe, our investigation in China would have been a total failure. But with Joe, and his guanxi, we've accomplished a couple of miracles. He found a nameless woman in a city with more than twenty million people. Now we're close to confronting her in Tibet. So when Pinky rants about our expenses, I'm going to tell him we did the right thing. We had to spend all that money to track down Madam Soong. And without those bucks, we never would have been able to restore the two million dollar dime to his client, Helmut Kaufmann."

"Hey, you don't have to convince me. It's Pinky you've got to worry about, and I mean worry."

Flo laughed and her boobs sort of jiggled. "Bear, that man is the cheapest person I've ever run across. He has a mansion that overlooks a golf course south of Carson City. I know from running his office a couple of years ago that Pinky has more money stashed away in more back accounts than King Midas has gold. A lost hundred grand wouldn't put a dent in those millions!"

"Babe, back home, while I was getting my haircut, I read an article in Playboy that claimed guys like Pinky got spooked by something when they were a kid. I'll crack a cold brew and give Pinky a call. Don't worry, I'll be with you while you're explaining all that squinchy stuff to the little fart."

"Bear, be honest. Did you actually read a Playboy article, or did you just look at the centerfold?"

"It was sort of both. Most of the haircut time I checked out Miss April, and then when the dude was trimming behind my ears I read some of the article. But I got to the part that explained all about the spooked kids. Now I'm pretty sure I know why Pinky's so super cheap."

Chapter Twenty-Five

Pinky—Carson City

The moment I reached my office, my phone rang. Lu answered it and informed me over the intercom that Flo was on my line.

Before I said a word, I painted a of touch of righteous indignation into my tone. "Florence, when you called me earlier, I was—"

"Stop ragging and listen or I'll hang up again and you'll never see that two-million dollar dime."

Circumspection took a firm hold of me as I said, "Go ahead. I will attempt to withhold any comment until you have completed your crass remarks."

"Thank you. But first, I need to explain the concept of guanxi, a Chinese cultural—"

"Cease and desist, woman. Unlike your ignorant ursine friend, I am not a young cub that requires training. I know, and understand the concept of guanxi. The Chinese have taken the old platitude, *it is not what you know, but who you know*, to direct and guide their lives. Now what does guanxi have to do with this call?"

Florence said, "Don't get snippy with me. Bear, you deal with him."

Bear said, "Boss, Joe got us the new name of Madam Soong. The broad is now traveling under the name of Zhou Jai Li. We're one hundred percent sure she's the woman with the big-buck dime 'cause I showed Soong's passport picture to the desk clerk where she just checked out and he verified that Soong and Zhou Jai Li are the same broad. And Boss, I had to give the hotel clerk a hundred clams before he'd even talk to us and then I had to give him three more Benjamin's to get the positive ID. But that's not all."

"Slow down my boy and give me a moment to think." Four hundred dollars to convince a simple desk clerk in China to look at a photo and nod? Capitalism must be alive and thriving in Mao's workers paradise. "Bear, do not even ask me to reimburse you for the four hundred dollar bribe. We have been through this song and dance before. What I need to know is—"

Again Florence interrupted. "Sorry Pinky, but here comes the bad news part. We are going to need another infusion of expense money. My guess is twenty-five thousand will cover our costs but that's just an estimate."

Dumbfounded, I demanded, "Have the two of you lost your minds? There is no way that you could have spent the first—"

"Pinky, I said, bad news, not end of the world news. Of course, if you want us to drop everything and come home, without the dime, so be it. You are our supreme ruler after all."

"Florence, do not say anything that you will regret later."

Bear said, "Boss, we need more money to get Soong back to Carson City or I'm afraid my old high school bud will end up lying on a gurney with poison dripping into his arm."

"My boy, you and Florence have given me

much to ponder. Hold your tongue and provide me with some peace and quiet so I can mull over the situation."

Somehow those two, the dolt and his female, have maneuvered me into another damned if I do, and damned if I don't, situation. Bear was correct, recovering Soong would be ideal, but capturing the dime had become paramount.

Then there was the Wilmington coin dealer who remained as a viable suspect, but the murky legal situation created by the dynamic duo's ham-fisted investigation made the eventual extradition of Botano to Nevada tenuous at best.

So my number-one priority remained the dime, quickly followed by a dazzling array of legal obfuscation by presenting Willow with not one, but two viable suspects for the murder of Ludwig Kaufmann. Granted, neither suspect was under arrest, nor within the State of Nevada's borders, but that minor detail was not within my jurisdiction.

And finally, the unexpected appearance of Gotthold had created yet another dilemma. Once I extracted Helmut from his jail cell, the possibility of splitting the inheritance in two presented a major quandary to me. It was a well known fact that a positive side effect of extricating a multi-millionaire from the specter of state execution was that the client's concern over a detailed accounting of his legal expenses rapidly faded into the background.

So once I convinced Willow to recognize the error of her ways, and she released my client, my next step would be to convince Helmut that

Gotthold, his supposed half-brother, was an impostor.

Finally, as Helmut's attorney of record, it would be my task to distribute the funds from his brother's estate to my client, minus any appropriate expenses and legal fees.

In the grand scheme of things, Florence's demand for an additional twenty-five thousand to cover their final expenses became a minor irritant, similar to my waiting a few moments each day for the coffee maker to complete brewing my first cup!

"Florence, I will approve your request, but I must warn you in advance that any future increase will be turned down sans discussion. And I will require a detailed accounting of all expenditures from this point forward. Have I made myself clear?"

"Yes, but all your bluster concerning future requests is just bull and we both know it. As of today, there are three of us working off the twenty-five thousand, Bear, Joe, and myself. We still have to pay for multiple airline tickets, hotels in Lhasa, and hotels in Beijing. Pinky, you don't have a clue what it costs to live over here. It's an expensive place for food, car rentals, bribes, hotels, everything required to live. Once we have Soong, and the dime, the four of us have to fly back to Beijing, and then there is the third airfare from Beijing to—"

"Florence, now you stop the blustering. I am well aware of your ability to cover your financial scams, so to speak."

"Pinky, I've learned from a master! For the moment, let's just agree that we are two people who know, understand, and respect, the other's ability to scam the less aware that exist among us. How about a deal? I promise to not inform the Nevada State Bar Association of your shady shenanigans concerning your excessive legal fees as long as you agree to supply the expense money needed to get us out of this damn country and back to Carson City. Are you part of the deal? Can you live with my promise that I'm not padding the books?"

No matter how desperate I might become in the future, it was now obvious to me that I could never again allow that woman access to any of my various bank accounts. "Florence, I agree. Now, go forth. Capture Soong and that damn dime."

Without a knock, Lu walked into my office. "Pinky, before you hang up, it's important I talk with Flo. The last time we spoke she asked me to give her a couple of minutes."

Chapter Twenty-Six

Bear—Beijing

"Flo," said Lu. "We need to talk."

"Okay, and just so everyone knows what's going on, I'll put this whole conversation on speaker! Lu, what can I do for you?"

Lu said, "Flo, it's not me. You said you needed to discuss something."

"Ah yes. I just have a couple of questions concerning female problems. What the hell, I don't care if the guys are listening if you don't. Lu, each month, just before that time, have you had any problems with—"

"Stop right there," cried Pinky. "I think it is time for me to return to the jail. I have a few more items to discuss with Helmut."

"Bye, Boss." I turned toward Flo and whispered, "Babe, do your female problems mean I need to leave?"

Flo shook her head and put her finger to her lips. "Lu, has Pinky left?"

Lu laughed. "Yes. He sprinted out the front door and I've never seen him move faster. What do you need?"

Flo said, "Lu, since we landed in Beijing, something about your uncle has bugged me. First he acted like a bumbling guy who couldn't drive a stick-shift car. But since that time, every day he seems less and less muddled and more in charge.

I'm beginning to feel like he's less of a helper and more like a puppet master. What do you know about your uncle's past?"

"I only know what my parents told me and the couple of times I talked with him when I set up your trip to China."

"Okay, give me what your parents told you."

"My dad was five years older than Joe and around 1966, my dad and his brother were physically separated, sent to different sections of China because of Mao's Cultural Revolution. My dad had just graduated from medical school when, as part of Mao's 'Down to the Countryside Movement', he was sent to a small farming village in the interior where he plowed fields, fed chickens, slopped hogs and was forbidden to use his medical education. Some years later, at the end of the Cultural Revolution, my dad finally returned to his home and started to practice medicine. Within a year, he heard of a program of advanced medical study in America and he applied. He was accepted and once he arrived in this country, he never returned to China.

"My uncle, on the other hand, wanted to become a member of the feared Red Guard. Before he could join, at the tender age of sixteen he was shipped to the Mongolian boarder where he spent years cutting wood. Once the Culture Revolution ended, and the universities were reopened, Joe attended a university. I'm not sure what he studied but he ended up as some kind of a big-wig in the Communist Party. Does that help?"

"I guess. I think that explanation explains what's going on. Two hours ago we just missed catching Soong at her hotel because Joe got lost finding the place. But I have a funny feeling that we weren't really lost and the time Joe spent driving around in circles allowed Soong to check out and head for Tibet.

"Before we left Soong's hotel, and after two phone calls, Joe informed me that we have travel permits to follow Soong to Tibet and I thought no westerner was allowed into Tibet unless they were a diplomat, journalist, or government official.

"Lu, I don't know about you, but I believe that most women have a sixth sense that tells them if a guy's a straight-shooter. That's where I am with Joe. My woman's intuition is warning me to look out. I'm beginning to think that we're part of some kind of trap—that your uncle isn't really helping us, he's using us."

Lu said, "I'm too far removed from your situation to offer real advice. In fact, I've never met my uncle, or stepped on Chinese soil. But it wouldn't surprise me that a retired government big-wig would have enough guanxi to do everything you've told me so far. I will leave you with this: just before he died, my father confided in me that once Mao's Cultural Revolution took him away from his parents and his home, and forced him to plow fields instead of allowing him to use his medical expertise, he stopped believing what Chairman Mao stood for, and that skepticism included his brother."

Chapter Twenty-Seven

Bear—Beijing

When Flo told Lu that she tumbled to Joe being something more than an old dork I got ticked off. I know everyone thinks I'm the dumb one, but it was me, not Flo, that figured out that Joe was more than Lu's uncle.

How did I know? When we were back at the hotel where Soong checked out, and after I dropped four C notes on that desk clerk, I saw Joe pull out a card. He flashed it at the dude behind the counter and the desk clerk dropped my four Benjamin's like they were made out of some kind of poison. That's when I figured out that Joe, and that little card he carried, packed a lot of weight.

What did I do with the extra cash? I never told Flo that I got the four hundred back, but that's okay 'cause a dude needs to have some walking around money that's all his!

As Joe fired up his Mercedes, he said, "Before I drop you off at your hotel, so you can pack for the flight to Lhasa, we have to make a quick stop."

I said, "Where're we going?"

"We take off in a few hours and as your guardian in China, it is my duty to take you to the Medicine Market."

"The what?"

"You will understand when we arrive.

While Joe drove through the streets of Beijing

197

my babe closed her eyes. I felt like doing the same. In fact, I was so pooped that every time I blinked, my eyelids scraped, like my eyeballs were covered with number six grit sandpaper. Somehow this vacation to Hawaii and China wasn't turning out to be much fun.

Joe slowed down and parked. All the stores on both sides of the block looked pretty tired and were sort of squished together. Across the street was the store Joe was aiming for. The big sign above the door said Medicine Market—in real English letters.

As we got closer I saw a bunch of boxes lined the store front. Once I stood over a box my mouth dropped open because it was filled with dried bats, and they were stuck on a sticks! That was about the nastiest thing I'd ever seen. Bats! Those creepy little animals that live in caves and fly around at night had somehow been snuffed, dried, and mounted onto a stick—like the store was selling dried bat lollipops.

The box next to the bats was filled with dried starfish. Yuck!

Another box with dried snakes. Double yuck!

Another with turtle shells, and more boxes and bags filled with all kinds of unidentified critters.

I grabbed Joe's arm. "Joe, what are you trying to do, gross out me and Flo?"

"Mister Bear, tomorrow we fly to Lhasa. The altitude at Lhasa is around 3650 meters. I am extremely concerned—"

"Joe, meters dosn't mean crap to me. Give me that number in a good-old American measurement, like feet."

He squinted, like his gears were working overtime. "I believe that converts to approximately 12,000 feet."

"Babe, how high is Denver?"

"About a mile high, that's 5280 feet."

"Jesus, Lhasa is almost twice as high as Denver."

Flo said, "Actually, more than double, but who's counting."

I thought for a second about Pinky, and how he's back, safe and sound, sitting on his butt in Carson City while me and Flo are heading into a town that's really up there. I said, "Joe, I've heard that guys, really tough dudes, have keeled over while jogging in Denver. Could that sort of thing happen to me and Flo in Lhasa?"

Joe smiled. "Now you understand why I have brought you to the Medicine Market."

Flo glanced at the bat sucker. "Would you care to explain how a box of dried Chiroptera is going to protect us against altitude sickness?"

Joe smiled again. "As usual you go directly to the point. First, you have to understand the differences between Western Medicine and Chinese Medicine. In America, if you were concerned about altitude sickness, your doctor would very likely prescribe Diamox. In China, I would go to my neighborhood medicine market and ask them to compound a medicine that would protect me against altitude sickness."

Flo said, "So which one works the best?"

Joe shrugged. "There are many factors involved with altitude sickness but the actual reason that some people become sick is due to less oxygen molecules in their bloodstream. Forty percent less to be precise. This happens because at 12,000 feet the barometric pressure is nearly seventy-percent lower than it is at sea level. With each breath, you place a great stress on your organs, and it's anyone's guess which organ could be the first to fail."

Flo said, "That's interesting, but you ignored my question."

Joe shrugged again. "To answer your question, I take both Diamox and the Chinese medicine they compound for me at this store. You see, it is difficult to determine who may be affected by altitude sickness since there are no specific factors such as age, sex, or physical condition that correlate with susceptibility. It seems that some get it because they are susceptible while others escape the symptoms."

Flo said, "Joe, do you have enough Diamox for Bear and myself?"

"I do."

Flo smiled. "Then let's go in and grind up some bat wings, snakes, and who knows what else. While were packing at our hotel, I'm calling Pinky to tell him he owes us a bonus for risking our lives for taking whatever concoction this place mixes up for us."

Chapter Twenty-Eight

Pinky—Carson City

My intercom buzzed. "Pinky, Willow's on line one."

At this point in my life I was beginning to understand the value of one true love, and Willow Stone, as I have stated more than once, was my favorite ex-wife. The one woman I should have never let get away. I grabbed the phone. "Willow, just saying your name sends chills down my spine. Besides my undying love and total devotion, what can I do for you today?"

"Pinky, I just finished speaking with Detective Spaulding from Wilmington, North Carolina. She's the police detective you conned into crossing the country to pursue the possibility that Carlo Botano was a viable suspect in the Ludwig Kaufmann murder."

"My dear, your term conned is derogatory to say the least. Based on the information supplied to me by my investigative team, Carlo Botano was—"

"Can it and listen to me. First, you had Bear take off with Helmut Kaufmann and skated on the edge of obstructing justice. Now—"

"My love, I do not want to sound as if I am splitting hairs, but you never had, nor will you ever have, a scintilla of evidence that I obstructed—"

"Now, according to Detective Spaulding, Bear and Flo told Botano that they were members of the

201

Carson City police force, thus they impersonated officers of the law. Pinky, this is an all time low, even for—"

"My dearest one, when Bear and Florence made their report to me concerning their investigation into Carlos Botano's activities during his stay in Reno, and his possible involvement with Ludwig Kaufmann's murder, they informed me that they were extremely surprised, if not shocked, when Mr. Botano made the incorrect assumption that the two were members of the Carson City police force. In fact, Florence told me that Botano was the one who blurted out, 'Oh my God, you're the cops!" My team never stated or insinuated to Mr. Botano that they were representing any law enforcement agency and I have no reason to doubt or question the honesty and veracity of Bear and Florence."

"Pinky, all that is easy for you to say, but I need to hear that from Bear or Flo and their statements must be made under oath. Now, you tell them to voluntarily come to my office this afternoon at three, or I will be forced to seek a warrant for their arrest due to—"

"Slow down my sweet and take a deep breath. You are the love of my life, and as such, I am shocked that you feel the need to use the authority of your office to threaten me or my employees. I would love to do as you asked, but as we speak Bear and Florence are in Beijing and at any moment they will be boarding a plane for a flight to Lhasa, Tibet."

"I don't believe you! You told me during our honeymoon that since marrying me, your new number one bucket list item was to visit China. You've been wanting to walk the Great Wall in Beijing, and observe the Terra Cotta soldiers in Xi'an, since you were a child. And you also mentioned the Potala Palace in Tibet."

"My love, your memory is, like your beauty, perfect. However, I do not understand why you would not believe that Bear and Florence are where I say they are."

"Because I know you. You went to Rome and Tuscany while Bear and Flo ended up in that hell-hole, Eureka, Nevada. You traveled to Quebec City while Bear and Flo were stuck in Los Angeles and Needles, California. Do you require any more examples?"

"My sweet, the fact that I, rather than Bear went to Rome, Tuscany, or Quebec City was pure chance. If you will recall, I was pursuing a viable lead in Kona when you decided to move up the arraignment of my client, Helmut Kaufmann. Had you not gone ahead with your irresponsible legal maneuver then I would be in China and Tibet pursuing Madam Soong. If you recall, she is the woman that I am positive pulled the trigger to cause the premature death of Ludwig Kaufmann."

"Pinky, it wasn't my fault that the arraignment date was moved up. The judge was going on a four week vacation and I felt that was too long to wait. But why didn't you tell me that you were going to miss your lifelong dream of China?"

"Because."

"What kind of an answer is that?"

"My love, I was on the Kona Coast of the big

island. My feet stood on the same sand that we walked on during our honeymoon. When you called, my only thoughts were—"

My intercom buzzed. "Pinky, Flo is on line two."

I understood the risk of allowing my employee to talk with Willow without a short period of, let me call it, fact finding. However, my precarious situation with Botano caused me to throw caution to the winds. "My love, Florence is on my other line. Would you care to hear her side of the Botano story?"

Willow hesitated for a moment, just enough to inform me that she had reservations concerning the impersonating an officer fiasco. "Yes, but conference the call so we can both hear her story."

I pushed the conference button. "Florence, I have Willow conferenced on this call so before you go into why you called, which could be privileged information, I would appreciate it if you would tell your side of the confrontation you had with Mr. Botano in Wilmington. Willow needs to hear, from your lips, that neither you nor Bear attempted to leave Botano with the impression that—"

"Damn it, Pinky," cried Willow. "Why don't you just hand Flo a script."

Florence said, "Because he doesn't need to. Willow, for a change, Pinky's telling the truth. Bear and I never, I repeat, never told Botano that we were members of the Carson City police force. Or any other police force. The dumb bastard came to that conclusion all by himself."

The tightness in my stomach relaxed. "Does that satisfy you my love?"

"For the moment. I'll discuss Flo's statement with Detective Spaulding and, excuse me, but one of my deputies just handed me a note. Pinky, I'll be back in a moment, but don't hang up, I need to ask Flo an important question."

Once I heard Willow talking to someone in the background, I said, "Florence, your statement a moment ago should be enough to avoid a messy situation for us all. For that I am grateful. Now, why did you interrupt my busy day?"

"To tell you we are about to board our airplane for Lhasa and that we have been warned by Joe that altitude sickness could strike us down at any moment. I don't know what Bear agreed to when he signed on as your underpaid investigator, but I'm not ready to cash in my chips and have my heart stop once we reach Lhasa because my bloodstream isn't carrying enough oxygen. In the past, Bear and I have put our lives on the line but I never had time to consider the situation. Also, we're going to Lhasa with Joe, a man who I actually trust less than I trust you. We both know that money and sex are your only motivations. What bothers me about Joe is I can't figure what's driving him. As far as I can tell, except for the dime, there's no money involved in tracking down Soong. And at his age I can't believe that sex is Joe's prime motivator. So there it is. I'm uneasy, and when I get that way, I end up scared. In case you missed my point, when you add my anxiety to the possibility of my sudden death, it's time for you to pony-up more cash."

As usual, Florence had exaggerated her situation and as usual, her incessant demands for money were over the moon. However, I required that woman and her dolt to recover that dime. "Florence, I will instruct Lu to deposit a ten thousand dollar bonus into your account."

"Not good enough. I want a written contract where you agree to pay Bear, and myself, as your investigative team, seven thousand a month."

I cried, "Have you lost your mind?" then I heard Willow's voice say, "I don't think so, but occasionally, with the stress of my position, I'm on the edge."

"My sweet, I was not talking to you."

Willow said, "So that leaves Flo. And that brings me to my next question. Flo, would you rather we talk in private, woman to woman?"

Florence said, "No. Go ahead and ask away."

"I'm expanding my investigative team and I understand you have the kind of computer expertise that my office so desperately lacks. And you combine an outstanding digital knowledge with the ability to think like a crook. The position would be full time with all the usual benefits—paid vacations—sick leave—health insurance, and a generous retirement plan."

Florence, for a change did not immediately respond, so I said, "Willow, I am dumbfounded that you would attempt to poach my star investigator. Unless you have more to discuss concerning the Wilmington affair, I believe our conference call has come to a conclu—"

Florence interrupted, "Would your offer include Bear? We've worked as a team for sometime now and trust me, that man's a lot smarter than most people think."

Willow, as if she had not heard my demand to

cease and desist, continued. "Flo, I'll take your suggestion about Bear under serious consideration. Now, think about my offer and call me when you return from China. Pinky, call me in an hour. I'm relieved that you, or your people, didn't break the law concerning Botano, and that allows me the freedom to discuss that personal item you wanted to talk to me about at lunch a few days ago—remember, the thoughts you had concerning that little box?"

For some reason, Willow felt the need to bring up my clumsy attempt to express my undying love for her, and in front of Florence of all people. Struggling to control my rising anger, I said, "Florence, stay on the line, and Willow, I will call you back. I have confidential instructions to pass on to my investigator."

My mind was spinning. Willow's offer of employment to Florence had placed me in an untenable position with my investigator. Perhaps my best option would be to encourage her to work for Willow when she returned. With Florence barging around the prosecutor's office, Willow's operation could be reduced to shambles in a month. But Florence might convince Bear to follow her and as troublesome as they were, in the long run, they were both controllable and affordable.

When I detected the telltale click that indicated Willow had done her damage and taken her leave. I said, "Florence, do what you can to avoid altitude sickness because neither you, nor Bear, have the time to come down with any sort of illness. My good woman, speed is of the essence concerning the recovery of that valuable coin so travel to your next destination with the knowledge that a contract guaranteeing thirty-five hundred dollars a month, for each of you, will be awaiting your signatures when you return to Carson City."

"Pinky, do you have any idea what an investigator for the DA's office takes home each month?"

I snapped, "Florence, I will not tolerate further questions of that ilk during the remainder of this conversation. You and Willow, your potential employer, can discuss those mundane details after you have returned to my office with the dime and Madam Soong."

"I had a feeling you'd say that and thanks for your unexpressed, but I'm sure heartfelt, concern over the health of your stalwart investigative team. Trust me, both of us will do our very best to hold off any fatal organ failure until after we find the dime."

Chapter Twenty-Nine

Bear—Beijing, China: Lhasa, Tibet

Before we hit the airport, me and Flo downed a Diamox pill, and then we choked down some nasty looking gray crap that Flo gave me after she mixed an envelope of that Medicine Market crud into a glass of water.

And that reminds me. According to Joe, as long as me and Flo are stuck in China, we can't drink any water—from a faucet—like we did back home.

And that goes for the whole damn country. Even in Beijing, with more than twenty million Chinese running around like a bunch of crazy ants, we can't drink the water.

Joe told us that in every hotel, from the five star joint we're leaving, to every other five star joint Joe'd put us into, we'd had to use bottled water to brush our teeth. Or down an aspirin. Or to make a cheap whiskey drinkable. And when me and Flo took a shower, we had to close our mouths when we'd spray our face 'cause Joe said if we didn't, we could get really sick. In fact, Flo got so spooked, she wouldn't let me into the shower with her 'cause she was afraid that in the middle of you-know-what I'd forget about Joe's warning, open my mouth and down a gulp of the nasty water and die, or something.

So holding a bottle of water in her hand, me

and Flo climbed on the plane to Lhasa. A few minutes after we took off, the plane popped through the gray, brown muck the people in Beijing call air and I saw the sun for the first time since we landed in Beijing.

Once the plane leveled off, one of those Chinese broads in a uniform, handed us a box. She said, "Special American breakfast. Very good. Five star. Inspected. Top notch."

I opened the box. It was filled with little packages but I couldn't tell what was in the packages. I opened the warm one and it looked, and tasted, like a cooked wedge of eggs with little hunks of bacon. It tasted good so I opened the next one. It was sort of like a hard oatmeal bar but it was okay. Everything worked until I hit the last package. I opened it and it smelled like something had really gone bad. That stink was like nothing I had ever smelled before and for sure never wanted to get near my nose again. I handed the package to Joe and said, "Hey, I don't know what this is but if I take one more whiff I'm going to barf."

Joe took a sniff and smiled. "Ah, one of our best Chinese pickles." He started to hand it back. "Are you sure you—"

I growled, "Don't let that thing come any closer."

I hit the uniformed broads button. She walked up and said, "Can I help you, sir?'

"Yes, bring me a couple of brews."

"Sir, will Tsingtao be okay for you?"

"Babe, I don't care what the name is. Any kind of brew in a can or bottle. Just give me something that tastes and smells like beer, not one of those damn pickles I just handed to Joe."

The uniformed broad looked at me like she didn't know what was going on but inside a minute she handed me two Tsingtao's and left. I popped the top, took a big swig. The broad was right, Tsingtao was beer, not very good, but better than water.

I said to Flo, "Babe, this beer's not much but it's a lot better than what's inside that smallest package. I think something crawled inside and died."

"You mean the pickle? I ate mine, and it was different, but very tasty."

I didn't know if she was putting me on so I finished the first brew and opened the second one.

After breakfast Flo kept looking out the window and bugging me with the same kind of talk she uses when shopping for clothes in the mall. "Bear, look at those mountains."

Or, "I wonder if that's Mount Everest?"

Or, "Put that beer down and look out the window. The Himalayan range is home to the tallest mountains on earth."

I took a swig and a glance. Shit, the mountains below our plane didn't look any different to me than the Sierra Nevadas above Carson City. But I could tell that Flo didn't want to hear that so I said, "Yup. They're cool!"

One brew later, we landed and as we walked through the little building, I noticed a counter with a dude selling stuff that looked like the same kind of big cans of hairspray that Flo uses. I grabbed Joe's arm and said, "Why would anybody sell cans of hairspray in an airport?"

"Mister Bear, those containers are not hairspray. They are filled with pure oxygen."

We stopped and Flo took one of the cans off the counter.

I said, "Filled with air? You're putting me on."

Flo said, "Not air, pure oxygen. It says right here on the label. Remember? Lhasa's altitude is 12,000 feet. We're still breathing air, but we're getting less oxygen then we did back home. Joe, do you think I should buy a canister or two?"

"Babe, I'm not buying one of those things. Hell, if we can't drink their water, why should we trust their oxygen?"

She set the can back onto the counter. "I can't argue with that logic. Joe, how far away is Lhasa?"

Joe said, "Thirty minutes. I have booked us rooms at the Tibet Hotel—five star—top class—very American."

I said, "And bottled water, right?"

"Yes. As I told you, bottled—oh, here is the man who will drive us to Lhasa."

Heading toward us was a big dude. I mean NFL football offensive lineman big. Around six-five, three hundred plus pounds, and not an ounce of blubber on him. This was a guy I'd want on my side if I lost my baseball bat in the middle of a Friday night rumble at the Old Globe.

The giant took a couple of steps in Flo's direction. I'm a good sized dude, but I'd need more than luck to take him down. I was trying to figure out where I could land one good punch when he smiled and pulled out of his pocket a white cloth thingie, like something my Grandma Zabarte would throw around her shoulders when she went to

212

church each Sunday.

Joe said, "Chen is offering Madam Flo a Tibetan prayer shawl. That's a traditional greeting most Tibetan's follow to bring luck and longevity to visitors to their city."

Then the big guy pulled out one for me and as he hung it over my shoulders I asked, "Joe, are all the Tibetan dudes this big?"

"Chen is not Tibetan. He's Chinese." Joe said a couple of words in Chinese in Chen's ear. Chen whispered back and Joe said, "In fact, most Tibetans have a much smaller physical stature. And you will note later, they have high cheek bones, and in my opinion, they facially resemble your American Indians."

I said, "Does Chen only speak Chinese?"

"He does. Why do you ask?"

"I'm just trying to figure out how he showed up right after our plane landed."

Joe's gaze dropped, like he was trying to figure out an answer. "Chen is a good friend."

Joe's answer stunk as much as those nasty Chinese pickles.

Flo said, "Where does your friend live, Lhasa?"

"Babe, take a gander at Chen's shoes. Those are cop shoes. Or maybe a government cop, like our FBI."

"Mister Bear and Madam Flo, I owe you both an explanation, but I am sure you are tired so first let us check into our hotel rooms. The Tibet Hotel has an excellent bar. I recommend that we meet after you unpack and allow yourselves a few precious moments to take care of personal needs. Over a libation I will explain what is going on, who

Chen is, and present to you my plan to capture Madam Soong and the dime that has eluded you."

I glanced at Flo and she nodded.

I said, "And once we get Soong we'll take her, along with the dime, and head back to America, right?"

Joe said, "As I said, there is much to explain. Even I cannot predict the ultimate outcome, but time will tell. Remember, Confucius says, 'He who learns but does not think, is lost. He who thinks but does not learn is in great danger.'"

By now I was tired of Joe's confusion bull crap so I took a step toward him. Guess what? His Chinese goon jumped between us.

Flo said, "Bear, calm down and listen to that last part of what Confucius said. 'He who thinks but does not learn is in great danger.' We are going to meet with Joe at the hotel bar, and there we will learn. Once we learn, we can think out what we are going to do next. Joe, am I correct?"

"Correct as usual, Madam Flo. Now, without further discussion, I will ask Chen to drive us to the Tibet Hotel. We have much to do before the sun goes down."

I didn't like where this deal was heading. Shit, we were a zillion miles from home, in a place where me and Flo don't speak the lingo. Now we're stuck in a place where we don't get enough oxygen every time we breathe. And for some reason, Joe has a bodyguard who's got me by a hundred pounds. Jesus, somehow Pinky put me and Flo into another shitty situation! I guess we have to go along with Joe and listen to what he wants us to hear. After that, maybe then I can come up with a plan to grab

214

Soong and the dime, and head back home.

I said, "Babe, that Confusion dude's name is weird. Pinky told me Zabarte is a dumb name but it's nowhere as stupid as Confusion. But if it turns out that the Confusion guy has given us the straight scoop, before we head back to America with Soong and the dime, we should ask Joe to set up a meeting with Confusion so I can buy him a cool one.

Flo flashed me a smile and said, "Joe, let's get this show on the road. Between your story and Bear's buddy Confusion, we can't afford to be late for our date at the bar."

Chapter Thirty

Pinky—Carson City

The envelope that contained the results of Zweibel's DNA test lay unopened on my desk. Inside was the answer that would prove, or disprove, Gotthold Zweibel's claim to half of the Kaufmann estate. I picked up the envelope and for a moment I considered opening it, but then I placed it back on my desk to weigh all my options.

The bottom line was that it made no difference to me if the DNA test results showed that Zweibel was indeed the half-brother of my client. My singular task was to convince my client, Helmut Kaufmann, that Gotthold Zweibel was a fraud. To accomplish that mission I required more background on the pretender.

But where and how will I come up with that information? Bear was not available wandering about many thousands of miles from Carson City. I sat back, closed my eyes, and searched my past for a possible name.

There was George Sterling, my drunken pro bono client. Could my problem be solved this easily? I picked up my phone and dialed his number.

"Hello?"

"George, Pinky Delmont here. I have a favor to ask of you."

"Pinky? I called you last week and Lu

answered the phone. Is she back with you to stay?"

"Yes, Lu is here for the duration. Now, if you feel up to the job, I have a short investigative opportunity to—"

"Hey, don't you remember? You still have my driver's license locked up in your office safe."

Damn! My sluggish thought process could be the result of extreme jet lag. "Ah yes, your driver's license. The last time I talked with the judge, he remained adamant that you not be allowed to get behind the wheel of a motor vehicle. George, ignore my call and my inappropriate offer.

"Pinky, don't you dare hang up on me. You've been promising to get my license back for years. When can I—"

"My good man, I will discuss your situation with the judge this afternoon and if he agrees with me, I will call you with the good news first thing tomorrow morning. Now, I am very busy so good bye." I severed our connection before he could say another word.

Every attorney worth his salt had a few pro bono clients. However, I discovered that the key to financial success was to find a pro bono client who took little, or none, of my valuable time. George Sterling was the ideal pro bono client. He is a heavy drinker, and after his third DUI arrest, George's license was suspended. The court agreed to let me keep his license in my safe to protect the law abiding drivers of Carson City. There was no way that any sane judge would allow George to drive again, so I will have to call George first thing tomorrow morning and give him the bad news. I also made a note by his telephone number to never offer George a job that would require him to drive a motor vehicle.

I sat back and again closed my eyes. Henry the guard's face popped into my head but that man feels out of his comfort zone when he ventures more than two blocks from the jail complex or his shabby apartment.

Other possibilities swirled around inside my head when the merry-go-round stopped suddenly on the features of a man who I recalled did exactly what he was told and asked few, if any questions. I buzzed Lu. "Check your Rolodex and see if you have a phone number for Jake Dudek."

"D U D E K?"

"Correct."

I sat back and remembered the last time Mr. Dudek had been present in my office. He was teaching Bear how to break into a floor safe that was hidden beneath the carpet in a ranch house in Northern Nevada. It so happened that I had the identical floor safe installed in my office, so Dudek used my safe as a teaching aid. Frankly, I was shocked to discover that it took Mr. Dudek, a man with a stainless steel hook in place of his right hand, no more than ten minutes of effort to expose my valuables to the light of day.

My intercom buzzed. "Pinky, Mr. Dudek's on line one."

I installed a delighted tone tin my voice. "Mr. Dudek. I trust I find you in fine fettle."

"Hey, we don't know each other well enough to talk about my fettle, whatever the hell a fettle is."

"I apologize, Mr. Dudek. Now can—"

"Call me Jake."

218

"As you wish. Jake, I want to talk with you concerning a job."

"Are you out of your mind? I don't talk to anybody about my kind of business over the phone."

"I understand. I just thought I would remind you about the first time we met. The day you taught Bear how to—"

"Jesus! Don't say another word. Can we meet somewhere?"

"Of course. Would my office work for you?"

"I'll see you there in five."

I buzzed Lu. "Mr. Dudek will arrive in a few moments. Bring him into my office and hold all my calls."

"Pinky, don't forget, you have a lunch meeting with Willow in forty-five minutes."

"Lu," I snapped. "There is no way that I would ignore the opportunity to linger over a glass of wine with my one true love. However—"

"Don't ever do that to me again."

"What did I do?"

"The tone of your voice. The one that sounds like you are talking to a child."

"My dear, I apologize. My pending meeting with Mr. Dudek made me lose sight of my manners."

Lu did not respond to my apology, but I was sure that I had spread oil upon the troubled waters. Before the man arrived I placed the sealed envelope in the top drawer of my desk. A moment later, my office door opened and Lu escorted Mr. Dudek into my inner sanctum.

I motioned to a chair and while Lu exited I struggled to pull my eyes off the shinny steel hook that thrust out from the right sleeve of the man's tattered denim jacket, a garment that matched his worn jeans. The legend, according to Bear, told the tale that Jake was attempting to open the door to a safe with a controlled explosion. Something went awry. The explosion popped open the door but it also blew off Jake's right hand.

Dudek was in his later years with wispy hair the color of snow that had almost melted away on a dirt road.

I started to thrust my right hand in his direction, to shake his hand, but caught my social faux pas in time. "Mr. Dudek, it has been a long time."

"It's Jake, damn it!" He squinted his rummy eyes. "Yup, it's been quite awhile. Could be four or five years." He glanced at his watch. "Don't mean to rush you, but I have an obligation to—"

"Escort the school children across Highway Fifty?"

"Yup, and it's an important job 'cause once, sometimes twice a day, a car, usually one with an out-of-state license plate, doesn't slow down enough so I have to get the drivers attention with my hook."

"Would you be so kind as to define, 'get their attention?'"

"I whack their windshield with the hook. One smack usually lifts their lead foot off the gas and doesn't always crack their glass. So what do you want?"

"As you know, Bear is my investigator, but at the present he is—"

"I don't need to know where Bear's hiding out.

In fact, the less I know the better. Damn it, what do you want me to do?"

"I seek an investigator to go to Elko to discover everything about a man named Gotthold Zweibel."

"Jesus, what a dumb moniker. And if I do the job, and after I figure out who he is, what then?"

"Return and give me the information."

"That's it? You don't want me to tune him up?"

"Tune him up?"

"You know, whack him around. Anything from a broken ear drum to a cracked knee cap."

"God no."

"And you should know that I don't tune up broads."

I felt as if I was standing on the edge of an extremely slippery slope. "I am truly pleased to hear you have high standards."

Jake glanced around the office and his gaze settled on the corner of the room, the location where the floor safe he had opened had been installed. "You still got that old AMSC B3800?"

"No. After watching you break in so easily, I changed to a much stronger wall model."

Jake stared at the wall behind me. "And you put the new one behind the picture over your credenza?"

"How did you guess that?"

"Look around the other walls in your office. Where else you gonna hide a wall safe? Okay, I'll do the job but it'll cost you five C's a day plus expenses. It's Friday so I'll leave today after I make sure all the kids are safe. I'll be back Sunday and give you the scoop Monday morning after school starts."

221

I smiled. This was going to be easier than I thought. "We have a deal. I will instruct Lu to cut you a check for one thousand dollars and you can submit a list of the expenses you incurred to—"

"Jesus, I may look dumb but I can count to three. If I leave our town today and come back Sunday, that's three days, so you're either dumber than I think or you're trying to screw me out of five hundred bucks. That's your first mistake so I'll put it off to simple stupidly, but if you try to cheat me again, I'll break both your arms with my hook."

An involuntary shudder crossed my shoulders. "Thank you, Jake. I guess we have a deal."

"Not so fast. I don't take checks! With me it's cash or nothing. I'll tell you what. Call that broad and tell her to give me two grand, in cash. I'll cover all my expenses. Hell, how much can a couple of nights in a dump like Elko cost me?"

"I will call Lu this moment and tell her—"

"Do that. She can give me the dough on the way out. By the way, is your new wall safe an AMSEC WS1214?"

"It is a WS1214! Does that mean you could not break into that safe like you did with my old floor model?"

"That baby's built like a brick shit house so it would take me at least fifteen minutes to get in. Back to this Zweibel dude. Why do you want me to check him out?"

Damn, that was the single question that I had hoped he would not ask. The more he knew about the potential inheritance, the greater possibility that Dudek would flip to the other camp if he thought Zweibel's side would give him more than my two thousand. "Let me say, at this point, the less you know the better."

"I understand that, but give me somewhere to start."

"Fine. Start with his birth certificate to his death certificate and everything between."

"Are you screwing with me?"

"No."

"Is this dude dead?"

"No."

"Got it. Birth certificate—school—family—friends. Right up to where the moke is hiding today."

"I will not require your last item."

"You know where he is?"

"I do."

"Is he hiding out?"

"No."

"And you're sure you don't want me to give him a taste of the hook?" He moved that hideous steel prosthesis across his neck. "Just so you know, if I go that far, it will cost you three grand more."

"Listen to me, Jake. I do not want the man hurt in any way! He is a client of mine. I need you to check him out—not to do bodily harm to the man."

He sat back and stared at the picture over the credenza as if he were planning his next safe-cracking job. Suddenly he sat forward and said, "Hey, I can relate to family problems. My dad was a worthless bastard. What kind of family problems does the dude have?"

"I can not go into details, but Mr. Zweibel's problems are similar to the ones you just described."

"Okay. But if I figure out that you're holding back something, it's going to cost you plenty, and I'm not just talking cash."

"My good man, we are both men of integrity and I never would intentionally mislead a colleague."

Chapter Thirty-One

Bear—Lhasa, Tibet

There were two bad things about Lhasa. The first? Flo told me that because we both could croak at any minute, there would be no more sex until we got below the altitude of Denver!

"Babe, I know that Joe warned us about that no oxygen thing, and how we could keel over any second, but—"

"Bear, I know you and when it comes to that sort of activity, once you get going there's no holding you back. Look, the quicker we get this job done, the quicker our sex lives will return to normal. Are you ready to go downstairs and meet Joe in the bar?"

"But Babe, we need to think about this no fooling around rule. Maybe Joe's—"

"Time for discussion's over. I'm leaving now. I'm sure that Joe will buy me a glass of red wine."

Shit!

"Babe, if any dude buys you a glass of wine it's going to be me."

There was one more bad thing about Lhasa, but once Flo laid down the law about our sex life, I forgot what it was.

We walked into the bar and Joe was sitting with his giant dude at a table in a dark corner near the back. As we got closer, Joe jumped up and pulled back a chair for Flo.

He said, "Please sit down and enjoy. As the host I will buy everyone a drink. Flo, Bear, what can—"

The Chinese giant tugged on Joe's jacket and Joe's eyes got real wide. "Bear, Flo, please do not turn around and attract any attention. I believe our target, Madam Soong, just entered the room and is sitting, alone, at the far end of the bar."

Flo pulled a metal doohickey out of her purse, that thing she uses when she wants to check her lipstick, looked into the little mirror and said, "I see her. What's next?"

"Chen will keep his eyes on her. Now, as I told you earlier, I owe you both an explanation."

I said, "Joe, before you start all that crap, my throat's as dry as hot desert sand at high noon."

"Of course." He waved and a broad wandered over and took our order.

"Now that your parched throat will be soothed, I will continue. My American niece, Lu, may have told you that I was close to Chairman Mao. That is true but that is only a small part of the whole story. In my youth I worked for the Central Department of Social Affairs which was the original intelligence wing of the Chinese Communist party. Today, that intelligence department is called The Ministry of State Security, or as we Chinese call it, The Guoanbu."

The broad served our drinks. I took a big swig of another crappy Tsingtao and said, "Come on, Joe, we need to get back home where they know how to make good beer. Cut to the chase."

"Bear, Flo, I haven't been totally honest with you since we met at the airport in Beijing."

"No shit." I drained the bottle and waved the empty at the broad for another. "Me and Flo figured that out a long time ago. The bottom line? We know you're not a dorky old fart that can't drive a stick shift."

Flo said, "Slow down Bear and give Joe a chance to explain."

"Okay."

Joe said, "I'm sure you are both aware of the Free Tibet movement."

I didn't have a clue, but Flo nodded like she was on top of what he was talking about so I figured she'd give me the scoop later.

Joe said, "Tibet was one of the few dilemmas that Chairman Mao and the Kuomintang had in common. Both sides in our long civil struggle agreed that Tibet belonged to China! Soon after we defeated the Kuomintang, and with the assistance of the Soviet Union, the forces of Chairman Mao liberated Tibet."

Flo snorted, "Liberated is an interesting choice of words. In my country we called what you did an invasion."

Joe smiled. "It is interesting that the accepted definition of a word depends solely on who wins the conflict, in my case, the Chinese civil war. Flo, to continue our discussion on a collegial level, let us return to Madam Soong and the reason the three of us are here in Lhasa. The Guoanbu has agents all over the world and that includes the Kona Coast of Hawaii. For years we've been aware that Madam Soong was a conduit to fund the Free Tibet movement but her involvement was limited to an insignificant amount of cash. Some weeks ago, I received information that Soong had in her possession a coin worth a large amount of money and that her goal was to carry that valuable coin to the Free Tibet group in Lhasa."

Jesus, Joe's story was beginning to sound like one of those cool James Bond flicks. I said, "And you're talking about the two-million dollar dime."

"Yes, I am."

"Joe, I hate to break this to you, but our boss needs that dime, and Soong, back in Carson City real soon. Trust me, I've worked for Pinky long enough to know that the little fart ends up getting what he wants. The boss may be a shrimp but he doesn't give a shit if he's up against Confusion, those come-and-go guys, or your buddy, Mao."

"Bear, as long as we can stop Soong from transferring the dime to her contact in Lhasa, you are free to take the coin to your superior."

Flo said, "Hold on, you said the dime. What about Madam Soong? We need her as much as we need the dime. She's one of two people who can clear a man accused of a murder he didn't commit."

"I'm sorry, Flo, but at this point, the Guoanbu has decided that Soong is an American spy and as such, she will be tried, convicted and executed before the sun sets tomorrow."

I could see that Flo was really pissed 'cause her face turned as white as the prayer scarves that big dude gave us back at the Lhasa airport. She said, "Sorry, but we can't go along with—"

Joe said, "Hold that thought. Soong just pushed her chair back from the bar." Joe turned and whispered some Chinese into the ear of his giant dude. Chen jumped up and followed Soong

228

out of the bar. Joe set some money on the table and the three of us got to the lobby in time to watch Chen, and a Chinese couple, follow Soong into the elevator.

Joe said, "My man will make sure Soong remains in the hotel. So I bid you a good night."

I said, "Sounds good to me. I don't know why but I'm pooped out."

Flo said, "Joe, you'll call us if anything changes?"

"Of course. From this point on, we go where Soong goes and do what she does. Shall we meet in the hotel restaurant for breakfast?"

Flo pushed me toward the elevator. "What time?"

"Assuming Soong cooperates, at eight."

As the elevator door closed, Flo said, "See you at eight."

The second my head hit the pillow I was gone until the phone woke me up. "Hello?"

"Bear, it is Joe. Soong just entered the hotel restaurant for breakfast. Chen and I are right behind her. Would you like me to order anything for you and Flo?"

I jumped up and shook Flo. "Yup. For me, coffee, three scrambled eggs and a pile of bacon. For Flo, coffee and three slices of unbuttered toast. Got it?"

Flo yawned. "What's going on?"

"We've got to get up or our breakfast will get there before we do."

We both threw some clothes on, damn near ran to the restaurant, and sat down next to Joe and Chen as the waitress brought our food.

Joe said, "Soong is sitting at a table by the window about ten meters behind you."

"Joe, I thought we agreed to give me that in feet?"

"That is correct. She is approximately thirty feet behind you. Now, judging from the food she has left to eat, you should have time to complete your breakfast. However, we must leave once she leaves."

"Got it."

I was chewing my last piece of bacon when Chen popped up. He left our table and a few seconds later Soong waltzed by.

"Once she's gone," said Joe, "We will stay back to avoid spooking her, but she will not get away because Chen is waiting for us in the parking lot. I also have a few cars waiting on the highway just in case she manages to lose us."

We got to the lobby just as Soong crawled into a cab. As soon as the cab's wheels hit the highway, a black SUV driven by Chen rolled up to pick us up. We jumped in, and while Flo scrambled with her seat belt, she said, "Where are we going?"

"The cab is heading in the direction of the center of Lhasa."

I asked, "What's there?"

"The main attractions are the Potala Palace and the Jokhang Temple. At this point, all we can do is follow the cab."

A few minutes later the cab pulled over near a big area that looked like a county fair back home without a Ferris wheel and short a merry-go-round. There were little stands selling food, and fancy souvenirs, tons of prayer shawls, and Tibetan people were all over the place.

Soong jumped out of the cab and walked past a pot-full of people who were lying on the ground with their hands and heads all pointing to the front door of a building. Once in a while one of the dudes would jump up, take a step forward, and then drop back down on the pavement. I said, "Joe, what the hell are those dudes doing? That ground looks hard, cold and dirty."

He said, "They prostrate themselves for hours before entering the temple. For Tibetan Buddhists, the Jokhang Temple is a very sacred place."

We watched Soong walk past the people on the ground and slip into a crowd moving through the front door.

Joe said, "Bear, Flo, you remain here. I fear two Americans would stand out but two Chinese won't be noticed."

Flo said, "You go right ahead. I'm going over to that colorful stand that's selling sweaters."

Shit, the last thing I wanted to do was go shopping with Flo. "Babe, I'm going with Joe. We'll catch you on the way back."

I watched Flo head to the sweater stall and on either side were stands that were selling jewelry and other junk. Trust me, nothing attracts my babe faster than that kind of stupid stuff. "Okay, Joe, let's go."

The three of us pushed our way through the front door and got stopped in our tracks 'cause the joint was stuffed wall to wall with bodies. I don't mean the place had a lot of people, the joint was jammed full—like we were those salty little fish and the building was a can. The wall of people in front of us moved to the left and started to shuffle along.

I said, "Joe, there's not as many to our right. How about we move over there and cut her off."

"No. In Lhasa everybody and everything moves clockwise. To go the opposite way in the temple could create a small riot."

It seemed dumb to me, but this ain't Carson City. "Okay."

After a few more shuffles I saw we were about five rows of people behind Soong but we couldn't get any closer if we wanted to 'cause we had to go with the flow. If we went too fast we banged into the dudes in front of us. If we went too slow, the guy behind would bump into our butts. As we moved through the tight hallway, I picked up a weird smell in the air and it wasn't just stinky people. In fact, I couldn't find any real air at all, just that weird smell.

"Joe, what the hell is that stink?"

"A blend of melted yak butter, incense, and body odor."

"Jesus, no wonder there's no room left for real air!"

The line turned left, and we shuffled into a side room. Along the far wall there were two weird looking statues, one blue, one white, and in front of the statues was a glass wall. Behind the glass there was a pot-full of money—mostly Chinese, but as I shuffled by I spotted a couple of C notes under a pile of coins.

I banged the glass with my knuckles and said, "What's the scoop there?"

Joe's eyes stayed on Soong. "One of the statues

232

is male and the other female. I believe the title of the pair is—"

"Hey, I don't give a shit about the statues. I meant all the cash."

"Oh! The pilgrims honor their favorite buddha with offerings of money. They also bring melted yak butter and pour it into those large containers with the candles."

I glanced to my right and there was a tub, maybe two by three feet and six inches deep. The damn thing was filled with some clear, yellow stuff and floating on the melted crap was a line of flaming candle wicks that were putting out a smelly smoke.

I jabbed Joe with my elbow. "Is that the melted yak butter?"

He nodded but never took his eyes off the prize, Madam Soong.

About then, I started to feel sort of dizzy. The air was filled with yak butter and smoke. I couldn't breathe and my stomach started to do flips. All of a sudden the top on that can of little fish started to close. I grabbed Joe's shoulder. "Hey, I've got to get out of here or I'm going to barf into that tub of yak crap. Meet you out front."

I turned, and pushed, and shoved, and fought my way against the river of pissed off people. Like Joe said, those Tibetans don't like people who walk the wrong way, so by the time I cleared the front door I felt like I'd just finished the fifteenth round of a heavyweight boxing match.

I staggered past the dudes laying on the ground and bent over so I could suck in some giant gulps of that skinny air they have in Lhasa. After a few minutes I stood straight and started to breathe like I do when I'm back home in Carson City.

About that time, Soong waltzed by me like she was the Queen of England and headed to a vacant cab parked by the curb.

A second later Joe grabbed my arm and while he pulled me, he said, "Chen will find Flo and meet us at our vehicle."

After we all got into the SUV, Joe said, "Soong talked to a monk at the far end of the temple and he handed her a piece of paper. She took one glance, handed the paper back, and bolted for a cab."

Flo said, "Bear, when we get back to our hotel room I'll show you all the cute things I bought. I'm so happy we came to Lhasa. They have some of the finest Cashmere wool sweaters, at the lowest prices in the world. By the way, Joe, where do you think Soong's going now?"

"My guess is the Potala Palace." He snapped off a bunch of Chinese to the giant behind the wheel. I noticed that when those two guys talked, they spoke real fast, and whatever they said ended up sounding like a weird song. Joe said words, but most of the time the words went up and down, almost like he was singing, but trust me, Joe's singsong wasn't close to the cool tunes that my buddy Garth Brooks records.

As Chen drove the SUV through Lhasa, I noticed that all the shops had the regular Chinese word pictures and some smaller, weird looking writing above. "Joe, what's that funny writing above the Chinese on those stores?"

"That's Tibetan."

Flo said, "I suppose you're going to tell us that the smaller Tibetan words are another great example of your 'liberation' policy."

I didn't have a clue what Flo was talking about, but I've known her long enough to recognize that was one of her nasty digs. About that time we'd closed to about a hundred feet behind Soong's cab. Joe said a couple of Chinese words to Chen. The black SUV slowed down and stayed behind the cab.

Joe said, "Flo, I do not appreciate your sarcasm concerning Chairman Mao's decision to liberate this land and bring it back into the bosom of China. Were you aware that the armed forces of Great Britain invaded Tibet in 1904 and the thirteenth Dalai Lama found refuge in Beijing?"

"No, I was unaware of that part of Tibetan history."

"And in 1907, Britain and Russia agreed to the principle of suzerainty of China over Tibet."

I said, "What kind of a Suzy are you talking about?"

Flo said, "Suzerainty is what happens when a large country has control over another state that is internally autonomous. In other words, in 1907, Great Britain and Russia agreed that China had legal control over Tibet."

Joe said, "Thank you, Flo. Once again, your superior intellect allowed you to understand the complexities of a difficult situation. Now, as you can see, Soong's cab has stopped and let her out at the curb below the Potala Palace. We will follow her and wait for the transfer of the dime that should take place very soon."

I looked up. The palace was a really cool looking place but it was way up there, maybe a thousand feet up. I said, "Joe, how many stairs will we have to climb if Soong goes up there?"

"Many hundreds. Perhaps a thousand. Why?"

I'm a big dude and strong and didn't want to sound like a wimp, but right now I felt like my legs where made out of overcooked spaghetti and I was having trouble grabbing a big enough gulp of air. "It's okay. I'm just a little rocky from all that melted yak butter and smoke."

Joe said, "I understand. We'll let Chen out. He'll follow Soong up the stairs while we drive up to the top using the back road."

Sounded good to me. "Thanks."

Flo grabbed my hand. "Hey, are you okay?"

"Just a little out of breath. I'll be good in a minute."

Joe pulled a u-turn and after a few minutes of driving up a little road, he parked the SUV by a door where two Chinese soldiers stood guard. Joe jumped out and flashed his squinchy card. The guys saluted and opened the gate. We walked past the door and stood on the edge of a big patio with hundreds of people milling around. Some of the crowd looked like American tourists, but mostly it was Tibetans waiting in a line that went to a big wooden door.

I said, "Joe, what's on the other side of that big door?"

"That door takes the devoted Tibetan Buddhists to the top floor of the palace, the place where the Dali Lama used to live."

I said, "The Dally who?"

236

Flo said, "I'll explain later."

Every minute or two, the door would open and a dozen people standing at the front of the line walked into the joint.

Joe said, "You two wait here in the shade. I'll be right back."

Me and Flo watched Joe walk past the line, knock on the door and when it opened, he showed a dude the same card he had used on the soldiers. I don't have a clue what that damn card said but it was like magic. He came back, took me and Flo by the hand, and we walked past the line of people and into the palace. Once inside, Joe found us a chair and said, "Sit down. While we wait for Soong and Chen to ascend the stairs, the guards outside will not allow anyone to enter."

Flo said, "What happens to them? Will the tourists and Tibetians be allowed to enter after Soong and Chen come in?"

Joe sighed. "I'll make sure no one will be denied access once we have finished our job. Now, when the guards let Soong and Chen enter, they will include a few tourists so everything will look normal." He glanced at his watch. "Relax, we have a few moments before the door opens."

Flo said, "How do you know when they will be coming through that door?"

"I know how long it takes to climb the steps and I've added a couple of minutes because this may be Soong's first assent. Now, if you will excuse me, I need to set up the next act in our little play with my operatives further inside the palace. While I'm gone, please sit down and rest."

Once I set my butt on a chair, I hoped Joe

would be gone a solid ten minutes.

Flo said, "Joe, before you leave, can we look around the room?"

"You can. This is the apartment where the Dalai Lama spent his time when he was a child."

I checked out some books that were sitting on a little table by my chair.

Joe said, "Bear, next to that desk in front of you is the spyglass used by the present Dalai Lama. When he was a boy he used to sit there and watch his people walk below."

"No shit!"

I got up, walked to the telescope, and stuck my right eye close to the lens. The people and cars down below were really small, like the fake ones that I used to make a little town next to my Lionel train set that sat under our Christmas tree.

Flo said, "This room is an absolute treasure. Look at that small bed and couch. Joe, did you say that this is were the Dalai Lama actually grew up?"

"I did."

I said, "That's a hell of a hike up that hill to go to school. Did the little dude have any friends?"

Joe said, "Not really. He was the Dalai Lama. He didn't leave this apartment and his days consisted of study, and prayer."

I shook my head. "No friends? Study and prayer? That's a shitty way for a kid to grow up."

Joe said, "Bear, I'm afraid that the life of a child growing up in the Potala Palace would be nothing like your childhood in Elko, Nevada."

"How do you know where I grew up?"

"From the moment you entered China, the Guoanbu discovered everything they could about you. Now, if you'll excuse me, I have work to complete. Look around but please don't touch anything."

After me and Flo watched Joe go through a door at the far end of the apartment. I said, "Babe, do you think those Gooboo dudes know all about you too?"

"At this point, nothing would surprise me."

I still wasn't sure what a Dalai Lama was, or what he did, but for a kid to spend his time looking through a cool telescope instead of having to go to school, his days weren't all that bad. I took a second look through the telescope, and this time I licked my finger and left a wet thumbprint on the lens. Like I said, I didn't know what a Dalai Lama did, but the next time he looked through this telescope he'd know Bear Zabarte had left his mark.

The door popped open and a dozen people walked in. Near the end of the line was Soong followed by Chen. The tourists and Tibetans milled around and said, "Oh and ah!" Then they were pushed through the door at the far end. Me and Flo got behind Chen who was behind Soong. After a couple of steps, Joe joined us. He whispered, "We'll follow her but don't get to close. We need to catch her in the act of passing the dime to her Free Tibet contact."

As we walked through the dark rooms, we passed a lot of giant jug-like things. They were about four by six feet and looked like giant flower vases painted with white and gold paint. "Joe, what the hell are those things?"

"They're called Stupas and contain the bodies of deceased Dalai Lamas."

"No shit!" Jesus. These poor bastards don't even know how to stick a body in the ground.

Finally the line slowed down when the tourists reached a Buddhist monk in his fancy yellow robes sitting behind a table. As we got closer I could see he was hawking some kind of thing. "Joe, what's he selling?"

"An amulet that proves you made the pilgrimage to the Potala Palace. All Buddhists will buy one because the talisman is supposed to protect them from harm and give them peace."

"Maybe I should buy one to see if it helps my stomach—" I shut up as Soong walked up to the table. The monk handed her an amulet. She pulled out a couple of bills from her purse and a few coins. I whispered, "Joe, I think this is it."

"I agree." He lifted his watch to his mouth and said something in Chinese.

Chen, who'd been right behind Soong the whole way, wrapped his big arms around her.

While Joe grabbed the Buddhist monk, I took hold of Soong's hands. She fought like a wild cat but between me and Chen, I forced her right hand to open and there was a coin sitting inside a little plastic thing.

A couple of the tourists started to come close to Soong, like they were going to help her, but Joe shouted something in Chinese, and then he said in English, "I am from the Guoanbu. The monk and the woman are spies." Before Joe got to the English part all the tourists had scattered like they didn't want to be around anyone from the Guoanbu.

Flo said, "Give me the coin." She pulled out the loopy thing and the coin book from her purse.

"Bear, let Chen hold onto Soong so you can give some light from your iPhone."

I clicked the flashlight app on. Flo opened the coin book, flipped to a dog-eared page and then stared through her loopy lens. "Move the phone closer so I can get more light." I did and Flo checked out the coin book page and then stared back at the coin. Finally she turned the coin over and looked at it again. "Joe, it looks like this is the real McCoy—the 1894-S dime."

I looked at the plastic holder. "Flo, we were lucky that Soong had a little plastic thing that fit the dime."

"Luck had nothing to do with it. That plastic thing, as you called it, is known as a coin flip." She looked at it through her loopy. "This one looks like the Saflip brand. They make museum quality storage units out of Mylar which is ideal for preservation and long term storage. Soong deals in rare coins and she would know that you can't throw a proof coin into your purse without doing some damage."

Joe said, "How much did you say this coin is worth?"

I said, "Around two million clams." About then my knees started to wobble. "Okay, Joe, we've got our coin. You've got your spy. How about we head back to the hotel so I can take a little snooze?"

"Excellent idea, but first, Chen needs to place Madam Soong in a cell. Then we should stop by my favorite restaurant in Lhasa for a celebratory dinner. Bear, I promise you'll love the yak steak."

Grandma Zabarte always told me that whenever she felt a little shaky, she had the collie wobbles. Now that I think about it, I don't remember how she cured her collie wobbles but maybe a good steak dinner would do the trick."Great idea. And I think we should let Pinky buy the victory dinner."

Flo said, "Sounds perfect to me and that might give me the time I need to convince Joe that we are taking Soong back to America with us."

Joe opened his mouth, like he was going to say something, then he shook his head. "Flo, you have your dime and considering what some would call your tenuous situation, I don't see how you can expect more."

Flo frowned. "Explain your use of the word tenuous."

I could see from Joe's pissed off look that this dude wasn't used to explaining anything to anybody. He said, "You and Bear are Americans and you are guests in my country thousands of miles from your home. I have just arrested Soong, also an American, on a charge of espionage. Tonight, during a phone call to my office in Beijing, I will have to explain to my superior why I did not arrest all three Americans. That my dear is what most would call a tenuous situation."

Flo stood up and poked her best attributes in Joe's direction. "I can understand your dilemma, but I have an ace in the hole."

Joe frowned, "An ace in the hole? That I do not understand."

I said, "Joe, when a dude plays five card stud poker, you are dealt one card face down, that's the hole card, and then four cards face up. Now everybody at the table can see what you have with the four up cards, but nobody knows what your hole card is. Let's say Flo has an ace showing and nobody has a pair, or anything higher than her ace. Flo's ace in the hole means she has two aces—that nobody at the table can beat her. Got it now?"

Joe looked at Flo and said, "Madam, I may have under estimated you. What is your ace in the hole?"

"Do you recall my friend at the State Department? I've been emailing him on a daily basis and he's willing to grease the wheels to bring Soong back to America, so she can face trial for first-degree murder in Carson City."

Joe scratched his head. "Excuse me but I still don't understand why you think your friend at the State Department is your ace in the hole."

"Because if you don't send Soong back with us, my friend will leak to the world that a brave Chinese-American woman infiltrated your country and was arrested attempting to help the Free Tibet movement with a coin worth two million dollars. I have no doubt that you can execute Soong for espionage, but the news coverage, from her capture to execution, will be a front page story, world wide, for weeks if not months. Now you have threatened to add two more Americans into your country's espionage scandal. Trust me, if Soong, a Chinese-American is a big story, two investigators from Northern Nevada should push the ratings over the top at CNN. Joe, due to your excellent work, the Guoanbu stopped the money from getting to the wrong people. You have the two monks from the Jokhang Temple and the Potala Palace under arrest and we all know that you have your ways to make them talk. One final thought for you to ponder. Nevada is a state with capital punishment. When we take Soong back to Carson City, she will stand trial for first-degree murder, and if she's convicted, she could pay the ultimate penalty. Either way, spy or murderer, Soong could end up executed."

Joe stood for a minute, and then he said, "Madam, I will consider your interesting suggestion over dinner. Bear, I'll take you up on the offer to let your superior pay for our celebration. However, you must allow me to buy a bottle of our finest red wine for the meal."

Flo said, "Thanks for the offer of the wine, but could you tell me the label?"

"Why yes, it's Great Wall Cabernet."

Flo said, "I'm willing to drink most any red wine, but I've already tasted it and Great Wall Cabernet is two steps below the worst Central Valley plonk."

I could tell that Flo's knock on a Chinese cabernet had pissed him off, but he forced a smile. "Flo, please choose any wine off the list."

"I'll do that. Thank you."

Ten minutes later we were sitting at a restaurant where Joe ordered the steaks. When I looked at my hot, sizzling hunk of yak, my stomach did a double flip. I jumped up and found the men's can. The john was just a smelly hole in the ground with handles. My stomach did a couple more rolls so I hustled back to our table. After a minute, the smell of cooked meat started to make me drool so I hacked away at my steak figuring no harm, no foul.

Flo said, "Joe, assuming you end up agreeing

with me, will China have any problem with extradition laws?"

"Has Soong been charged by your authorities?"

"I'm not sure, but I don't think so."

"Then in the eyes of my government, Soong is just another American tourist. However, keeping her quiet during the flight home could present a problem for you."

Flo shook her head. "I don't think so. The woman has two choices. She can stay in China, be convicted of espionage, and be dead before the sun sets tomorrow, or she can come with us and face a charge of murder. With a good lawyer there's always the possibility that she could escape the death penalty."

I swallowed a hunk of steak and said, "That's true, but if she uses the Public Defender she stands a better chance with Joe."

The yak steak tasted great, but I figured that I better slow down. My stomach was still rumbling.

Flo paid the bill and Chen drove us back to our hotel.

Joe, who'd been on the phone since we left the restaurant, grabbed Flo's arm as we waited for the elevator. "Flo, it's all set. You are free to take Madam Soong back to Carson City. Your plane leaves Lhasa airport tomorrow morning at nine and you will connect with a non-stop flight from Beijing to San Francisco followed by a connecting flight to Reno, Nevada."

Jesus, that meant that me and Flo, and that Soong broad will be in the air forever but we were going home. Pinky will get his damned dime. Willow will get another murder suspect. Everybody will get everything they wanted except me. Like a dork, I forgot about that air thing—that missing forty percent that Flo had warned me about in Beijing.

When I crawled into bed I knew I must be pretty sick 'cause I couldn't keep my eyes open long enough to watch Flo take off her bra. But for me and Flo, the night didn't end there. What happened? I don't have a clue so Flo will have to tell you what went down during that last night in Tibet.

Chapter Thirty-Two

Flo—Lhasa, Tibet

Bear asked me to explain what happened after
he passed out from altitude sickness. I'll do that
but first you have to understand that my man
damn near died during our last night in Lhasa.

With all the running around following Soong
in the Jokhang Temple and the Potala Palace, we
were both exhausted, but before I crawled into bed,
I packed our bags because I could tell that my man
looked a little pale. I turned out the light and
figured that his white face was the last thing I
would see before our wakeup call at six. The
minute my head hit the pillow I fell asleep. A
couple of hours later, I woke to the rasping noise of
Bear gasping for air. I turned on the light by the
bed and his lips had taken on a tinge of blue.

I grabbed the phone and called Joe. "Joe,
Bear's really sick. I need your help."

He said, "I'll be there in a moment and I'll
bring Chen. As soon as I hang up call the front desk
and tell them you need an oxygen generator."

"Got it."

I hit the button for the front desk. "Yes?"

"I need an oxygen generator in room 212."

"I will ask the bell captain to bring you an
oxygen generator first thing in the morning. Good
ni—"

"Hold it right there, buster. My man needs

that oxygen generator now. If someone isn't knocking on my door in two minutes with that damn thing I will personally come downstairs and kick your ass."

I slammed the phone down and heard a knock on the door. I rushed over. "Joe, is that you?"

"It is."

I opened the door and Joe rushed in as he fired off a few words of Chinese to Chen. They moved to Bear's side of the bed and Joe forced Bear's eye lids back.

I heard another knock at the door. I opened it and a sleepy-eyed man walked in carrying a little box the size of a big kitchen toaster. At one end I spotted a rubber hose and an electric cord dangled from the other. The man plugged the thing in and it started to make a soft chugging noise. As the man left the room, Joe grabbed the end of the rubber hose and sat down on the bed next to Bear. He held the hose under Bear's nose and said, "Bear? Can you hear me?"

My man groaned.

"Good." Joe grabbed Bear's hand and moved it to the end of the hose. He closed Bear's fingers around the hose and said, "Hold this under your nose and take deep breaths."

Bear groaned again.

"My man, grip tight, hold on, and breathe. Your life hangs in the balance.

Joe got up, took my arm and led me away from the bed. "Flo, it was close, but I think we started the oxygen in time. Tomorrow morning Chen will bring him a couple of bananas to eat on the way to the airport." His eyes scanned the room and stopped on our suitcases sitting by the front door. "Are your bags all packed?"

"Yes."

"Good, because you and Bear must be on that plane at nine. Once the craft's wheels lift off the ground, the internal pressurization of the plane will adjust to about five thousand feet. Trust me, you will see Bear return to normal with each passing second."

I looked at my man's face and it was the color of an Old Globe bar rag. "Joe, he looks bad. Are you sure he'll be okay?"

"As long as he continues to breathe in the oxygen from the hose, yes, I believe he will."

Chen and Joe exchanged a few words. Joe nodded. "One final thing, my car will be waiting for you two at the hotel entrance tomorrow morning at six. If Bear has any problem making the walk downstairs, call me and I will send Chen up at five-thirty so he can be of assistance."

I glanced at the clock and it was three-thirty. It didn't seem possible but only an hour had passed since Bear woke me. I said, "Joe, we thank you and Chen."

"You are very welcome. Our chance meeting has altered my view of your country. As the Bard of Avon so beautifully expressed: 'All the world's a stage, and all the men and women merely players; they have their exits and entrances, and one man in his time plays many parts.' Good night, Flo."

Joe's recitation from Shakespeare surprised me! To hear that he was erudite enough to see that each side, capitalist and communist, had their roles to play was refreshing.

Sad to say that was the last time I saw Joe. I understood from talking with Lu that her father and uncle had never reconciled due to political differences. In my opinion, after working with Joe over the past few days, Lu should ignore all that political crap and reconnect with her uncle. God knows Joe's not getting any younger. My take is that he played his part with Chairman Mao's party line and judging from his many kindnesses, self-preservation taught him to toe the chairman's political mark. If Lu doesn't want to claim him as her uncle, then I want first dibs on him.

The next morning Bear still looked like death warmed over, but his lips were no longer blue. He managed to hold down two bites of banana on the ride from Lhasa to the airport. When we arrived at the terminal, Chen commandeered a wheelchair to roll Bear from the SUV to a security check. He flashed a card, the guards let us pass onto the plane where we set Bear into his seat. Once I had Bear's seat belt on, Chen guided me to a second car in the parking lot where Soong was waiting. She had been handcuffed to a ring in the back seat. Chen took off the right cuff and attached it to my left wrist. Like it or not, the two of us were going to be seat partners all the way home. Chen walked us through security and onto the plane. As I stood by him for the last time, I shook his hand and said, "Chen, Bear and I thank you for all your help."

For a moment, the inscrutable Chen's dark eyes stared straight ahead. Then he glanced down at me. He didn't smile. He didn't frown, but he gave my hand a short squeeze, and I knew he understood my thank you.

The plane took off and inside of five minutes, just like Joe had promised, some pink returned to Bear's cheeks. Three minutes later, he clicked on the light for a flight attendant. When she arrived, he said, "Babe, you've got to get me something to eat. Anything but those nasty pickles will work. And don't forget to bring me a couple of cold brews."

I sat back and relaxed for the first time since Bear woke me last night. I tapped Soong's shoulder and said, "I feel very lucky today because my man dodged another bullet!"

Soong hissed, "I trust you understand that because of you and your man, the Free Tibet movement might not survive."

"I'm curious, was the Free Tibet movement worth murdering a man?"

"Mao murdered millions."

"Sorry, what Mao did decades ago doesn't come close to you shooting a bullet into the forehead of another human being."

Soong said. "I do not agree. Now, the handcuffs are hurting my wrist."

I said, "Lady, the second you pulled that trigger and murdered Ludwig Kaufmann, you lost the right to complain about anything." I jerked the chain and a flash of pain crossed her face. "As you've noticed, we're chained together. That means we'll have to eat together, sleep together, and go to the bathroom together. But this chain doesn't mean I have to listen to another word about Mao, or your Free Tibet movement, so shut up!"

Soong got the message and she stared out the windows of three different airplanes during our flights home.

As much as I disliked that bitch for putting my man's life in danger, I couldn't help but feel a little sorry for her. She had put two million bucks, and her life, on the pass line, rolled the dice and the bones up came snake eyes. Now she was facing a minimum of twenty-five to life in a Nevada prison, or if things went really bad, the last thing she'd see would be the needle being stuck into her arm.

Chapter Thirty-Three

Pinky—Carson City

"Pinky, Mr. Dudek is here to see you."

"Please send him in."

The door opened and Jake Dudek entered. His severe expression did not offer me any indication of his success or failure.

"Mr. Dudek, please sit down."

"It's Jake, damn it. I'm getting old but the last time I was standing here I told you to call me Jake."

"My good man, I stand corrected. Please sit down and bring me up to speed concerning the result of your epic trek to Elko."

"Did you just say, 'I stand corrected?'—'Bring me up to speed?'—'Epic trek?'" Dudek slammed the tip of his stainless steel hook into my solid mahogany desk top. "Damn it, start talking like a real man or I'm leaving."

While I struggled to control the quiver on my lower lip, I calculated the cost to repair the damage to my desk. "Jake, sit down. Excuse me but I forgot to give my secretary an important message. When I return you can tell me what you discovered about Zweibel."

As Jake sat down I jumped up and left my office. When I reached Lu's desk I whispered, "Call the police but don't send them in until I buzz you a long buzz. If I give you three short buzzes, that means I overreacted, everything is fine, and you can send the police away."

Lu stared at me as she picked up her phone and dialed the police.

I returned to my office and sat down. Jake, as he wished to be called, was sitting in the chair with his eyes closed, as if he were taking a short nap.

Before I spoke I checked the results of his wrath and estimated the damage his hook had made was a quarter inch diameter hole with, at present, an undetermined depth. I cleared my throat and said, "Jake, I have returned, so please continue."

His eyes popped open. "Sorry about the desk. You can fix that hole real easy. I'll kick in twenty-five bucks to help you buy a half-sheet of mahogany veneer at Home Depot. Now, I went to Elko to find out what I could about the dude named Zweibel. He went to school there. He actually went to the same high school that Bear went to. His mom made a living cleaning some of the town's businesses after hours. Actually, that's about everything except . . ."

I perked up. "Except? Except what?"

Dudek sat up, dug into his right nostril for a second, and then flicked a piece of something onto my authentic persian rug. "Pinky, I think I found the answer you were looking for, but it's going to cost you a couple of grand more."

"But Jake, we had a deal."

"I know it looks like a chicken-shit move, but my expenses ended up a lot higher than I figured. Two grand more or I walk and if I walk, you'll never find out what the good part is."

Why was it that every Tom, Dick, and Jake of

this world had the impression that attorneys are made of money? For a moment I considered giving Lu the long buzz. The police would barge in. I would show them the evidence of Jake's attack on my desk, and they would drag the criminal from my office. But if I did that I would never discover the information this miscreant held in his twisted brain.

"Jake, Lu will give you an additional two thousand dollars as you leave, but the information you give me has to be worth the extra expense."

"And who decides if the info is worth the two grand?"

This man was testing the limits of my patience. I stood and as I leaned forward to indicate my total resolve I slipped my index finger over the buzzer button to call for my immediate rescue. "My good man, I decide, and if that does not meet your warped criteria, so be it!"

"Jesus, I'm not sure what you just said, but I guess it's okay."

Crisis passed, I slipped my finger off the buzzer button and sat down. "Please go on."

"Okay. Here's the secret poop. This guy, Gotthold Zweibel, was born in Hawaii, in a naval hospital that sits up the hill from Pearl Harbor. His dad was a sailor named Gunter Zweibel. The dad and mom got divorced soon after Gotthold was born. The mom returned to her home town of Elko, Nevada, and she raised the kid there, all by herself, with some bucks kicked in each month from the dad. One final thing. The word on the street is that the kid's smoke doesn't make it to the top of his chimney when it comes to dealing with people that piss him off."

"Excuse me?"

"He has two arrests on his record. Both were for assault with a deadly weapon."

"Was he convicted on either charge?"

"Nope. But I checked out one arrest report and he had shot so many holes in an apartment that the cop wrote the ceiling looked like swiss cheese."

"And did the record indicate the reason for his anger?"

"Sort of. He claimed he caught his old girlfriend with another guy. Pinky, between you and me, this guy's skating on the wrong side of the ice. I don't see how he dodged a couple of years in the funny farm. Okay, was my info worth the extra two grand?"

"Jake, you are amazing. Now, I have a question for you."

"Fire away."

"How did one man, over a weekend, come up with information that covers two states? And you had to access confidential records for much of that information."

His eye lids lowered. The hook moved toward me, and hovered very close to my nose, as he growled, "Pinky, I don't ask how you do your lawyer job so don't ever ask me how I do mine."

I forced a pleasant expression to mask my fear. "How silly of me! I will make sure I never ask that sort of question again. Jake, I would go so far as to say your information is worth the two thousand, plus an additional five hundred, minus two fifty to repair my desk."

Jake stood and offered me his good hand.

"Pinky, doing this job for you was not so bad after all. I heard all kinds of scuttlebutt around town that you were a chicken-shit bastard but obviously the word on the street was screwed up." He moved the hook across his throat. "You can count on me to do whatever you need. All you have to do is ask."

I pressed the button three short buzzes and prayed that by the time he exited my office, Carson City's finest would have left the building. I shook his hand. "Jake, I will be sure to call you again. But first, I must call Lu to approve your extra fee of two thousand, two hundred and fifty dollars. Is that amount correct?"

He nodded. "You got it."

I hit the intercom button. "Lu, Mr. Dudek is leaving and you are to give him two thousand, two hundred and fifty dollars."

She said, "Pinky, the cops just left but I can get them back if you're in some kind of trouble."

"No trouble whatsoever my dear. I owe him that money to pay for the transaction we just concluded. Goodbye."

Jake said, "Hey, if fixing the desktop comes to more than my two fifty, let me know and I'll cover some of the rest. I don't want nobody in this crummy town saying that Jake Dudek don't hold up his end."

He jerked up from his chair and walked out of my office.

Alone, I reached into the top drawer of my desk and extracted the results of the DNA test. I opened the envelope and read that the test proved Zweibel was not related to my client.

I glanced at my watch. Bear, Florence, and the

dime should have landed at Reno by now. I grabbed my phone. "Lu, as soon as Bear and Florence hand me the dime, I will visit the jail to give the good news to Helmut."

"Your schedule is clear for the rest of the day. Perhaps you should take Bear and Flo out to dinner. To celebrate their success."

"Sounds like an excellent idea. Would you be free to join us? From what Florence told me, nothing would have worked in China if it hadn't been for your Uncle Joe."

"Thank you. I would be honored to join the celebration. Hold on, Mr. Zweibel just walked in. Her voice dropped to a whisper. "Do you want me to tell him that you are out?"

"Send the villain in. It is time that someone stood up to that hoodlum and I am just the man to do it!"

Chapter Thirty-Four

Bear—Reno Airport

Finally, somewhere over the Pacific, one of those broads in uniform handed me an American beer. Actually, any beer's better than nothing, it's just that all of those Chinese brews tasted more like canned panther piss than the good old American stuff I was use to.

Flo expected Pinky to pick us up at the airport. In fact she told me that he should be treating me like some kind of hero—I think she called me a congering hero.

But she still doesn't get the part that the boss is a what-have-you-done-for-me lately sort of dude. Flo thinks that showing up with the two million dollar dime and the broad who snuffed Ludwig Kaufmann, would make the shrimp happy.

But like I said, I know him better than she does. Shit, if he was here, he'd put his hands behind his back, start walking in a circle, and say, "Bear, I do not want to complain, but it has been a good two days since you have accomplished anything of merit."

Anyway, the second we got off the plane Flo called Pinky's office and shook her head. "I got a recording asking me to leave a message. That's strange. It's two in the afternoon. Either Pinky or Lu should be in the office."

She tried again. This time she left Pinky a

nasty message 'cause he'd stiffed us at the airport, thirty-five miles from home, and Flo was still cuffed to that Soong broad.

I said, "Let's rent a car. Pinky'll pay for—"

"Damn it! Don't you understand? I have to get clear of this woman."

"Calm down, Babe. I'll call Willow's private line." After a couple of rings she picked up her phone.

"Yes?"

"Willow, I don't know what's going on with Pinky, but me, Flo, and that Soong broad are waiting for him at the Reno Airport."

"Slow down, Bear. You, Flo, and who?"

"That Chinese coin broad from Kona. You remember, Madam Soong? The one that snuffed Ludwig? The broad that me and Flo found in Beijing and followed to Tibet?"

"I find your last statement hard to believe. There's no way that you could find that woman in a country as vast as China, much less capture her in Tibet and smuggle her out of that country without creating an international incident."

"We had a little help."

"That has to be the understatement of the century! I'm almost afraid to ask, but did you also find the dime?"

"Yup."

"And you slipped a two million dollar coin past the Chinese authorities?"

"That was the easiest part. Flo hid it in her bra. At least it was there the last time I checked."

"Wow! You'll have to excuse me but . . . hold on. Did you say that Pinky was supposed to pick you up?"

"Yup. Joe called Lu when our plane took off from Beijing to be sure Pinky'd be on time to meet our flight."

"I'm getting confused again. Who's Joe? And what does he have to do with—"

"Hey, I'll fill you in on the whole scoop later. Flo's getting desperate 'cause Soong's been cuffed to her since we left Lhasa. If somebody doesn't get here real soon, packing some keys for the cuffs or a bolt cutter, I'm afraid Flo will kill Soong before you get the chance to execute her for the Kaufmann murder."

"I understand. I'll send a Deputy Sheriff at once."

"And me and Flo'll need a ride too."

"It's against regulations to transport civilians, but considering you've brought me a prime murder suspect all the way from China, it's the least I can do. The deputy will leave immediately. By the time you've collected your luggage, and the three of you have walked to the arrival area, the deputy should be waiting for you."

"Tell him to hurry. Flo's getting that trapped animal look in her eyes. She seems about ready to chew Soong's arm off at the wrist."

"Oh!"

"And keep checking around town for Pinky or Lu. As soon as me and Flo get back, we'll head to the office to see if we can come up with something."

"Hey, don't worry. Perhaps Lu became ill and had to go home. Or Pinky had a doctor's appointment."

"You're right. Like my Grandma Zabarte use

261

to tell me, 'Bear, you're always making a mountain out of a mole hill.' And thanks again for sending the cop to pick us up. Bye."

I fed Willow that bull about mountains and mole hills, but we both knew that Pinky'd never, I mean never, ever, leave his office without being sure there was somebody left to answer his phones.

About ten minutes later, a sheriff's van pulled up. A giant cop, about an inch shorter and maybe five pounds lighter than Joe's right hand dude, Chen, jumped out and ran up to us with bolt cutters in hand. The cop tried to unlock the cuffs but the keys didn't work, so he used the bolt cutter. By now a bunch of people were standing around to watch the show. The cop separated Flo and that Soong broad with a single snap of the cutter blades.

As the cop grabbed the dangling end of Soong's cuffs, Flo sprinted back into the terminal. "Have to hit the Ladies room," she yelled. "Be back in a few minutes."

The cop slapped a set of American cuffs onto Soong's other arm, read the broad her rights, and placed her under arrest for the murder of Ludwig Kaufmann.

Chapter Thirty-Five

Pinky—Carson City

I seldom made errors concerning peoples' psyches, especially those among us who had indicated they possessed a touch of criminality in their nature. However, in the case of one Gotthold Zweibel, I made a miscalculation that nearly cost the lives of two people.

The man barged into my office and demanded, "I've been trying to see my half-brother for days and they told me that you won't allow anyone, including me, to see him. What the hell is going on here? This is America, and you can't get away with that sort of crap!"

"Calm down, Mr. Zweibel."

He clenched his fist. "I'm long past calming down! He's my brother and we've got a lot to discuss!"

"As Helmut's attorney, I am prepared to dispute that fact."

"What the hell does that mean?"

"Mr. Zweibel, I have advised my client, Helmut Kaufmann, to not accept your claim to the Kaufmann inheritance."

The young man's expression shifted to full-blown anger. "I'll hire a shyster and fight you in court for my rightful share." He moved closer and lowered his voice to a whisper. "Or you and I could make a deal right now. Grab a piece of legal paper and write out one of those settlement things that gives me a hundred grand and I promise that I'll never ask for more."

"My good man, I have—"

Zweibel's face flushed as he pounded both fists on my desk. "Are you deaf? This is your last chance! Just hand over the cash, or else."

I maintained my stoic expression. "Or else? Mr. Zweibel, did you just threaten me?"

"You could say that."

It was now obvious to me that between Zweibel, and Dudek, an immediate review of those allowed access to my office was required. I made a mental note to run the problem by Bear when he returned to Carson City. I casually pressed the buzzer one long time while praying that Lu would recall my signal for help I had set up earlier when threatened by the man with the stainless steel hook.

"Mr. Zweibel, I just noticed from my calendar printout that I am late for an important meeting with the DA. I understand your concerns but you cannot walk into my inner sanctum, without an appointment, and expect Northern Nevada's top attorney to drop everything because you—"

"Shyster, what is it that you don't understand?" Again he pounded my desk, as if that action would cause me to backdown. "I want the money from my inheritance and I want it now!"

It was time for the moment of truth. I opened my center desk drawer, removed the DNA test results, and slid the envelope across my desk. "Perhaps you should read that first."

He extracted the single sheet from the

envelope and I watched his eyes scan from top to bottom. "A DNA test? But that's illegal. There's no way that you could have—"

I interrupted. "You may not recall, but during our first meeting I offered you a cup of coffee, and you took a sip. That single touch of your moist lips on the edge of the cup provided the lab with your DNA. Next, all I had to do was get a sample from Helmut and as you have just read, the DNA samples do not match. Mr. Zweibel, as an officer of the court, I am required to inform you that you have committed a crime. In legal terms, you falsely represented yourself as the half-brother of Helmut Kaufmann and as such, you used a false pretense with the intent to defraud Helmut Kaufmann of his rightful inheritance. If you do not vacate my office at once, I will be forced to call the authorities."

My office door opened and Lu walked in. She glanced at Zweibel, then back at me. The expression of concern on her face informed me she understood that something was amiss. Then, in a casual manner that I had not realized Lu's high moral standards would allow, she constructed a verbal scenario that provided me with a plausible reason to leave. "Pinky, you are due in court in ten minutes for the George Sterling case and you must not keep the judge waiting. I have the Sterling file waiting for you on my desk. Would you like to go over that information before you leave for court?"

Zweibel said, "Hey, he's not finished talking to me."

Lu frowned at the ruffian. "Excuse me, I apologize for my interruption, Mr. Zweibel, but I have a duty to keep Mr. Delmont informed of his pending court appearances." She continued. "Pinky, if you need me, just push the buzzer one time. By the way, I will be doing inventory in the supply closet, so you may have to buzz me more than once."

Obviously, Lu had missed my first coded plea for help, but now she recognized that my situation was growing more precarious by the second. I had no doubt that once she reached her desk she would immediately contact the police and we would soon be rid of this thug. "Thank you, Lu. That will be all. Please close the door on your way out so Mr. Zweibel and I will have two minutes to conclude our confidential discussion."

But I had underestimated the young man. He moved to his left and blocked Lu's exit.

Lu said, "Please excuse me, Mr. Zweibel. I have work to complete."

He laughed. "Sorry, but you two should have told me the same story. Shyster, you told me that you were late for a meeting with the DA. The broad tells me that you have to be in court for some Sterling character. It seems to me that you don't have to go anywhere." He pulled a pistol from his jacket pocket and pointed the weapon at me. "Relax Delmont, I'm not going to kill you. At least that's not my plan, but you never know because I'm not a very good shot." He aimed the pistol a foot from my left hand. "Give me a hundred grand or, with any luck, you'll just end up minus a thumb. If that doesn't get you to cough up the money, then the next bullet will take care of the other thumb. By that time, if you're still holding out, the third shot will remove your right index finger. Tell this broad to hand over the cash or start kissing some of your favorite body parts adios."

Earlier Jake Dudeck had informed me that Mr. Zweibel had exhibited criminal instability when it came to dealing with people.

My mouth became so dry that I had trouble moving my tongue. "Mr. Zweibel, calm down and listen to me. I do not keep that amount of cash in my office."

My mind raced as I glanced at my desk clock. Bear and Florence's plane should have landed by now. I scanned the calendar printout that Lu placed on my desk each morning and noted that Bear and Florence had promised to turn over the two million dollar dime to me when I picked them up at the Reno airport.

However, with Bear and Florence out of the picture, and the authorities ignorant of our situation, if Lu and I were to break free from this madman, the plan of escape would be left up to me and me alone. "My good man, your threats have caused me to take stock of my situation and I see that agreeing to your demands is my only alternative. As I previously stated, I do not keep that much cash in my office, but to circumvent the IRS, I have a rather large sum hidden at one of my Lake Tahoe condos."

When Zweibel looked to the ceiling for a moment, as if to ponder the intricate details of my offer, I grabbed a pen, scratched B F L T C on my calendar printout. Satisfied, I dropped the pen in my lap and held the printout close to my face as if to read the small print.

Suddenly, Zweibel cried, "Hey, what the hell

are you doing?"

"Nothing. I was just checking the printout to make sure that my meeting with the County Sheriff was not this afternoon, but tomorrow afternoon. I have a feeling that you would not want to bump into him as we walked across my parking lot."

He glanced around, gave me an exasperated stare, and said, "Okay, let's go. You drive your car, and the broad goes into the trunk. If you even think of doing anything stupid, she dies."

Lu cried, "Pinky, I can't do that. I'm claustrophobic. If he puts me in that trunk, I'll lose it."

"Mr. Zweibel, I have a much better idea. Place Lu in the front passenger seat. That way you can sit behind her and hold your weapon against the front seat. If either of us do anything wrong, you can pull the trigger and she will die."

Lu glared at me. "If those are my two alternatives I would rather go crazy locked in the trunk."

Zweibel said, "Forget the trunk. I like the shyster's idea. Now let's head to Lake Tahoe."

As my 1985 series 3 Sovereign Jaguar cruised up Highway Fifty, taking us from Carson City to South Lake Tahoe, I scanned each intersection for a sign of a police car, any police car, but to no avail. By the time we reached the summit, I knew my days on this earth could be running short. Part of what I had told Zweibel was true. I did own two condos, and I was heading to the one on the California side, but there was nothing inside the dwelling more valuable than a bottle of aged

Scotch.

However, all was not lost. I calculated that for us to escape from our psychopathic kidnapper, we would require approximately two hours. One hundred and twenty minutes should allow time for Florence to discover, and decipher, the clue on my calendar printout, followed by Bear's mad dash up the hill to rescue us.

So what scenario could I concoct that would expend that much time and still look plausible to Mr.Zweibel?

It was then that an off-handed remark by Lu sparked me to consider our first life-saving scenario.

"Pinky," she screamed. "You almost hit that car."

My God, Lu's admonishment was a potential solution! A simple motor vehicle accident. Both cars would have to pull off the road. We would have to exchange insurance information, and with any luck, a police car would show up.

However, I was sitting behind the wheel of my beloved Jaguar and there was no way I could allow myself to intentionally destroy this pristine vehicle. I realize that few, if any, could comprehend my dilemma. I was guiding the wheel of my 1985 British racing green Jaguar Sovereign sedan—not a cookie-cutter Lexus or Mercedes, which any low-class buffoon could purchase off a showroom floor.

Through the windshield I watched the line of cars in front slow down for a red signal. All I had to do was to hesitate applying the brakes for a millisecond. However, against all of nature's instincts to maintain life at any cost, I gently pressed on the brake pedal. There had to be another way to survive than through the demise of my beloved Jaguar!

At that moment, a kernel of a plan germinated. As I drove past Harvey's, the first casino hotel built on the South Shore, a fully fledged flower bloomed—my mythical cache of money would be incased behind the rocks and mortar that make up my floor-to-ceiling fireplace!

I realized that my plan sounded like a cheap TV series pilot for the FOX network, but I was positive that I could sell it to the madman in the backseat.

Three blocks past the Nevada/California state line I turned right and carefully steered my Jaguar through the gated entrance. A moment later the three of us walked into my condo.

Zweibel glanced around. "Cool place. I like the view of the lake. Where's the cash?"

Lu stood at my side as I said, "It's all here but it will take some effort on your part to uncover the container."

"What do you mean my effort?"

I walked over to the dramatic wall of rocks and smiled. "Behind this solid wall sits a metal box and inside that container is one hundred and twenty-five thousand dollars in cash."

Zweibel joined me and tapped the rock wall with the butt end of his pistol. "Okay, shyster, get your tools and go to work."

"You don't understand. I do not have any tools here. In my home I have every tool a man could—"

"What kind of crap are you trying to pull?"

"My good man, I'm not in the habit of—"

"If you call me 'my good man' once more I'll shoot you right between your beady eyes."

I took a deep breath to clear that unpleasant mental image from my mind. "Mr. Zweibel, you will have to purchase the required tools from the local hardware store. There is one located about—"

"What kind of an idiot do you take me for?"

"Before you interrupted me, I was about to address your concern. This condo, along with all the others in this development, was built for both personal use and as a potential rental. Each dwelling has a lockable closet so the owner can secure personal items during its use as a rental." I reached into my pocket, pulled out my key ring and removed a key. "This is the key for that closet, which is situated directly behind you." Zweibel turned toward the closet door. "I propose that you lock Lu and myself in the closet. Then you can drive to the hardware store and purchase a star drill, a hammer, and a pair of safety goggles. I have at least fifty dollars in my wallet and that should cover the cost of the tools. Once you return with the tools, you can let us out of the closet and I will begin the demolition of the rock wall."

Zweibel nodded. "Shyster, you are good. Okay, both of you get into the closet, and don't get too chummy. I'll be back real soon." He started to close the door, and then stopped. "Hold on, I'll need your car keys."

Oh my God! There was no way I would ever let that cretin sit behind the wheel of my Jaguar. "Mr. Zweibel, lock Lu in the closet. I will personally drive you to the hardware store."

"And the next thing you'll tell me is that you

won't yell for the cops while we're waiting in the check-out line." He pressed the business end of his weapon into my spine. "I told you to hand over those keys. Don't make me pull the trigger."

That was the moment when I realized that as much as I loved my treasured Jaguar, a motor vehicle, no matter how beautiful, was not worth my life. I turned over my keys.

From the closet I called, "Please drive carefully." A moment later I heard the front door close.

Lu said, "Pinky, did you make up that baloney about star drills?"

"Not at all. A star drill is a foot-long hardened steel rod with a five-eighth-inch diameter. When I was nine-years-old, my grandfather taught me how to use a star drill to cut through a section of concrete pavement in his garden. Grandfather Delmont instructed me how to place the sharp, star-end point on the concrete. Then he taught me where to hold the metal rod in my hand and how to tap the flat end with the hammer. The process may sound primitive, even hazardous to a thumb or index finger, but the system is very effective. Working with a star drill is a slow, methodical process, but I am positive that it will do the job on the masonry or grout around the rocks. When our kidnapper returns, I will recall my grandfather's instructions and go to work."

"Pinky, there are times when your vast pool of knowledge goes far beyond my expectations, but—"

"But what, my dear."

Lu clutched my hand. "So you take down a wall of rocks. How is that going to save us?"

"The rocks will not save us. That is Bear and Florence's job."

Lu shook her head. "Explain the Bear and Flo part later. First, what about the metal box full of cash behind that wall of rocks. I still don't understand what's going on. Do you really have to destroy your beautiful fireplace?"

"Yes, to buy time. I left a clue for Bear and Flo on my calendar printout. They will need some time to rescue us. By my calculation my demolition effort must use up at least ninety minutes. That is why, once our captor returns, I will pretend to work as hard as I can while I actually accomplish very little."

"When did you leave a clue for Bear and Flo?"

"Just before you saw me pick up the calendar printout you leave on my desk each morning."

"So there is some hope for us?"

"You are correct."

Lu frowned. "But what happens to us if Bear and Flo don't show up in time? Eventually, you will have removed the last rock and—Oh my God! There's no box full of money behind those rocks."

"My dear, let us hope that our kidnapper is not as bright as you are."

Chapter Thirty-Six

Bear—Carson City

I asked the deputy to drop us at Pinky's office.
I figured if Pinky and Lu were both gone, Flo could
con a ride out of Willow to our apartment.

The front door was unlocked! I carried our
bags into the office and called, "Lu? Pinky?
Anybody?"

Flo said, "I don't like this."

"Me neither. Let me check out Pinky's office." I
pushed the door and peeked in. To tell the truth I
half expected to see the shrimp's body slumped over
his desk, or lying on the floor with a knife in his
back. "Babe, it's all clear in here."

"That's good news, I guess. I'll check the
restroom." Flo stuck her head in the can and said,
"Nobody here."

I said, "Let's go into Pinky's office. We can sit
down and try to figure out what's going on."

"And we can take a couple of hits from Pinky's
super expensive brandy."

"That too." I walked around Pinky's desk,
pulled out two glasses, the bottle of brandy and a
bottle of scotch. I'd much rather have a beer, but
Pinky didn't keep brews behind his desk, just fancy
booze and I liked scotch better than brandy. I
poured a full glass for me and Flo. "Here's to you,
Babe. We did one hell of a job in China!"

Flo lifted her glass. "Here's to Joe, because

without his help we would have never found the cleanest bathroom in Beijing."

"Right. Four star. Top notch. Very American." I downed the scotch and set the glass down on a paper sitting on Pinky's desk. I knew if he walked in and saw me put my glass directly on his fancy desk he'd have a shit fit. When I picked up the glass, for a second shot, I noticed some big, handwritten letters on the paper. "Babe, while I pour me another, take a look at this."

Flo looked over the paper and shook her head. "B F L T C. Humm. A BLT means bacon, lettuce and tomato sandwich, but the other letters don't make any sense to me. How about you?"

I downed my second shot. "Nope."

Flo sipped her brandy and kept staring at the paper with her lips moving. She was doing that thing she does when she tries to figure out those weird license plates, like the day she told me that BUTTMAN was the license plate for a doctor of proctology, whatever the hell proctology meant.

About the time I was downing my forth shot, Flo cried, "I've got it! Bear, Flo, Lake Tahoe Condo. Pinky left us a clue. He's at his condo and I'll bet a month's pay that Lu's with him."

"Babe, why would Lu go with Pinky to his condo? I know we've been gone a long time, but not that long."

"That's a good point. We've been gone so long we don't have any idea what sort of mess Pinky's gotten himself into."

"We need to call Willow." I hit her number on Pinky's phone.

She answered, "Pinky?"

"Sorry, Willow, it's me and Flo again."

"But the phone number on my screen indicated this call came from Pinky's office line."

"I know. Like I tried to say, the deputy dropped me and Flo off at Pinky's office. Flo just figured out that—"

"Give me that phone." My babe held the phone so we could both hear Willow. "This is Flo. First, Pinky's office is empty.We've been stuck in China so long that we don't have a clue about what's going on back here. Is there any reason for Pinky to hide out? Is he in trouble with that Vegas mob-boss again, or is somebody else gunning for him?"

Willow said, "Over lunch he did mention that he's doing an investigation into a man who claims to be Helmut Kaufmann's half-brother. Other than that, I can't think of anything new."

Flo said, "Thanks. By the way, we're looking for a ride back to our apartme—hold on, I just noticed that Jake Dudek was Pinky's first appointment today. Willow, did Dudek pop up on your radar screen for any reason?"

While Flo listened to Willow's answer, she whispered, "Call Jake."

I said, "You mean Jake Dudek?"

She glared and started yapping with Willow about some girl stuff. I left Pinky's office to call Dudeck on Lu's phone. "Jake, this is Bear. How's it hanging?"

"Thought you were in China?"

"Was, but I'm back."

"Bear, you're not pissed off at me for doing that little job?"

"What job?"

"If you don't know, forget it."

"Jake, we've been buds a long time, but if you clam up on me, I'll come over and kick your ass."

"You and what army?"

"Come on, Pinky's missing and we don't know where to start looking."

"Why didn't you say so? Pinky hired me to check out the background of a dude named Gotthold Zweibel."

"What the hell was that?"

"You know how it is, I can't say much over the phone, but I can tell you this much: He's a nasty little shit and once he gets pissed off you'd better be careful."

"How nasty?"

"A couple of assaults with a deadly weapon. Likes to pull the trigger, make a lot of noise, and scare the shit out of people. The problem with that kind is they usually get tired of scaring people and start killing them."

"Thanks, Jake."

"Bear, when you have a little time, stop by. I'll buy you a beer and get your view on China's evolving political situation. I'd be interested to hear your take on the slow transformation from Communism to Capitalism."

What? "I'll do that. Got to go. Bye."

As I headed back to Pinky's office, Flo came out. She said, "What did you find out?"

"Jake did a job for Pinky by tracking a dude named Godsomething Zweisomething and it turns out the guy's a bad apple. I'll bet you a dinner at the Golden Nugget that Pinky, Lu, and this Zweisomething dude are at Pinky's condo."

"Okay! Now we know where to go, but our truck's parked at our apartment."

"Lu's car is parked outside."

Flo ran over to Lu's desk and dug through her purse. After a second or two, she waved a set of keys in the air. "See! That's what I told Willow. You're a lot smarter than most people think."

"Babe, is that good?"

"It's so good that our boss and Lu are going to owe us both a lot more than a dinner at the Nugget."

I got what Flo just said, but trust me, I'd rather the boss took us out to the Tuesday Night buffet at the Nugget! Hands down, the Nugget's got the best buffet spread in the whole damn state of Nevada.

Me and Flo ran to Lu's tired Escort and jumped in. While I figured out how to start the thing, I said, "Babe, we've got one problem left."

"What's that?"

"Pinky's got two condos at Tahoe. Remember? One's on the Nevada side, and the other's on the California side. Which one do we head to?"

Flo reached into her purse. "I'll flip a coin. Heads it's the Nevada side. Tails we drive to the California one."

The coin went up, hit the headliner of Lu's car and dropped onto Flo's lap.

I said, "If I was tossing with a dude and we were betting big bucks on that flip, if the coin hit something else before it hit the ground, we'd have to flip over. But there's no bucks on the line so it's your call."

She said, "In case you've forgotten, I'm not a

dude, and I don't care about the stupid flipping rules you guys live by." She picked up the coin. "It's tails. Head to the California condo."

"Right."

Chapter Thirty-Seven

Pinky—Lake Tahoe, California side

The moment Zweibel left the condo and headed toward the hardware store, I felt we had a real chance to survive. However, Lu seemed to have a different opinion concerning her future. While I slid my hand over the dark walls of the closet seeking a light switch, she said softly, "It feels like my world's closing in, and it's very dark."

In our present situation, I could not afford a panicked female. About that time I discovered the light switch and turned on a dim forty-watt bulb. "There, I trust that will help."

Her breathing was shallow and labored. She said, "What will happen to us when he discovers there's no money behind those rocks?"

"My dear, close your eyes, calm down, and let me remind you what I told you. Before we left my office, and while Zweibel's attention was diverted for a moment, I managed to scribble five letters on the daily calendar printout. By now, I have no doubt that Florence will have discovered the letters and knowing how her mind works, she will have solved the puzzle. Then, Bear and Florence will drive up Highway Fifty to this very location and rescue us from the villain."

"But what happens if Zweibel shoots us before they arrive?"

"They will arrive in time."

"And if they don't, we're dead."

"Didn't those two track Madam Soong from Kona to Beijing to Lhasa, capture her, recover the valuable coin, and escape from the Chinese authorities?"

"Yes, I'll give you that. But when they were in China they had the assistance of my uncle Joe."

"I agree, but now they are back in America, a country where at least Florence understands the language, and Bear knows how to drive from Carson City to our present location."

That was the instant when I recalled I own two condos on the lake, and based on my Lake Tahoe Condo clue, there was no way that Bear and Florence would know which condo fit the clue. Should I inform Lu that our hope of success had dropped to a fifty percent guess? I think not. If I had any hope of pulling off my star drill masquerade, I required that she be in complete command of her emotions.

Lu's voice broke through my moment of foreboding. "Pinky, I understand what you've been trying to do and I thank you for your concern over my mental well-being, but I remain less optimistic than you are."

"My dear, each of us is entitled to our own opinion. However, I cannot allow your pessimism to weaken my confidence in Bear and Florence. If you have a better plan, this is the time for you to make your presentation. I am all ears."

Lu sobbed. "Sorry, no plans. Bear and Flo will arrive in time or our fate is left in the hands of a sociopath with a gun."

"Lu, I believe that you have summed up our

situation. Now, I suggest we sit down on the floor and rest our legs."

Some time went by, and when I heard the key enter the closet door lock, I glanced at my watch and was shocked to discover that only fifteen minutes had passed since Zweibel had incarcerated us.

He opened the door. "Okay, everybody out."

The bright sunshine that streamed through the windows caused my pupils to constrict. I shaded my eyes. We needed to waste more time. I said, "Excuse me, but I have to make a short trip to the bathroom to urinate."

Zweibel blocked the closet opening and did not allow Lu to exit. He closed the door and locked it. "Make it snappy, shyster. The broad doesn't get out until you get back."

Lu's muffled cry came from behind the door. "Pinky, please hurry! I can't take being trapped in here much longer."

I ran to the bathroom but my task took longer than anticipated because I have never been able to perform that natural chore under pressure.

I returned to the fireplace. "Zweibel, let her out!"

He opened the door and Lu rushed into the room.

I demanded, "Now hand me that star drill and hammer."

He did.

I hesitated a moment, waiting for him to produce the pair of safety goggles. "Hold on. I told you to buy a pair of safety goggles. Did you forget them?"

"No, I didn't forget. Trust me, little man, a few flecks of concrete in your eyes are the least of your problems."

I resisted the urge to throw the star drill at his head because if I missed he would shoot us both. My only hope was to hammer away at the fireplace long enough to allow our rescue team time to arrive.

"As you wish."

Lu said, "Now I have to go to the bathroom."

Lu may not have an alternative plan but she seemed to understand my stall-for-time-operation.

"Jesus! Shyster, get in the closet."

As I entered the closet I slipped the star drill into my pocket and prayed that the sharp end would not create a hole in the pants of my exquisite Armani suit. My new outfit had arrived from Italy a few weeks ago and to ruin a pair of pants at this stage would be inconceivable.

A few moments later Lu returned and the closet door was unlocked.

"Now, no more bullshit. Start knocking those rocks out or I'll shoot the broad."

With the initial tap of the hammer onto the drill, I could tell that unlike cured cement, the mortar holding the rocks was much softer than concrete. I shifted my shoulder to block Zweibel's direct observation of my activity, and hit a rock rather than the mortar. After a few minutes of moving the drill a quarter inch and then hitting the end with the hammer, I had loosened one rock. I said, "Mr. Zweibel, you will be pleased to note that one rock is about ready to come out."

He rushed over, ripped the star drill and

hammer from my hands, and said, "Back off, shyster, and let a real man take a whack at this."

Obviously, Mr. Zweibel's grandfather had not provided his grandson with any star drill lessons. He stuffed the pistol in his back pocket and rather than take a controlled tap, he took a mighty swing with the hammer, missed the end of the drill, and smashed the hammer head onto the tip of his digit.

"Shit!" screamed Zweibel. The hammer and drill crashed to the floor . As he jumped around the room, the carpet became spattered with the blood that shot from his split thumb. He dropped to the floor, rocked back and forth, and bellowed, "Shit— Shit—Shit."

For an instant, I considered jumping the wounded thug, but before I could make my move, Zweibel forced himself to stop screaming, jumped up, and pulled out his pistol. "Shyster, pick up that damn hammer and get back to work."

Luckily for us, Zweibel's amateurish attempt at doing my job had made my effort to slow down the rock removal much easier.

After a few moments he growled, "Shyster, you're dogging it! Get your ass in gear and move those rocks."

I stood back from the fireplace and offered him the star drill.

He shook his head. "I've had enough."

That was when I noticed Bear's big head peek into the room from the sliding glass door that led to my patio and the lake. I did not know what was going to happen, or how it was going to happen, but I knew that somehow my ursine friend and his woman had arrived in time.

Chapter Thirty-Eight

Bear—Lake Tahoe, California side

Me and Flo got to Pinky's condo and I was super happy to spot Pinky's fav Jag sitting in his parking place. "Babe, the coin toss idea worked." I opened the car door to get out and then stopped. "Hey, you don't think there's any chance that we're walking into one of those Pinky and Lu kiss-kiss things do you?"

"Are you kidding me? Lu is a refined woman. Pinky talks like a gentleman, but he's a lot further from being cultured than you are."

Damn! She keeps doing that to me. I don't know if I should be happy or get pissed off. "You stay in the car. I'm going to nose around."

"Okay, but don't be gone too long. If Jake's right, and that Gotsomething guy is a loose cannon, we've got to do something before he does."

"Right."

I walked around the corner of the parking lot so I could head to Pinky's place from the lake. As I got close, I slowed down and looked into the living room. Jesus, what a sight. Pinky was standing at the fireplace holding a hammer and a steel bar. Every couple of seconds, he'd stick the end of the steel bar against a rock and hit it with the hammer. The boss's hair was gray from the mortar dust, his fancy dark suit jacket looked like he had the worst case of dandruff in the world, and the shrimp was

285

sweating like a pig!

About then I caught Pinky's eye. He gave me a little wink so I was sure he saw me. I moved in a little closer and saw a dude standing a few feet behind the boss. He was between twenty and thirty, held a pistol in his right hand, and his left thumb looked like he'd stuck it into a running garbage disposal.

I gave Pinky a thumbs-up, backed away, and hightailed it back to the car.

Flo said, "So?"

"I got to a spot next to the sliding glass door that goes to the lake."

"Come on. Did you see Pinky or Lu?"

"Spotted Pinky and for some weird reason he's trying to knock down his rock fireplace."

"He's doing what?"

"Babe, don't make me go through that again. So what do we do next?"

"Is Pinky alone?"

"I didn't see Lu but I did spot another dude and my guess is his name is Gotsomething."

"Was he helping Pinky destroy his fireplace?"

"Nope. He was pointing a gun at the boss."

Flo sat back and closed her eyes.

"Babe, like I told you, the dude has a gun. You can take a nap later. Right now we've got to—"

"I'm not taking a nap. I'm trying to think." She sat there for a couple of seconds and then her eyes popped. "Here's a plan that should work. You go back to the sliding glass door and wait for a couple of minutes."

"Okay, but what are—"

"Let me finish. Once you're in place, I'll knock

on the front door."

"What are you going to say? 'Hi, would you like to buy some Girl Scout cookies?'"

Flo flashed me her stink eye. "Are you finished?"

"Yup. Go ahead."

"I think the man holding the weapon can't afford to let Pinky or Lu answer the door. Assuming I'm right, the man with the gun will come to the door. When that happens you open the sliding glass door, sneak up behind the guy with the gun and deck him."

"You still haven't told me what the hell you're going to say to the dude."

"I will inform him that I am from the condo owners' association and we are taking a short survey."

"What if he doesn't fall for that line?"

Flo sat up, wiggled her assets, and said, "Trust me, he'll fall for the line."

Hell, she was right. As long as the dude stayed close to those babies he wouldn't care if Flo was reading names out of a phone book.

"Right. Give me two minutes and then lay on the doorbell."

I got back to the glass door with about fifteen seconds to spare. I saw Pinky working away but he didn't see me. About that time, Flo rang the door bell and the dude with the gun grabbed Pinky and pushed him into a closet. He disappeared for a second and then I watched him shove Lu into the same closet.

After he locked the closet door I heard him yell, "I'll be right there!"

Now all I had to do was walk in, take down the dude with the gun, and rescue the boss and Lu. What the hell could go wrong?

I found out quick enough. The first thing that went south was the damn sliding glass door was locked. I grabbed a bowling ball sized rock from Pinky's patio and bashed the handle.

Now the door handle and lock were gone, but I still couldn't get the damn door to slide 'cause some dummy had dropped a dowel in the slot where the thing moved back and forth. I was trying to figure what to do next when I glanced up. The dude must have heard me smash the door handle 'cause he was running toward the glass door and pointing his damn gun at me.

I jumped to my left and almost all of me got behind a skinny patio wall.

Bang!

The bullet popped a hole in the glass about shoulder high and I heard it whizz by.

For a second, we stared at each other and tried to figure what to do next. The bastard couldn't get out and shoot me and I couldn't get in to break him in half.

Bang!

Shit, that one caught some of my arm. The next shot would have my name on it. Before he had time to aim his third shot, I grabbed Pinky's redwood picnic table, and aimed the heavy table at the two bullet holes, the weakest spots on the door. Crash! The table, a million pieces of broken glass, and me landed on the dude. He let out a yelp, sort of like a wounded rabbit, pushed me off and ran for the front door. I yelled at Flo to clear the way and

288

jumped the bastard just as his feet hit the front porch. We both hit the ground real hard, but my landing was a lot softer 'cause the poor bastard got squished between me and the concrete walk.

While I lay there trying to figure out that I was okay, I said, "Flo, Pinky . . . and Lu are inside locked in a . . . closet."

Flo disappeared and in a minute I heard the boss say, "Thank you, Florence. You arrived in the nick of time."

Before I rolled off the dude I checked him out. He was still breathing but somewhere in la-la land. I grabbed his gun, laid on my back, and stared at the clear blue sky. "Babe, how'd you get through the locked closet door?"

Pinky said, "My boy, she did not have to unlock the door. I smashed the mechanism from the inside with my trusty star drill."

I said, "Your what?"

Pinky said, "A star drill. An important part of my intricate plan."

I stood up, saw Lu, and said, "How are you doing?"

"I'm fine, but I need to apologize to Pinky for not believing in him."

Flo said, "Why?"

"He came up with what I thought was a ridiculous idea, but he carried it out. Here we are and both of us are still alive."

I said, "You're kidding me. The boss came up with a plan that worked? Damn that's a first. Did that star thing have anything to do with your plan?"

"Why yes, it did. My boy, many years ago my

grandfather instructed me in—"

Flo interrupted, "I'm sure we'll be interested in hearing the details later, but first we need to take a look at my man. Bear, are you okay?"

"I think so. Why?"

"Because you have a load of scratches on your face and there's blood coming from a deep gash on your left arm."

I glanced at my arm. Now I knew why that second shot felt like it hit me. "It doesn't hurt much."

Pinky said, "In fact, all the wounds look superficial to me. I'm sure Bear's minor injuries can wait until you take him to the Carson City Clinic where I have an account."

Flo said, "We'll have his arm, and those cuts tended to at a twenty-four-hour medical facility I noticed near Harvey's. And Pinky, considering that you and Lu are still breathing, I'm sure you'll happily pick up the bill."

Pinky started to say something but Flo flashed him her evil eye and his mouth closed.

I said, "Babe, did you notice that I had to make a few changes in our plan?"

"I did, but why did it take you so long to get inside the condo?"

"The damn sliding door was locked."

Pinky said, "That door is kept locked when the condo is unoccupied."

I brushed a little drop of blood off my lip. "Are you the dork that put that dowel in the slot so the door wouldn't open even after I bashed the handle?"

"I am! Anyone with half a brain would do— hold on, you broke the handle? Is the whole sliding glass door destroyed?"

I said, "Boss, that dude took a shot at me! When the second shot hit my arm, I could tell it was going to be him or me. I grabbed your big picnic table and smashed the glass."

Pinky's face turned white. "My beautiful door is gone?"

"Yup."

"And what about my pristine redwood table that you used as a battering ram?"

"It's pretty much down to kindling for your fireplace."

"My boy, normally, I would dock your pay for the damage. However, under the circumstances, I will let this one pass."

"Thanks, Boss."

Flo jumped in, "Thanks, my ass! Pinky, as I said, you and Lu are alive because Bear saved your butts. This wounded and bleeding man put his life on the line for you and all you can say is you won't dock his pay?" She shook her head. "Speaking of pay, I'm still in negotiations with Willow concerning her offer of two investigative positions with the DA's office. Bear and I haven't made up our minds yet because I wanted to be sure that the offer you made me, the one over the phone of thirty-five grand a month for each of us, remained on the table."

Pinky said, "Of course my offer still stands."

Flo said, "And your offer includes paid medical and dental insurance?"

The cheap shrimp was starting to squirm. "Ah—"

"And includes three weeks paid vacation?"

Pinky said, "I agree to the health coverage and the vacations. However, the first week of each January I will post a vacation schedule that will allow one, and only one, of my valuable employees to be off in a given week."

"Not good enough! Three weeks of vacation without restriction as to the time of the year, or to the number of employees allowed off."

"But all three of you could choose the same week."

"That's why businesses like Rapid Replacement are busy year around."

Seeing Flo and Pinky go at it was a lot more fun than watching TV where a couple of dudes hit a tennis ball back and forth.

"Florence, this time you have gone too far!"

Shit, nobody in this world knows better than me that sometimes my babe could be a giant pain in the ass. But that's Flo. She always pushes things too far! So Pinky might as well give up now 'cause he had a better chance of getting a Royal Flush off a poker machine than talking Flo out of what she wants once she's made up her mind.

Pinky sighed. "I will agree with your vacation stipulation."

"And a month's free use of this condo each summer."

Pinky said, "One year only and I will pick the month."

Flo shook her head. "Not just one year, damn it. Every year and we will select the month! And I know I've told you this more than once. I'm not 'your dear', and will never be 'your dear'. In the future cut out that crap or the three of us will walk.

Lu will find a new position with an employer who has integrity, and Willow will have herself two new investigators."

Pinky brushed off some of the gray crap from his shoulders and said, "Florence, do you have the coin in your possession?"

"I do, but what's that got to do with this negotiation?"

"My de—Florence, once you hand over the two million dollar dime, I will agree to all your employment demands."

Flo said, "I will need a moment of privacy to get it. Lu, come with me and I'll show you what a two million dollar dime looks like."

A couple of minutes later Flo handed Pinky the dime. The boss never asked her where she'd hid the dime, and I wanted to keep it that way 'cause that little hunk of silver spent a couple of days cuddled between my babe's boobs and that's my territory.

About a month later, after all the scratches were gone from my mug and the gouge on my arm was healed, me and Flo got our first big paycheck from Pinky.

The next day, while I spent the afternoon at Jake's joint downing a couple of brews, my babe did some big-time shopping. A few days later, IKEA delivered a new living room set, a new bedroom set, and for me, a cool-looking leather chair with a little built-in refrigerator to keep my beer cold.

But that wasn't all. The next day, me, Flo and Lu went to the Ford dealer in town. After the usual haggling, I traded in my old bucket of bolts for a new F150 STX truck. While I signed the paperwork, Lu took Flo for a test drive in a brand-new, bright red, Mustang GT Convertible with a 420 horsepower V8 engine. When they got back, Lu bought the Mustang. On the way home, me and Flo agreed that every time Pinky parked next to Lu's hot new muscle car he'd go a little nuts.

Two days later, my babe capped off what she called our mad buying spree when she bought me a brand-new, Samsung sixty-inch TV complete with a flock of surround-sound speakers.

A day later, a dude installed the TV and speakers, and before he left, he helped me move my new leather chair to the perfect spot in the living room.

I filled the little refrigerator with bottles of beer, sat down, turned on my new TV, leaned back and yelled, "Flo?"

"Yes?"

"Thanks."

"For what?"

"For helping me, a dumb Basque bartender from Elko, make enough money so I could afford a new pick-up. And how from now on, my beer will always be cold, and my Red Sox will always look great. Trust me Babe, a dude's life can't get much better than this."

She called from the bedroom, "You're welcome. Now, stop talking about your new truck, your beer, and your Red Sox. Turn off the new TV, come into the bedroom and show me just how grateful you really are."

Like I said, life doesn't get much better!

Chapter Thirty-Nine

Pinky—Carson City

We had just completed a delightful al fresco lunch at a new French bistro a block from my office. The restaurant's ambiance was splendid and the cuisine magnificent. The wine, a crisp rosé from the Loire valley, enhanced our entrees. So what was holding me back? I gazed at Willow, her extraordinary countenance was highlighted in the early afternoon sunshine, and considered my personal quandary. Once again I had the ring in my pocket, but what kept me from asking her the ultimate question? Frankly, I was concerned that my frail ego would not survive her refusal.

Willow smiled. "Pinky, a penny for your thoughts."

It was now or never. I pulled the diamond ring from my pocket and said, "My dearest, before I go on, you need to know that you, and only you, are the one person in this world that I—"

My cell phone buzzed and I glanced at the screen. "My love, please excuse me, but this is a call that requires my immediate attention."

I pushed my chair back and walked away from my intended. "Yes?"

Lu said, "Pinky, assuming he's on time, Helmut Kaufmann arrives at your office in three minutes and I expect he plans on finding you waiting for him."

"Did you complete compiling the billing hours for his defense?"

"I did."

"Give me the total."

After a moment Lu said, "$480,000."

"And handling the Kaufmann estate?"

Another hesitation. "$140,000."

"Make up a final bill for Mr. Kaufmann, but do not show the billable hours. Combine the murder defense and the estate work together. The total sum for both will come to $840,000. The expenses for both cases will total $155,000. The final bill for all the legal services I provided to Helmut Kaufmann, including expenses, will come to $995,000."

Lu gasped. "But that's $355,000 more than the previous total, and if I delete the billable hours there would be no way for the client to know if his bill is correct."

To this day I do not know why it took me so long to discover a simple fact of the employee, employer dynamic. While walking past Lu's ostentatious display of motor vehicle decadence in my parking lot, I finally understood the benefit I gained from over-paying my staff. I was counting on Lu's concern over her excessive car payments to allow her exalted ethical principles to slip down a few pegs.

"Lu, I believe that we have gone through this before. My job is to give legal advice and your job is to support those activities. Am I correct?"

"Yes, you are correct."

"My dear, to help solve your moral muddle, please recall that a week ago Mr. Kaufmann was bankrupt, incarcerated, and had no future beyond a life in prison or execution. Today he is a free man with an inheritance in excess of two million dollars. Once his legal expenses are settled, Mr. Kaufmann will end up with more than a million dollars in his bank account. Prepare the bill and inform Mr. Kaufmann that I will be a few minutes late for our celebratory meeting."

God I love the law!

I ended the call and returned to the table where Willow remained with an expectant expression on her lovely face.

I pulled the bauble from my pocket and presented the ring to her. "My love, please accept this as a sincere token of my affection."

She took the ring, and we both watched as the sun's rays danced off the facets.

My heart pounded with anticipation.

She said, "There's so much about you that drives me up a wall, but regardless of that, I find that I think about us all hours of the day."

"Does that mean you will marry me again?"

Willow's expression vacillated between a smile and a frown. "Pinky, I . . ."